For the Children

David Laws

BLOODHOUND
— BOOKS —

In memory of David Laws

Chapter One

The audience step gingerly into the studio, both daunted and fascinated by all the cables, cameras, gantries, spotlights, podium and their own tightly terraced banks of seating jammed into the middle of the muddle.

This is TV at its most exciting, the feeling that you are part of a great show; nervous but elated and wondering what will happen next. Where's the great master of ceremonies, the larger-than-life bouncy host who fronts up this show that most of us have only ever viewed from the seclusion of our living rooms?

Today, in the studio's green room, sitting nervously and balancing cups of tea on best-dressed laps, we'd been soothed, organised and cajoled by a team of well-groomed, smiling young women assistants, but there's no sign of the great man. 'You'll meet him on set,' they say.

Not long to wait. Dark figures flit about, as if in a trance, tending to the tangle of wires and gadgets, vague forms peopling the shadows of this intriguing place. The banks of equipment look like an electrician's nightmare, but the director is a slick fellow, full of effusive arm gestures, as if orchestrating his spec-

1

tators, keeping us in tune. 'Hello, everybody, hello and welcome to the show. We have a really great performance for you today... an astonishing episode of history brought to light by the actual participants.'

This episode, he tells us, is to be called *Helen's People*. This much we already know. We are Helen's People. Most of us, if not all, spring from just fifteen little kids who got out just in time. But got out of what? That's the point of the programme; that's why we're gathered here today.

Now for the preliminaries, all the dos and don'ts: no coughing, no interrupting and respond clearly when asked. Just like the actors in the theatre we, the audience, have our part to play.

And then, without any of the expected fanfare, there he is, ambling unannounced from a side door, giving us that crinkly, grizzled grin, the foppish hair bouncing on the familiar brow, the epitome of laid-back style. Always liked him, the nice easy way he has, gently prompting his subjects, none of your nasty TV inquisitorial interrupters here.

Finally, after a couple of false starts, the performance begins, the cameras roll and we hear the familiar silky baritone voice. 'Hello and welcome to another edition of *Never Forget* and this is Alex Hunter, your host for the evening, welcoming you to your favourite programme.'

Applause.

'This is the show that brings you great deeds, great heroism, great stories of yesterday. As we say each week, you ignore the past at your peril. We aim to demonstrate that history matters, that yesterday is today and today is your tomorrow.'

A pause and this is clearly for a close-up shot. 'In our troubled world of dictators and warmongers, the heroism of the ordinary person shines through in the face of violence.'

A wide sweep of the arm points at the audience. The cameras zoom in. 'Here today are people anxious to give thanks for their lives and celebrate the remarkable achievement of their survival. Look at their faces, ladies and gentlemen, and you will see whole families, grandparents, parents and the young, who would not be here today were it not for the remarkable acts of courage, daring and fortitude of one person in the face of dire threats and perils.'

Cameras pan along a line of embarrassed faces. We look around at all the wrinkles and grey hair. Some are recognisable. There's Daniela Lewandowski – I remember her, she once came to tea, and then there's that big-time businessman Kowalska who's been in the news. What will they say on camera? I look around carefully, examining all the faces, and recognise Marta and Beata. This is a wonderful reunion; even Friedrich has made it to the studio.

Our host is in full flow. 'Whole families, several generations are gathered here today to give thanks for their very existence, due in no uncertain terms to acts of heroism. This is history close up. First-person history.'

He's looking in our direction, at Eliza and Gabriella and me. We can expect the spotlight, the microphone and the questions, to re-run that strange episode of our early childhood.

What do we remember?

For goodness' sake, I was eight at the time. Just fleeting shadows. All I know is that something ominous happened back then – a wall of noise, a violent vibration – that made me fearful of any kind of travel, followed by an overwhelming sense of insecurity. Later, however, there came light; playing games with that little boy who's now an eminent professor. I spot him in his seat two rows away. Will he remember me, with my violin, or Gabby, or Eliza? Do I detect a twinkle in his eye?

Even later, of course, clearer impressions: school, friends, career, family. I'm Zofia, by the way, you'll hear more about me later... much later.

At this point Alex Hunter moves adroitly up a gangway close to the audience and sits on the only unoccupied seat. He extends the microphone to our man with thinning sandy hair and the winning smile I remember so well.

'Professor Peter Fairfax, you're an expert on 20th century history at the University of East Anglia and you have a very special tale to tell, a very personal tale. Would you like to explain?'

We lean forward in anticipation. Most of us have never really heard the full unvarnished story, the complete picture, just little titbits, but now perhaps we are about to be told.

The professor – my old friend Peter – nods. 'I grew up with this history,' he says in his gravelly kind of growl. 'All through my childhood I heard it, saw it, lived with it. How young children were rescued from grave danger, came to Britain to begin new lives, and thrived–' He waves an arm around the sea of faces.

Hunter interrupts. 'And you know the person responsible for saving these lives? For making possible today's reunion?'

'Of course I do. She's my mother.'

Hunter is beaming his beatific smile. 'And what's more, ladies and gents, we have enticed this marvellous lady all the way from her care home, so that she can share with us the celebrations of her 90th birthday.'

He gets to his feet and raises his arms in accompaniment to a roll of drums from somewhere off camera. All eyes swivel to follow the spotlights which now focus on two large studio doors. These open slowly, thanks to unseen hands, and an elderly lady in a wheelchair is pushed centre stage followed closely by two supporters in nursing uniforms trailing red, white and blue balloons and glitzy party hats. From another direction comes a trolley. It carries a huge cake with icing and candles.

The applause is deafening.

Amazing! Of course I recognise her! It's Auntie Helen!

She seems bewildered at first, then breaks into a grin. That's when I note; obviously, she's been prepared; her hair is done and lipstick applied.

The applause dies down and Hunter crouches by the wheelchair. 'Welcome, Helen Fairfax, thank you so much for being here and sharing your big day with us. Can I ask? What was your greatest wish on your 90th?'

Is he expecting a significant or evocative answer? If so, he doesn't get it. 'A nice cup of tea,' she says in a quavering yet firm voice.

Laughter and more applause.

Despite admonitions to the contrary, Eliza and I holler and shout and make a connection. Auntie spots us and waves back in recognition. We give her the thumbs up. It's a message from us to her; we three girls, Eliza, Gabriella and me. We're all of retiring age now but we came good, made something of our lives. At Sadler's Wells, the London Symphony and the BBC, we kept our promise to do good things. All that peril and action, Auntie – it was worth it!

Ever the showman, Hunter says, 'And now, before we join the party and cut your birthday cake, we'd all like to hear the story of the rescue from your very own lips.'

'But it wasn't just me,' she says, 'there were others involved, I wasn't the only one.'

'Modest to a fault,' Hunter says.

'And it wasn't all daring derring-do,' she insists. She's not intimidated by the occasion or the place; insistent on getting it right. 'There were some very tricky, frightening and scary moments, and, to be honest, some rather shaming moments.'

'Of course, of course.' Hunter is anxious to smooth over her regrets and get to the point. 'But there's no one better to tell this story. We already have that from your son. This...' Here the wave of an all-encompassing arm that takes in audience, studio and show. 'This is essentially your story. The time for modesty is over. Succeeding generations need to hear this.'

He puts his hands together, as if in prayer. 'Please!' It's a heartfelt plea. 'Will you tell it to us now?'

I hold my breath and look at all those props that provoke troubling images: the nose section of a plane, looking oddly cut off and rather menacing, and the scary photo of a giant rocket. I recall the rather stiff man from the Ministry of Defence talking in the green room about 'setting the scene' and some back-up actors with gas masks, fashion-on-the-ration suits and paint-on stockings.

So the process begins. We're being taken right back to how we all got here, right back to the very beginning. Back to the days when I was a mere stripling and Auntie was in her early thirties navigating the scary days of the Blitz. They were worrying times those, full of fears and uncertainty when our whole future was in doubt: survival, victory or defeat?

It's a tough story with a very dark beginning on a dusty London street...

Chapter Two

Tuesday 2nd July 1944

Helen Fairfax put her head down, closed her ears to the clamour all around her and stepped out towards the station as fast as her well-muscled legs would carry her. She'd have run if it wasn't so shameful.

Her focus was on the road ahead, blocking out all the shrieks and signs of distress around her.

It was a pivotal moment. Everyone for themselves.

She skipped over some bricks and skirted a couple of baulks of timber, detritus from someone's bomb-blasted roof. She was seized by a single idea that blanked all others.

Get to the station; get out of the city; get to safety.

She was vaguely aware of others around her, intent on the same purpose; most on foot, carrying suitcases and children in arms, some with prams, a few with bicycles, all seized by an atavistic instinct to flee the source of danger, ignoring wreckage in the street, brushing aside obstacles. Helen stepped over a scatter of smashed roof tiles and that was when she almost cannoned into the woman.

Probably a young woman – but prematurely aged. A turban skewed about her head, ragged clothing, spread-eagled on the pavement, waving her arms in signals of surrender and wailing in a loud voice, 'I can't do it, I can't go on.'

This brought Helen to an unintended halt, shocked, her act of flight stalled. Sitting on the pavement next to the woman were two young children. Toddlers, just out of babyhood. Frightened eyes, the beginning of tears. All around them flowed the detritus of an upended pram, the contents rolling and flapping against the grimy flagstones; blankets, pots, clothing...

A deep breath, an even deeper sigh, an urgent resolve to calm down. Helen made her decision. She was ashamed of herself; ashamed, in fact, for all of them. Where was the famous Blitz spirit?

She stooped to upright the pram, picking up a couple of pillows and a bedraggled doll, smiling at the children. 'Come on,' she told the woman, now silent, body lolling, eyes vacant. 'It can't be that bad. Up you get!'

'I can't, I can't cope. He's left me all alone, the bastard, all by myself in this lot.'

'Pick yourself up. Let's get going.' It was a sympathetic tone, but one touched, nevertheless, by alarm. Helen put out a hand as a gesture of friendship to the children, sneaking a quick glance behind, drawn by the sound of fire bells and a rising column of black smoke just half a mile to the rear. 'We don't want to be hanging around.'

It took a couple of forceful minutes of urging but finally she succeeded in getting the three of them on their feet, pointing in the right direction and mobile, albeit at a snail's pace, inquiring about the cause of the trouble and getting the lowdown on the family's plight. 'He's gone missing, left me with this lot, bombed out and nowhere to go. I told him we should never have come back to London but he wouldn't listen.'

They were being overtaken by the rush, frightened people

fleeing not just the latest bomb blast but fearful of all the others they expected were about to rain down upon them.

Now they were passing another bomb site, the crater still smoking, houses scythed in half, bathrooms and bedrooms exposed, beds teetering on the edge of a damaged upper storey, wallpaper flapping.

The woman, who announced herself as Ethel, was once more voluble. 'Bloody 'Itler! Look at it! What's he wanna do this for? Someone ought to do him in.'

Millions have already left the city, Helen knew, and now another million were on the road. Flocking northwards in a race for safety. This, she acknowledged, was V-1 panic caused by the new Hitler super weapon – a chugging pilotless buzz-bomb being launched from France – and she had disgraced herself by giving into it.

She swallowed. This was not the person she was meant to be. Not how she thought of herself. Not how her beloved Hank would have expected her to act.

Ethel seemed to have regained some of her spirit. 'What's Winnie doing about all this, that's what I wanna know.'

At first Helen was completely focused on getting this family out of the danger zone but as they stepped urgently northwards with Ethel lagging, she found herself warming to her new role as substitute mother, clutching these little hands, urging the girls forward. Tilly and Tina had stopped whimpering and were chattering about their dolls, one of whom had a leg missing.

When they reached the pick-up point for the evacuation buses, a huge disorderly crowd spilled across the circus, blocking pavements and engulfing the terminus. Uniformed figures with clipboards were furiously shouting, frustrated in their attempts to impose order.

Ethel was still talking. 'Did you see that last one, the one that hit Goodge Street? All them bodies laid out on the pavement... before they covered 'em up.'

Helen made shushing noises but there was no stopping this story.

'All minus their limbs and some of them had no heads.'

Helen did her best to push her little party to the front. 'She's in a bad way,' she managed to tell a bus inspector.

'So are they all.'

Vehicles edged their way through the crowds, loaded and left. One after another. Ragged queues formed, faces upturned to the sky, fearful they might be caught even at the point of departure.

Helen decided she couldn't send her trio on their way with a hurried and peremptory goodbye. Absurdly, she experienced pangs of illogical sorrow at the parting. For a very silly moment she entertained the ridiculous idea of taking them home with her – until she remembered that she wasn't going home.

Instead, when the girls complained of hunger, Helen felt in her pocket for the precious bar of chocolate she had been saving for her young son and brought out the cheese sandwich wrapped in greaseproof paper intended for her journey. 'You'll need these,' she said, packing them on to a bus.

Finally they went, minus the pram but still clutching the most vital of their possessions.

Helen resumed her journey to the station, praying the trains were running, that the line to Hatfield was still open.

The bomb that had set her running had devastated three houses and damaged many more. She'd heard the phut-phut of its pulse jet engine, stopped in alarm at the sudden silence that meant it was falling, and took shelter in a doorway. The blast, just a few hundred yards distant, had been the most overwhelming experience of noise, terror and rain of debris, causing her temporary loss of control.

Never mind, she told herself. *Today I'm a frightened rabbit fleeing the fox, but tomorrow I'll be biting back. Doing my bit to thwart the enemy. Ferrying warplanes, keeping the system ticking over, backing up the fighter boys.*

She ground her teeth, still ashamed of her earlier lapse, and decided that this homily was not good enough. Instead, she made a vow to take the fight straight to the architects of such appalling destruction. She owed it to the memory of a very special person. She also owed it to her son to live up to the heroic image he had of her. She was no longer willing to accept a minor role; she wanted a more direct way of hitting back.

As yet, she didn't know how, when or where... but somehow she would find a way.

Chapter Three

The station was hardly better than the bus terminus. Chaos, changes of platform, contradictory announcements, rising frustration. Helen caught sight of a departure for Cambridge with a few spare seats and for a moment she was tempted. A change on to her local line? Back home to Peter by evening?

No! A firm if reluctant shake of the head. Duty called. She had to get back to base. Of course, she was being pulled in two directions, she knew that only too well, but this was her decision. While single women and mothers with teenage children were conscripted into national service, mothers like her were exempt – but then Helen was answering a call that could not be denied.

Eventually she found a train for Hatfield and was surprised to recognise Owen Trelawny, one of her father's friends, now looking considerably older, being pushed and prodded about in the hustle to find a seat. He'd been something in the motor trade, she recalled.

'What a lovely surprise,' he said, when she found two places for them by a window and they inevitably began a catch-up session on their lives.

'A little boy,' he exclaimed, amazed at the maturing of the young girl he once knew, and she filled in her son's details: big blue eyes, good at reading, his features perceptibly changing and developing by the week.

'And the father?'

Helen glanced out of the window and did not reply.

The conversation quickly moved on to the reason for their hasty exodus from the city. 'It'll only get worse,' he said. 'You know what's coming next? Some new weapon Hitler's got. Even worse than the buzz-bombs.'

'I've heard,' Helen said shortly.

'No warning this time, no chance to stop it, just bang, wasting a whole city block at a time.'

Helen wondered if they should be talking openly on this subject, since there has been no public announcement from the government, but then people were much more relaxed these days about 'walls have ears'.

'It's what I'm hearing from my friends in the know,' Trelawny was saying. 'When people in the city realise what's coming the stampede to get out will be even greater. Much worse than the Blitz. No more space in those Tube stations. And shelters are useless against the devastating power of this new wretched thing.'

She sighed. The war had reached a stage where the scent of victory was in the air. How ironic then, that the Germans were about to launch on them a devastating new weapon born of a technology vastly superior to the Allies.

'I suppose you'll be doing something equally spectacular for the war effort, eh?' Trelawny asked.

Helen laughed but did not enlarge.

'Something daring, I'll be bound, lots of daring young women about these days, and especially you... you with all those long flights, I don't know how you managed it.'

'All in the past now,' she said, making a gesture as if to whisk the past away. 'I'm a conventional housewife now.'

Not quite true, of course, more the weekend mother, she admitted silently to herself. She smiled back, knowing her aviation exploits were extraordinary to him; that she, a mere girl, had flown solo across endless tracks of desert and barren landscapes, making her name as a pioneer back in the early thirties. In Trelawny's world women didn't simply stay in the kitchen; they held soirees, attended races, concentrated on looking elegant. The notion that they might get their hands oily and fingernails blackened delving into an aero engine in a grubby workshop was beyond his comprehension.

She didn't resent him for that. His was a different generation, old school, trying to get a grip of this fantastic wartime era. Besides, she'd always thought of him as a bit of a toff, with his walking cane, panama hat and pink cravat; a square peg in the rough trade of the motor business.

'Actually,' she said, 'that was why I was in town today. Meeting the person who was my supporter back then. Reawakening the old friendship. Re-living all those difficult days and all the tremendous back-up he gave me.'

'But good times, yes? You loved all those old string-bags.'

'Yes, they were good times...' Her voice trailed off, reflecting on her almost manic quest for breaking distance and speed records and flying the flag for women in the air. Now all those carefree skylarking days were gone. The likes of Adolf Hitler and Hermann Göring had turned the joy of flying into a menace and a threat.

'Met my friend in the Café Royal quite by accident,' she said, keeping up the fiction of the chance encounter with Ashley

Devereaux, once her aviation supporter and now senior civil servant at the Air Ministry. In fact, she'd contrived the meeting to indulge in some special pleading. And that was how she knew all about the imminent peril of the V-2 rocket bomb that was shortly to be launched against the city, its power thought to be so devastating that the government feared it might have to leave the capital altogether. No news had been given out publicly but intelligence in Whitehall was privately predicting huge craters, massive explosions, unlimited numbers sent over every day, enormous casualties, the new blitz expected to begin at any moment.

Her mind returned to that café rendezvous. She'd been shocked by the statistics and stunned by the images Devereaux had created for the impending apocalypse: roads blocked by rescue vehicles; civil defence overwhelmed; a logjam of ambulances; gas, water, electricity and sewer services disrupted; and serious health problems. Ten thousand killed every day and twenty thousand badly injured.

The horror of these statistics had so shocked her that they transformed into a nightmare vision. The scene in her head was the worst she could imagine: attending a morgue to identify her family laid out on a slab.

No! She tried to push the image away but it returned cruelly as she peered down at them, the whole family, every one of them, bruised and battered and showing evidence of suffering, including Trelawny and all the people she had ever known and cared for. This was truly a vision from hell.

It would not go away. Wouldn't fade. Kept playing on her mind. Beyond tears, beyond any normal concept of grief.

These were her demons. They so enraged her that she promised herself to do very much better than a mere pledge to hit back at the enemy.

As Devereaux urged her to get out of London – 'as fast as

you can, before this all kicks off' – she vowed personal vengeance on those responsible for sending death and destruction flying across the English Channel.

Chapter Four

Wednesday

Helen was perched on an uncomfortable chair in the ferry hut, a ramshackle building right next to the de Havilland aircraft factory, waiting for the dockets to arrive, the little bits of paper that contained the details of the next job.

This was the hub of the women's section of the Air Transport Auxiliary at Hatfield; the task was to deliver new and repaired aircraft from factories to front-line airfields.

Just now all the talk was of the weather. She could hear the other girls saying it, accompanied by the inevitable wagging finger.

It's much safer to wait for the weather to clear.

Helen, however, was thinking about the night before: about the scare of the V-1s, about Devereaux's frightening take on the V-2 blitz that was shortly to burst upon the city, and the reawakening of their former close friendship. Theirs had been the partnership that led to her long career in aviation, piloting early biplanes to distant places, in particular, setting the record, yet to be beaten, for London to Peking. This was her history. She loved flying. It was what she did. It was in her soul.

Since those early days, however, their friendship had

cooled; he had married and a burgeoning civil service career had taken off. Their meeting the previous day in London had been to press the case for women flyers to attain a higher role in the war; if she were honest, it had also been a desire to rekindle some of that earlier warmth.

Now she was anxious to get on with the business of the day, already dressed in fleece-lined Sidcot overalls and big black fur-lined flying boots. The chatter continued all around her as she went to the tea bar for a refill. The new girl was there, searching her pockets with a hunted expression. 'Sure I came out with it this morning...'

Helen laughed and pushed some more copper across the counter. 'Here, have it on me.'

'Thanks.'

The two of them settled at a window seat, nursing their drinks, Helen refusing the offer of a cigarette while Maude was anxious to talk. 'How's your little boy getting on?'

Everyone in the ferry hut knew about Peter.

'Fine. Playful, inquisitive, loves his gran. Just as well, since I can only get back at weekends.'

'Must be hard, being away.'

'Doing my bit. I like to think this is what I'm good at.'

'I wish I were as confident.'

Helen knew Maude was just out of training and facing her first flight that morning as part of a group of Tiger Moths due to fly to Prestwick. Normally she tried not to wear her experience on her sleeve, disliking other 'veterans' who formed cliques and adopted superior attitudes. Nevertheless, she decided to offer some advice. 'Don't fret, just remember your basic flying skills and follow the others,' she said. 'Don't lag behind, keep tight on their tail and you won't get lost.'

Someone coughed, a door banged and her friend Violet walked in followed by a gust of unwelcome wind. She sat opposite and said, 'You're looking pretty peeved this morning. Bad night?'

Helen shook her head. 'Just frustrated, all this waiting around, all the talk of bad weather, and a bad batch of compasses. It's nonsense. Just the usual wail.'

Violet chuckled. 'Always the impatient one.'

'Just because of a little bit of mist the whole darned ferrying operation is paralysed for twenty-four hours, everybody sitting about, twiddling their thumbs and no new aircraft delivered to where they need to be.'

Violet, who was no slouch in the cockpit and ferried four-engined Lancasters and Stirlings, looked dubious. 'Frustrating, sure – but foolhardy to ignore the weather, surely? Have you seen outside?'

'I have.' Helen, grasping her helmet, goggles and gloves, was peering at the mist-shrouded sky outside. 'Not that bad. Some little gaps.' She stared hard, balled a fist and made a decision. 'I'll find a way.'

Violet snorted. 'We know you've got tons of experience, Helen, but the fog is still a killer.'

'I can smell my way through it.'

'On your head be it.'

Helen wouldn't say it, of course – that would be bragging – but with her history of years of flying early aircraft around the globe she reckoned she was entitled to make such a judgement.

Just then her name was called. A docket had arrived to reveal that her allotted task was to deliver an aircraft to Weymouth on the south coast. 'Right, I'm off,' she said, aware that several frowns followed her out of the room.

Later, of course, she would have to acknowledge that this attitude was one of complacency, of over-confidence, foolish even, but at the time she was firmly of the opinion that she knew best. She didn't want to sit about, wasting another day and there was a very personal reason for her impatience. She was anxious to get home for her son's birthday at the weekend. Her mother would happily fill in for her absence if there were a delay, but Helen was determined to get back home by Saturday, as was usual, this time to see Peter cut his sixth birthday cake. Of course he'd want his mother there.

Outside on the airfield she looked up again at the mist and the cloud. Not that bad! Signs of it breaking pretty soon. Might be a bit hairy, might scare those faint hearts back in the docket room, but she'd find a way through. She would not allow what she regarded as excessive caution to spoil Peter's birthday party.

The aircraft was wheeled out of the hangar, sleek, pristine, brand new from the factory. A mechanic told her that the compass was working. 'I've put a new one in,' he said for the third time, which – strangely – was less reassuring than if he'd said nothing.

The Mark 12 was a magnificent beast and she was one of a select group who'd passed the conversion course to be allotted Category Two status: competent to fly single-engine fighters. And what an aircraft!

She unlatched the cockpit half-door, leaned in and grabbed the far side, then stood on the seat before sliding down inside. Snug. It felt very snug. She smiled in anticipation as if wrapping the fuselage around her. The power trolley was hooked up and the engine fired first time. Good omen. Right hand on the stick, left on the throttle, her take-off as smooth and silky as it was meant to be. That's how you flew; you only changed hands to retract the undercarriage.

She dodged and weaved, looking for gaps and holes in the mist, confident of her ability to find a way through. It had taken a long time for the ferry girls to be recognised by the RAF. Initially, they had been confined to open cockpit Tiger Moths – and almost froze to death – but eventually authority relented and now the best pilots were allowed to ferry the latest and the largest. Violet was Category Five. Flying the Lancaster bomber, she told everyone, was 'just like driving a car'.

Admittedly, all their routines were simple enough: straight and level flight at 2,000 feet, keeping land firmly in sight, navigating by map and landmarks.

The trouble was: no land was in sight.

Helen peered intently into the murk. It would clear soon enough. She was confident. It was instinct. This was what had taken her all the way from London to Asia in those early record-breaking days when other flyers regarded crossing the English Channel as a most daring feat of aviation. Her record, and the dextrous way she now handled the Mark 12, was a matter of pride.

She identified a valley topped by mist but could still see the walls of the hills and the roadway at the bottom, taking the aircraft down low so that trees and bushes could be seen flashing by to the side and above.

She laughed briefly, thinking of all the others still stranded and idle back at Hatfield, then gripped the stick more tightly as the valley began to narrow and close in.

Perhaps this was not so clever after all, the gap to fly through shrinking with each second. Lower and lower was the only way.

Careful of those trees. Perilously close to the telegraph poles. One tiny error at this speed...

A loud thwack and the Mark 12 shuddered and slew sideways towards the hill on the starboard side.

Shock and an instinctive reaction. That's how she corrected and kept on course. Must have been something unforeseen, a chimney or stray wires.

Another crack and the aircraft was bouncing, barely under her control.

The smell of cordite did it.

Those stupid trigger-happy ack-ack gunners. This was ridiculous. She was about to be shot down by her own side.

Anger flared in her as she jockeyed the bucking aircraft, a victim of the curse of the crazy gunner, known to shoot at anything that moved.

Couldn't they tell the difference between a Spit and a Messerschmitt?

Chapter Five

Only option – over the top.

Strictly forbidden, of course, and against all the rules, but needs must in an emergency. She had to get out of this before they pulverised the aircraft.

She eased the stick back, increased the throttle and climbed steeply through the thick gloop of the cloud, furious with the people on the ground but also angry with herself. She must have strayed too far off course. The rule was to stay well clear of anti-aircraft positions and barrage balloons. Those long balloon cables! Sudden death awaited anyone flying into them.

She held her breath. No more explosions, and suddenly without warning she burst out of the cloud into bright sunlight, the grey mass of cloud below her. She eased the control column back on track, peered anxiously all around the aircraft and spotted a patch of ragged metal on the port wing. Little fragments of metal trailed in the slipstream with scorch marks all around. The aircraft had climbed well enough but would it manoeuvre? Several gentle turns reassured her. Phew! Thank goodness for bad shots.

She checked the plot again and made a small adjustment to

the flight path, veering slightly to the west to line up with the West Country.

Admittedly, flying without sight of land and relying on the compass would be problematic. Still, what really bugged her most was the ridiculous ruling that Auxiliary flyers were not allowed to have radio sets, robbing them of an easy way to check their navigation. Her destination was a fighter airfield almost on top of Portland Bill and they urgently needed this Spitfire Mark 12. They were down by three machines after being jumped on a patrol over Calais the day before.

She glanced again at the compass, confident now that she would make it to Weymouth. The Merlin engine was performing as it should and she ignored several unfamiliar noises. There were bound to be a few aches and pains after being pasted by the gunners. She was conscious of being alone in an enormous sky empty of aircraft and no sign of a break in the cloud.

Still a way to go and Helen's concentration began to wander back to her family and young Peter and the life they led at the sprawling farmhouse in Suffolk. Last week she had been particularly piqued by Ursula – the Hon. Ursula, the one with all the swagger and the exotic bouffant hair-do – who had made conversation in the ferry hut and asked her in her seemingly innocent way how her son was progressing at school.

Helen wasn't fooled. A barb disguised as concern. An unspoken accusation masquerading as interest. A sub-text that read: what are you doing in Hatfield? A mother should be at home with her child.

'Loves his school.' Helen's reply. 'A really happy little boy – but then at home he has the run of my parents' place, any boy's idea of paradise.'

Paradise. That was a key word. And the image in Helen's mind at that moment flickered away from the Suffolk farm to a garden path along which strode the bronzed figure of a pilot officer in the RAF's Eagle Squadron, his cap set at a jaunty angle, the boundless confidence of an American volunteer, complete with Clark Gable grin. A portrait of past happiness backlit by a rosy sun.

But the Hon. Ursula broke the spell. There had always been enmity between them. 'But wouldn't it be better if your son had his mother at home?'

'Weekends,' Helen replied defensively. 'Something really to look forward to. For both of us.' The image of the elegant man on the garden path faded in favour of the Suffolk farm, to a picture of Peter having fun. 'He's fine,' she said. 'Doting granny, crazy grandpa, exciting uncles and a great playground. Swords to make, sheds to hide in, streams to jump, old cars to sit in.' She smiled at the thought, refusing to be fazed by Ursula and others who just didn't get it.

A small concern broke her train of thought. The compass was telling her to make another change. Furrows at the brow! Should she have checked it herself before take-off? Some of her colleagues, of course, would have advised turning back at the end of that cloud-enclosed valley; others would say that she should never have taken off. She might be the only 'Attagirl' flying today but she was going to make it. She'd have the last laugh. Wouldn't she?

Then she was back to introspection, back to thinking about her past, hurt when she recalled how some of her contemporaries had accused her of arrogance. Really! So untrue, so unfair. She'd done her best to fit in. Not a trace of the prima donna. She considered herself an absolutely normal person. Nothing out of the ordinary. Loved the country life, being with her son, working in the hangar on the engine of her Gipsy Moth, helping to serve dinners at the Bury orphanage, going to dances, dressing up, parties. She freely admitted it; she was a romantic. She'd only known her husband for a proverbial five minutes before taking the plunge. At this point she was fully into self-justification... *I'm shy and modest by nature. Only when it really counts am I assertive. I want what any other mother wants.*

But first and foremost, of course, there was that over-riding sense of mission to fulfil; a duty to the war, the urge to get back at a cruel and ruthless enemy but also a duty to herself that was intensely personal.

Still thoughtful, she peered out at the cloud once more... and realisation finally came to her. She'd been so deep in her past she hadn't been paying attention. Her eyes flew to the fuel gauge. She drew in a sharp breath, glancing quickly at the clock. Damn it! She swallowed and admonished herself for losing concentration. She'd lost track of time, flying nearly to the limit. Should be there by now.

Time to get down again. A careful, gradual descent. Down, down, down – and finally, at last, breaking clear of that darned cloud, searching for landmarks.

Oh my God! I'm over the sea!

Chapter Six

Helen swallowed and looked at the waves and the cold, cold water and the endless dark depths below. The cockpit was just above freezing, despite the big fleece, and her eyes weren't quite focusing. The hand of fear had gripped her.

Deep breaths and think! Don't panic, she told herself. *Don't go to pieces. Just use the compass.*

Then reality finally dawned. She had been using the compass – and this was where it had got her.

The fuel gauge was hovering close to empty and when she turned her head to look back to the right and then the left there was neither smudge nor smidgen, not even a miniscule dot of land. What she had been dreaming of a few minutes before had been a pristine horizon. Now she had it, and it was shorn of all human trace.

Instinctively, she reckoned she must have overshot the coast and left land far behind. Behind – the opposite direction to the way she was flying! So, holding her breath, she nosed the aircraft round in a gentle circle, heading back the way she'd come. The way she thought she had come.

Please, she pleaded with an animated version of the coast in her head, *Show yourself!*

But it didn't.

Impatience, pride, ego. She admitted these had been her downfall. Don't wait for the weather... Don't waste time getting the compass checked... Just get on with it! In a painfully penitent mood, she confessed her errors. Any minute now the fuel would cut and the plane would glide for a short time before stalling. Now was the moment to face up to the sheer ghastliness of her options.

Over land, she might have been able to bale out with a half decent chance of survival, but the sea was cold and who knew when – or if – rescue might arrive. On the other hand ditching the aircraft in the sea was not recommended. The bible for ferry pilots, the blue book of Pilot's Notes, advised against it. The aircraft, they said, did not possess good characteristics in water. What they meant, of course, was that if you put your nose in first, as you might well do in a sea that was not as calm as a mill pond, you'd probably do a submarine and dive straight to the bottom. But if you were in luck and could get your tail down first to break the worst of the shock and cut the speed the machine might just survive and float – for a short while – but would also probably turn turtle and trap you upside down under water.

She looked ahead. Still no sign of land and the needle on the gauge was dead on empty.

Time to make the decision: *jump or ditch?*

The decision was jump. Even in a funk, Helen could be decisive.

First, she needed height, pulling the nose up, heart pounding, praying the fuel didn't cut off before the aircraft was high enough for the parachute to work.

She looked down inside the cockpit working out the mechanics of the next few seconds. Good job she'd insisted on having a dinghy pack as part of her parachute kit, citing proximity to the coast as justification, despite opposition. It must have been an unconscious premonition of disaster.

Now she swallowed and tried to remember the escape drill.

Check the chute and release the straps... Right, done!

Now jettison the canopy.

Whoof! With this gone the air flow whacked her in the face and she instinctively shrank back to re-consider. Perhaps a ditching after all?

Get a grip! An internal voice shouted at her from somewhere behind her skull. *Don't funk it! Let go of the stick!*

She swallowed, tensed, then did it. This bunted the aircraft into a sudden dive, instantly shooting her into space. A massive shock as the Spit dropped away.

The terror of empty space, of having no purchase on anything, of shooting helplessly through the sky. Roaring in the ears, wind slashing like a knife across the face, hands outstretched like a human fly. *Don't react, wait, time it, just like on that other occasion, then pull the cord.*

Crack! The biggest jerk and sudden arrest you've ever imagined. The wind knocked out of her.

And then a great silence. No engine noise, no shouty sergeants. Floating down on a gentle breeze, the sea coming up to meet her, closer and closer.

Just before hitting the water, release the parachute straps – she remembered that much from training so the dinghy pack could detach from the chute.

She expected splashdown to be cold but it was worse, like hitting an iceberg. She came up like an angry walrus, snorting and blowing water from her nose. The chill shock of it was beyond expectation. Jumping into the swimming pool back in Southampton, during dinghy drill, was nothing compared to reality. She was overwhelmed by the sheer immensity of the sea. Of course it was immense, but close up, with her head just above water, her vulnerability sent a chill stab of panic to the brain.

Then the folds of the chute flopped down into the waves all around her, like some giant skirt and parts of it covered her, so she had to fight her way clear. The dinghy had inflated automatically, thanks to an attached CO_2 bottle, and was held close by a short cord. But how to get in? She desperately searched her memory for the right way to board without her bodyweight tipping the thing on top of her. She paddled frantically, fumbled in the cold, splashed and struggled, remembered vaguely about a water-filled counterweight, grabbed the side and finally, with a huge expenditure of panting effort, wriggled and dragged herself over the side and in.

Hideous, simply hideous. She was shivering and shaking. *But you've made it down*, she told herself. *Now cope with the next ordeal. You're aboard, a vast achievement, immediate danger denied.* Her mind flicked back to that other parachute jump – the one she'd made in her teenage years, answering a challenge from her brothers, and when they'd congratulated her on landing smoothly she'd given them her special derisive stare; The Stare, that said 'Anything you two can do, I can do too'.

Now she lay back, panting, trying for distractions, telling herself to think of something wonderful. Pink ice cream, marmalade sandwiches, reading *The Wind in the Willows*, dinner at the Regal, hide-and-seek with Peter, walking up the aisle.

How she wished to turn the clock back to those good times. Were they gone, or might she see some of them again?

There was a slight swell and a small wave broke over the side of the dinghy, soaking her again. That was when she realised her boots had gone. An absurdly odd thought: when – or if – she got back to the depot and they asked her how she coped, she could tell them with a rueful if truthful smile: 'Well, I got my toes wet.'

The Spit had vanished, swallowed up somewhere beyond her vision, and she was fearful of the swell, remembering another tale they told in the ferry hut about a ditched pilot who swam for nearly two hours before being rescued from the sea. However, she didn't rate her chances if a sudden wave tipped her out of the dinghy.

Instead, she tried to think of other things. Of nicer things. Of Peter joyful at her arrival on a Friday night, of doing crazy stuff together, exploring a tiny island 'looking for cannibals', bargaining with market traders holding a sixpence, of daring rides in the park and a cowboy film at Bury's Plaza.

And then that other figure who was never far from her mind. She saw his image again, quite clearly defined, as if he were sharing her ordeal in the dinghy, could hear the timbre of his voice. There were tears in her smile as she played out the scene in her mind; his sparkling eyes, his height and stature and his implacable determination to get in the air to help 'your plucky little island to fight off those vicious Nazis'. She laughed out loud, realising there was no one to hear her, just the sea. And then she cried.

Saturated feet and sloshing water forced her to start baling. What had happened to the RAF rescue boats? Did they patrol this part of the sea, whichever part of the sea this was? How long could this dinghy stay afloat?

Questions, questions. Better to think back to flying expeditions long past. Tehran, Baghdad, Calcutta and goodness knew where else. Just as well she was comfortable in her own company. Served her well on all those tedious flights across endless trackless territory with only a compass and a novel for distraction.

Don't mention the compass!

She considered, without arriving at any answers, the prospect of a long period tossed about in the Channel. The tide seemed to be pulling in one direction, so she must arrive somewhere soon. Surely?

Then an awful thought: the wide open Atlantic?

For a time her mind went into a kind of suspension in which there were no thoughts at all. And when something in the sea jerked her back to full consciousness she refused to accept the possibility of obliteration. She said it out loud: 'I'm too young to die.'

Instead there were optimistic images of frantic planning sessions at some highly organised and efficient rescue centre. The RAF were ordering out their rescue boats, though she had no idea if they covered this far down the Channel. She visualised a crowded room full of men in sou'westers working at chalkboards and coloured diagrams. They were shouting her name and an estimate of her last position.

Pity about the absence of wireless. Pity about that compass.

Then a sudden doubt. *Be realistic!* This was probably all wishful thinking. At this fraught time of the conflict, men drowned every day and planes crashed on a daily basis. It was war. It was normal.

Another wave swamped the bottom of the dinghy and brought her back to the stark reality of her predicament. Would she ever see her son again? Or mother, father, brothers Thomas and Nat. How would Peter cope without a mother?

Her eyes were moist as she thought about her boy. Never seeing him again – that brought an acute pain to the chest. Surely, cutting short the joy of motherhood was the ultimate cruelty. Never again seeing Peter in the back garden kicking a football, wearing his Bury Town shirt, his inexhaustible energy an amazement to her; never seeing him write so beautifully in his homework book with its little stick-man drawings; never hearing him piping up, perhaps stumbling a little, over his eight times table.

If only Hank had survived to see the fast-growing boy's progress; how wonderful it would have been to see him in action as a father.

Memories were both a pain and a pleasure, distracting her from the discomfort of the dinghy. The action-packed weekends, days of attention and tutoring, the spelling bees and the counting sessions were all part of it. 'I don't want to write any more, I want to go out to the meadow' was met with stern advice: 'You've had all week to play, now you must work to become a clever boy, to make the best of yourself.'

Had she been too harsh, too eager to compensate for her weekday absences? Mothers and daughters didn't always see eye to eye, particularly over parenting.

'Leave off, he's only a little kid,' said her mother.

'But you indulge him...'

Episodes from Peter's past floated into mind: the day he went missing and the whole family searched frantically, fearing he had fallen into the river, only to find him at the old tower that had once been a windmill and now occupied by a wizened old man the local kids called a wizard; or the time he spent hours watching the riverbank hoping to catch a glimpse of fox cubs playing outside the earth.

'You told me to love nature,' he'd explained at the time. He loved to throw her objections back at her. And later: 'I'm exploring, I'm on adventure, like *Just William*.' Or when disappearing once again on his Fairy bicycle, 'William never asked his mummy first.'

Helen decided then the moment had arrived to change the storybook. The William stories were giving him too many ideas. And how had the childless author Richmal Crompton become so uniquely insightful of young boys?

Her mind wandered again, this time about herself, asking: is this what I'm doing, going on the adult version of a *Just William* adventure? Is Peter like me; am I like him?

'Supposing you got lost?' she demanded of her young son at the conclusion of another adventure.

'I'd ask a policeman.'

This boy had all the answers; six going on sixteen.

Gradually time ceased to have meaning and her eyes fluttered with fatigue. She lay back in the dinghy, her thoughts reduced to a kind of fine mist and she was ready to take whatever fate had in store, this being a situation she could do little about. No point in paddling because she had no idea which way. The sea was making the decision, taking her inexorably in one direction. Night had fallen, though there was still light enough to see.

How long could a person last without food or water? Would she float for ever on the ocean until reduced to a starved skeleton, destroyed by exposure, cold, hunger, thirst, or the next big wave which tipped her into the deep?

She felt like a human iceberg. Had never been so cold, couldn't feel her feet, must have done something dreadful to them, trench foot or decay, her body stiff and difficult to move.

Later, much later, when daybreak arrived, she sensed something about the sea had changed. Seemed calmer, smoother even, and she raised herself just enough to look out at the horizon.

A shock, the unexpected. What in fact she had dreamed of – land, and surprisingly close. A long smooth sandy beach reached right across her line of vision. And on the beach were human figures and animals.

Even in her battered state of half-aware consciousness she was mystified. She was looking at a completely lonely spit of land unbroken by any permanent trace of normal activity, nothing to nail it down, no clue as to where she might be. It did not seem to be a place where people came to swim or paddle or play with their children; no umbrellas, no seaside chalets, just a vast open expanse of sand peopled only by these strange figures.

She looked again, closer and more concentrated, all drowsiness gone, and established that these people were riding and exercising horses.

She blinked in disbelief. No, not people as she had first thought, but just one person, a male rider, active and galloping, with a second figure stationary and waiting, holding two more animals, as if in readiness.

Helen rubbed her eyes, taking in a scene she never expected to see.

Chapter Seven

S tiff and painful as it was, Helen levered herself upright and attempted to paddle with her hands towards the shore. Her efforts were not immediately effective and she soon gave up when it became obvious the dinghy was drifting shoreward.

As she came closer she could see the man, now dismounted, his attention fully fixed on her imminent arrival, waiting for the dinghy to come within reach.

Her rescuer.

She tried to stand but pain seared through her shoulders and her legs gave way, flopping her back into her watery seat. Just before the dinghy grounded, she grunted with a huge effort and forced herself to try again.

This man – medium height, middle age, close cropped fair hair – stretched out a hand as she staggered once more and fell. He had almost to drag her out of the dinghy before bringing her upright.

'Where am I?' A hoarse voice, which she hardly recognised as her own.

He chortled. 'Jersey, of course. My private beach. Now,' he added, 'can you walk? The house is just over there.'

Of course she couldn't walk. She'd spent the whole darned night and untold hours of daylight stretched out like a frozen lump of polar flesh in a brutally uncomfortable canvas monstrosity that someone had the nerve to call a boat. She felt paralysed and incapable. And now it seemed she'd ended up in the Channel Isles.

'No, of course you can't walk,' he conceded and turned around to yell at the other figure some way behind. 'Hans, bring the Kubelwagon round.'

This piece of dialogue was a slap in the face sufficient to wake the dead. Slowly, even in her brain-fogged state, she put it together. Hans? Kubel-thingy? Memory and realisation came together. This man wasn't some ordinary Mr Nice Guy, even though he spoke perfectly unaccented English. A nasty little fact registered: the Channel Islands had been conquered by Hitler, occupied by the enemy. This was Nazi territory!

He was looking puzzled at the dinghy, as if he'd never seen one before, and then at Helen and then at her sodden and bedraggled overalls. 'You're not local, are you?' he said with a frown, like he'd just unearthed a rare fossil, and it wasn't really a question. 'You're English!'

She should have protested. Or at least made some defiant statement. Perhaps asking what he thought he was doing on British territory, prancing up and down one of His Britannic Majesty's beaches, exercising his horses where mums, dads and kiddies should have been digging in the sand with buckets and spades, but she was not sure she was capable of putting the words in the right order.

'You're in a bad condition,' he said, stating the blindingly obvious. 'We should get you indoors, dried out, fed, watered and rested.'

'To the PoW camp,' she muttered sourly.

'No, no,' he said, smiling broadly, 'you'll be my guest.'

Helen closed her eyes at this. Was she dreaming?

She could not believe in this man or the situation. She couldn't believe his friendliness, nor his factotum Hans, who seamlessly eased her into a seat on this strange jeep-like truck. She clutched for a handhold, frightened that in her weakened state she might fall out.

The vehicle was driven up the beach and into a highly tended garden, where a strange old house came into view. It seemed to be made up of several different buildings bolted together; turrets, towers, dormers, vast tiled roofs, tall chimneys and a grand columned entrance which in a moment of complete irrelevance she decided was a pompous architectural affectation.

This place which, in more normal circumstances, might have appealed as a curiosity, now took on a dark and forbidding ambience, threatening even, like some potential house of horrors. A chill went through her, worse than the damp reality of her condition. She was in enemy hands; this was to be her Strangeways, her Dartmoor. Would she ever emerge from it alive, as a person recognisable as herself? Everything was clearly set for a painful incarceration, perhaps torture, perhaps mental manipulation. Who knew what demonic new techniques for personal destruction they had invented. This ancient heap would be her nemesis.

She swallowed hard, made a conscious effort to pull herself together and ditch the quavering in her stomach. A loud warning voice resounded around inside her head: *Don't fall for this man's line in soft soap, Helen, don't collapse.*

More stern talking-to. *No relaxing, tighten your lips, stick out your chin. He mustn't think he's won you over, lulled you, got you under control.*

The truck stopped and she heaved herself painfully out of the seat before embarrassingly helpful hands arrived. Then she tried for a dead-eyed hostile glare, a no-nonsense, no-thank-you aggression in response to his playing the gentleman.

Never show fear. She knew that right enough. Fear was what bullies fed off. Hadn't she seen enough in the past? Base-wallahs who thought women couldn't fly.

But when she faced this man on his own threshold she could only manage a mild-mannered, almost sickeningly polite, 'Who are you?'

Instantly, the words hardly off her tongue, she beat herself up. Where was the woman who could jump out of an aeroplane, fly to Calcutta and pilot a Spit? She swallowed. The uncomfortable truth was, right now, she didn't feel brave at all.

'Friedrich Winter,' he answered evenly, despite her ungracious tone, 'and you're very lucky you landed on my private beach. Anywhere else on this island and you'd now be enjoying the dubious company of our Mr Wolf whose manners, I regret to say, are not quite up to scratch.'

She looked at him blankly, confused and puzzled by the ease and usage of English idiom, which surely meant dual nationality or split parentage. She looked down. Her shoulders sagged. Keeping up an aggressive front was just too much effort. Her lips were sore, her body felt it belonged to someone else, her limbs a torture. Fatigued and powerless, the last remaining dregs of strength were draining away. Willpower sapped. She stopped observing or thinking and just let things happen.

Guiding hands helped her up a wide creaking wooden staircase, lest she stumble or fall. No more protests. And here was a massive bathroom with old-fashioned gilt taps and a bath full of steaming hot water. Towels, soap and oils. All the amenities provided by the all-encompassing helpful but silent factotum Hans. Now, in his absence, a blessed relief. Wonderful warmth, beginning to feel her body again, feet once more part of her. A robe, a chicken sandwich, even a glass of Liebfraumilch.

This is how they soften you up, Helen, make you thankful, grateful, vulnerable. Remember who you are. Remember who he is.

Remember these are the people who kill and bomb and deprive you of your loved ones.

Chapter Eight

The bed was vast, a bliss of soft relief, impossible to refuse. Impossible also to leave. Even when she awoke, without any idea of how much later, mind and body would not give it up. A refuge, a safe haven, her sanctuary, hiding from this strange new world she had just entered, a topsy-turvy predicament for which she was ill prepared.

The bed was a deep and comfortable retreat. She shrank into its soft and embracing touch and ignored several intrusive sounds from outside the room she did not wish to hear: a clink of metal which might have been a spade on stone, the distant thudding of horse hooves and later the drone of an aircraft, reminding her of her own foolish mistake.

No hustle, no call, nothing to disturb her, so eventually she emerged with great reluctance from her semi-conscious stupor, sat upright and confronted her new reality. Despite the warmth and comfort, she began to shiver. And then it got worse and wouldn't stop. It wasn't the cold. Common sense told her it was shock. She knew the symptoms well enough, seen enough cases of trauma, the Blitz had been a continuous horror.

Tears blurred her vision. Would she see home again? Was

this the result of her determination to fly? How stupid to land herself in this mess! Careless, foolhardy, complacent. A massive blot on the big aviation reputation. Right now they'd be trashing it back in Weymouth. And escape? Idiot! Jersey was an island.

Worse; was she about to turn her son into an orphan?

The thought of never seeing Peter again was a horror and she buried her head in a pillow.

Later, realising she couldn't hide for ever, she discovered a set of dry clothes put out for her, consisting of trousers and a shirt. She shrugged and put them on and went to examine the room. This only made her more depressed: no obvious exit or escape route and the sheer luxury of her 'prison' was confusing to her. The bathroom, with gold taps and several huge basins, was roomy enough for her old school hockey team to perform their ablutions.

In the corner of the bedroom a mahogany writing desk with candlesticks caught her attention. She began to fiddle absent-mindedly with it, discovering the secret of a false front and a hidden compartment which, alas, proved to be empty.

She shuddered at a hideous ornamental musical clock dominating a side table alongside a couple of figurines and knew just enough about antiques from her mother's dabbling at fairs and the Jakes and Hardisty Emporium in Bury's West Outgate to guess at Louis the 14th.

The headboard had a double scroll and next to it an expansive beechwood wardrobe supported a floor-to-ceiling mirror. She looked away, not wanting to confront the diminished figure she had become.

Instead, she peered from the window to see extensive well-manicured gardens. A man was working in the far distance. She wondered about the nature and wealth of the family who lived in this house before the occupation and their subsequent fate. Anything, in fact, to avoid thinking about her next move.

There was that strange entrance she had seen on arriving at the house, its medley of styles and the pompous columns; how she hated fake grandeur added to inappropriate buildings. More avoidance, more reverting to past pleasures; to happy memories, to pink ice cream, yellow roses and ice skating at Richmond on Christmas Eve.

She was putting off for as long as possible the unpleasant task of facing up to the consequences of her perilous situation. Part of her wanted to continue the pretence of being treated as an honoured guest at a country house party. Part of her wanted simply to climb back into the luxurious bed, remaining there indefinitely, telling herself this was all a bad dream. She looked longingly at the warm, inviting sheets – and stopped.

A new resolution. *Get a grip!*

She stopped thinking about creature comforts. She was a pilot officer and officers were expected to confront reality, not hide from it. Flying unfamiliar aircraft, blazing new routes, even climbing mountains or racing cars, these were what she knew, but finding herself unexpectedly at the mercy of the enemy, how did you cope with that?

Then another reminder: only days before she had vowed vengeance on those responsible for engineering death and destruction on a massive scale.

Finally, a deep breath and a new determination. Time to confront the enemy. Time to confront the man downstairs.

Chapter Nine

S he found Winter seated on a chintz sofa in the lounge, another essay in luxury. Over the fireplace a huge painting was strangely reminiscent of a Constable scene – was a Constable, she discovered later. Adding to the impression of luxury was an elaborate candelabra and a decorative white ceiling bearing a family coat of arms.

How should she play this? One word out of place, she cautioned herself, just one misjudged phrase might be sufficient to cause a sea-change in her reception; from hospitality to hostility in double quick order.

She studied the open face of her captor, the relaxed features, the smile playing at the corners of his mouth and decided there was no way of wrapping up the obvious questions. So she took a deep breath and plunged straight in. 'Who are you really, and what is this place?'

He grinned and dogs ran freely around the room, dashing crazily about, chasing one another in an excitable pack, the advent of a newcomer creating something approaching canine frenzy. Her strange host ignored all this, leaving his sofa and ploughing right through the pack. It clearly did not occur to him that his 'guest' might not be a dog-friendly person.

Fortunately, dogs were as common as sheep on her Suffolk farm and now a particularly appealing black Labrador marked her out as a new friend.

'That's Tiggy,' he said, standing before her. 'Loves women.'

This alerted her to another mystifying fact about this household. No evidence of a female human presence. The ever available loyal factotum Hans seemed to be the only other occupant, bar a gardener and another presence she recalled from outside – someone dealing with the horses: in the Kubelwagon they'd passed a low building which might have been a stable.

She was determined not to be thrown off track. 'You're not in the military?' she ventured, not having seen any uniforms.

Winter merely smiled and indicated a chair. 'Feeling better now? Rested?'

She nodded, emboldened enough to consider inquiring about his immaculate English, his adroitness with the vernacular, speculating on a multi-lingual family background, yet a cautionary impulse told her this would be pushing familiarity too far. *Remember who he is! These are the people who rampage around the world bombing and massacring.* By rights she should hate him and hold his kind in contempt, but it was quite difficult to hate the flesh and blood Friedrich Winter.

She almost asked him – wanted very much to ask – about his family. There were no women here, so was he married; did he have children, how did he feel about their survival prospects in the war, how did he feel about sudden death?

She thought then about her own prospects, entertaining a sliver of hope, despite her situation, that she might survive, even possibly escape.

'Been here long?' she asked, restarting the conversation.

'Long enough.'

'You live here in this big house almost alone, save for all these dogs and horses to keep you company?'

'That's been my life.' He smiled. 'Dogs, horses and, of course, the land.'

His emphasis on the last alerted her. Perhaps he was some sort of landed aristocrat with a vast estate back in Central Europe peopled by respectful tenants doffing their caps. She went ahead and said it. 'You strike me... well, you seem to be almost like a gentleman farmer.'

'That's because I am,' he said. Far from being offended by her remark, he seemed pleased with the description. 'In peacetime life, I am a gentleman farmer.'

The easy-going nature of this conversation disturbed her. She had been full of rage and an impulse for vengeance when she'd been bombed and blasted by the V-1 in London, but this meeting seemed to be on a different level. When you came face to face with your enemy and he wasn't wielding a sword or making threatening gestures – wasn't even exhibiting the faintest hint of a snarl – how should you react to his humanity? How long did hate last?

'So tell me,' she said, almost confidentially, 'who are you really?'

And when he told her she almost fell out of her chair.

Chapter Ten

S he felt her senses go liquid and a sudden constriction of the chest when he informed her matter-of-factly, almost casually, that he was the deputy commander of German forces on the island of Jersey.

Her hopes of survival took a steep dive. She clenched a fist until the knuckles went white.

However, Friedrich Winter's mission, he would have it appear, was to be as British-friendly as it was possible for an enemy to be. 'We plan to run the perfect occupation, that's our aim,' he said, 'to show the rest of the English just how fair-minded we can be.'

She wasn't so quick this time to melt in the face of his geniality. Was this too good to be true? She was on her guard against trickery or propaganda.

'Actually,' Friedrich Winter said, demonstrating once again his command of the language, 'your arrival here at this time is extremely fortuitous. I can foresee a useful role for you. Consider yourself my guest.'

She didn't react. Instead, she would demonstrate that she was no easy conquest, that she knew a thing or two about foreign occupations. 'So tell me, commander, how do you treat the natives around here?'

'With civility and due respect for their rights.'

Not what she expected to hear. She snorted in disbelief, quite forgetting her earlier caution about being careful with her words. 'But you're the representative of a very aggressive warlike nation.'

'Not here. Not in the Channel Islands.'

'Not so gentle in France, I hear.'

'Over that I'm afraid I have no control.' He looked at her as if desperate to persuade her. 'Look, I have to say, I personally very much hope to see an end to this conflict. I would like to see peace restored to the world.'

She wasn't sure she was hearing correctly. 'Do you broadcast this message of peace and goodwill across the world?'

He smiled but didn't answer, emboldening her to go further: 'Do the rest of your gentlemen at arms concur with this philosophy?'

Again, he didn't answer, and that phrase came back to her... *one wrong word...*

Then another thought, another dark possibility; if he had any plans for a secret dalliance, turning her into his private sexual plaything, he could think again. She could fight. She would fight. Fists, nails, knees, anything sharp to hand.

However, calming down, Helen had the sense that this man was above and beyond mere self-indulgence; that some other factor was at work.

'As it happens I have more guests arriving tonight. For a meeting. And it's quite possible they may wish to meet you.'

She was speechless. This was getting crazier and crazier. Note the word *wish*, not *demand*. And for a guest, it was a mighty strange arrangement.

When she entered the bedroom once more the key rattled in

the lock behind her. That gave the lie to the effusive flags of welcome, now revealed as the gestures and generosity of a polite jailer. A big welcome mat, but one she couldn't step away from.

For a locked-in guest, surely, there was only one answer. Escape. Getting right away from this lunatic place.

But then she didn't feel up to the role of the intrepid escaper. She felt lonely and abandoned, facing an uncertain future with no one to consult and no source of advice on how she should react. For all the courtesy and kindliness of the man downstairs, the prospect of a dramatic change of fortune would not recede from her mind. The dreaded spectre of the Gestapo and the brutality of the Nazi security state festered away in her imagination, gnawing at her self-control.

Her eyes flickered. How would her brothers have coped? How would he... her Hank? She thought about them, all of them, longing for their presence and their insight, trying to guess their reactions.

The answer when it came was simple.

To use the only thing she had left. Her wits.

Chapter Eleven

The windows of the bedroom were shut tight and probably fixed and there was no obvious way out, so Helen sat on the bed to examine minutely the red and white patterns of the vast bedspread, while facing up to the frightening prospect that she probably wouldn't be seeing home again.

Her doleful reverie was interrupted by the sound of many arrivals. None of the windows gave on to the front of the house or the main driveway but car doors were slamming, heavy boots were biting gravel and indistinct voices floating up to her. She also heard footsteps on a nearby staircase and began to wonder about Friedrich Winter's guests and what they could possibly want with her.

Nothing more happened for at least an hour, then came a tap at the door and the voice of the arch factotum Hans: her presence was requested in the dining room.

Should she refuse? Make a bolt for it?

Instead she followed the man down the stairs, captive to intrigue but fearing that her status was about to change. She was led through a long, narrow book-lined room, noting the English titles and wondering again about the fate of the previous occupants. Elaborate chandeliers, mock medieval fireplace, Delftware dinner service, a long case clock, a huge carved Flemish table. All this spoke to serious wealth, confirmed when she entered a huge reception room which had become a smoky, noisy male den. All voices ceased as she was shown to a seat.

Never show fear was a fine exhortation – but difficult to maintain under the intense scrutiny of half a dozen pairs of unfriendly eyes. She could sense a hostile curiosity, felt them stripping her bare, savouring what lay ahead, like predators glimpsing prey.

Friedrich Winter was seated close to another massive fireplace topped by an elaborate Italian clock and faded portraits. He was still in civilian dress and she was not introduced. Next to him, a stiff unbending elderly man wore a strange set of clothes suggestive of a deerstalker and to whom clear signs of deference were extended.

On the other side of a long table, a middle-aged figure in field grey stared unblinkingly at her, a contemptuous smile playing around prominent lips, and she was conscious of a haughty swagger about the two younger men in air force blue.

She crossed her arms, hands clutching the upper sides to stop the shakes, and forced her right foot hard into the carpet to still a jumping nerve.

If the ensuing silence was designed as a form of intimidation, she would meet it with a stern gaze. She kept her expression as rigid as she could make it. False bravado, of course; she was trembling inside.

She would dearly love to slink away, back to the bedroom to drink coffee and eat cake, and not have to sit like a star exhibit on display, but she stuck to her resolve, despite the dry mouth and the clammy hands. She was acutely conscious of being a single helpless female in a roomful of men; she had no rights, no protection, was completely at their mercy.

51

Horrific images of abuse, humiliation and violation plucked at her consciousness but she forced herself to keep control. There was one notable consolation: no black uniforms. Perhaps the island was free of Gestapo and the SD. The earlier relaxed state of her 'host' had suggested this.

Suddenly it struck Helen that this was like a viewing session at the zoo and she occupied the wrong side of the wire. The spectators studied her with unabashed attention, unaware that the 'animal' on display viewed them in equal measure of curiosity and disdain. Did this lot smell? Eat strange food? Wear strange rags? Two species eyeing once another in a state of mutual incomprehension.

A mistaken phrase could seal her fate. She feared the nod or the glacial glance that might signal her doom; the sentence of death that might spill from cruel lips.

Chapter Twelve

Friedrich Winter was acting like a master of ceremonies. After some preliminaries she did not understand, the grilling began. They all appeared adept with the language of their enemy, but were intrigued and sceptical that women were allowed to fly, even more so when mention was made of the Spitfire. Women in fighter planes? They couldn't credit it.

'Don't you have enough men to go round?' asked a uniformed colonel – she'd recognised his badge of rank from all those lectures back at base. 'Are the Allies running so short of manpower they now have to use women?'

'We use our feminine resource rather better than you do,' she said. 'Could cost you in the end.'

'In bombers too? Surely not on operations?'

She looked out of the window unwilling to be too ready with the answers.

How did she manage to become so lost, they wanted to know, didn't she use a compass? The colonel persisted: 'How is it possible to be so far off track, across such a large area of sea? An awful long way to drift...'

'Serious mechanical and navigational malfunction,' she said. 'You can cover an awful lot of sea at 300 miles an hour.'

The question and answer session took on a lighter touch when they heard about her pre-war flying exploits. Her reputation here seemed to settle their doubts. A young air force lieutenant piped up about his pre-war experiences in Africa, flying a similar aircraft and with this the atmosphere lightened. And all this time she was aware of a little guy in the corner with smarmed down hair, the third person in the room who didn't rate a uniform, and he had been staring hard in her direction. Not saying a single word.

Eventually Winter invited her to 'Leave us now and return to your room.' Coffee and cakes had been provided by the ever-reliable Hans and were apparently already in place.

By now some of her fear had dissipated and she had the distinct impression that she had passed some sort of test.

But what kind of a test? And what was the hidden issue?

Chapter Thirteen

I t was a parade of all the good things in her life that she would never get to experience again. A kaleidoscope of horror.

The optimistic note of the strange meeting did not last long. Locked once more in the bedroom, her mood swung violently in the opposite direction. Tears welled, her chest heaved and she closed her eyes, trying to blot out a spinning whirligig of images from her past that tortured her present. Her brothers around the big old oak table in the farmhouse kitchen, urging her on, daring her to fly further and faster; Pa hammering furiously in one of his many sheds, repairing a jalopy; Mother baking an apple pie and, dearest of all, Peter dressed in his cute new school uniform reciting his times tables, proving what a fine young man he promised to be.

She gulped, seeing him amid the much cherished clutter of his room: bunk bed, books, toys, a clock with huge figures and hands, photos of him as a baby as if he needed reminding, a bucket full of coloured wooden bricks.

He was her flesh and blood. He was part of her and she had vowed to enjoy and treasure his childhood, thinking how short it might be, fearing he would grow away from her, dreading the time when he reached maturity and another woman became his Number One. She knew other mothers kept their adult son's bedrooms ready for a return or treasured artefacts of a long-departed personality. Sad, very sad.

And now it would all be cut short for her. She wouldn't be there to guide her boy, to help him and to love him.

Interrupted by a summons to the ground floor, Helen managed to arrive dry-eyed, anxious and furious all at the same time. Her distress was such that she overcame her forebodings to seek a proper explanation of her position. She felt – enemy or not – that Friedrich Winter was a decent man. She'd expected to be confronting a bully, but in fact he seemed almost avuncular. In the moment that followed he merely smiled and promised she would be told everything in due course, adding archly that she had arrived on the island 'at a most opportune moment'. In the meantime he pressed her to meet 'someone I think you will find quite interesting'.

She was wary. Why should she?

'No pressure,' he said, like some slick salesman – she could hardly believe this treatment – 'but I think you'll like him. He's an engineer.'

She shrugged and waited, as asked, in the lounge, wondering what was next in this weird set-up when in walked the little man she had spotted at the meeting. The one who said not a word. Small, with slicked down hair, staring eyes. Eyed her the whole time while the others did the talking. Never a comfortable feeling.

He extended a hand and said his name, which she didn't catch, but in an accent that seemed strangely mid-Atlantic.

'You're an engineer.'

He nodded.

'In what?'

'I worked on the rockets.'

She gasped. Was he talking about the hated V-1 his dreaded compatriots were sending over from the launch pads in France? 'Not... the doodlebug? The buzz-bomb that's killing our people in London?'

He swallowed. 'No, not the V-1... This, I'm afraid, is more powerful. It's a rocket, maybe you don't know about it yet.'

A deep freeze moment between them.

'We know it,' he said, 'as the V-2.'

'Then you're no friend of mine. Why the hell would I want to talk to you?' she spluttered in indignation and rose from her chair. She would walk out. She wasn't staying in the presence of this wretch. How could they expect her to talk to someone responsible for spreading death and destruction around the capital these past few weeks? The doodlebugs were bad enough – and now she knew from her talk with Devereaux that worse was to come.

'You!' she accused, standing over him, pointing a finger, preparing to walk out, 'you and your grisly friends nearly killed a friend of mine. And worse, you've killed dozens with your damned buzz-bombs, d'you realise that?'

He nodded and looked down. 'I know. I bitterly regret it.'

'Only last week dozens of people died in London.' Suddenly the memory of it returned full blooded and red hot. 'Dozens, simply dozens! Bodies all over the place. Carnage. You'll have to do more than just regret it. You should be strung up.' She turned and marched towards the door, ignoring the fact that she had nowhere to go.

'Excuse me.' A strangely diffident tone. 'Please come back. I need to talk to you.'

She swivelled and faced him from by the door. 'What can you possibly say that I would want to hear?'

'There's something I have to say.'

He seemed so docile, so lacking in aggression, so un-German that she hesitated, took a deep breath, and slowly returned to her seat.

'It's because it's all so horrible that I want to make amends,' he said.

For a moment she could not find a response, still outraged that Winter thought she would want to talk to this man, but she stayed silent, contenting herself with a hostile glare. Slowly, however, as he began to speak, she became intrigued by the story he was telling. 'I'm a German-American, came to this country...' Here he looked out of the window at the Jersey countryside and corrected himself. '...to Germany when I was just a young kid. Hail from Wisconsin but my dad was one of the first returnees.'

'Returnees...?'

'Back home to the Reich. It's a slogan. A Hitler message to all German immigrants in the States. Lots accepted and left the US and went "home" to Germany. Only my dad was one of the first, right after the Nazis came to power. Didn't wait for the official announcement. So I came over at the age of fourteen and went to school in Germany, went through college, did my qualifications, did my training, got a job at the research station.' He made a face of regret. 'Have to admit it, overjoyed, at first I loved it. Playing rockets to the moon, spaceships and all that. That's how we pretended to ourselves. It was all about science, not war.'

Helen sighed. Did she really want to hear this man's excuses?

But an hour later, she was still listening as Leo Beck, as he announced himself, had such an intriguing story to tell she could feel her hostility dissipating. He was making a big impression. He was sincere, of that she was certain, hated the war, desperately wished he could do something to end all the horror.

Still sceptical, she said, 'For the life of me I can't believe you were so blind you didn't know what you were doing. Making a vast killing machine... that's horrible!'

He swallowed, all regret. 'It was exciting science. Completely new. So we blanked from our minds the real purpose. What we didn't want to know we ignored, pretended it was somehow not relevant.' He sighed and looked down. 'How we fool ourselves...'

He asked if she had any English cigarettes and when she said she didn't smoke, he produced a pack of Ecksteins, asking again if she minded him lighting up. This was new. When did any smoker ever ask if his habit was acceptable?

Later they got to talk about his childhood in America and what he remembered of it. 'A little church,' he said, 'lots of singing, kids at school, several friends I had to leave behind, New York harbour on the way out, leaving behind the Statue of Liberty... kind of gross that, don't you think?'

'And now?'

'Out of it. A gradual awakening. Volunteered instead for Todt and they have an overwhelmingly urgent need for engineers.'

The Todt organisation, she learned, were the builders of bunkers, the spreaders of concrete, the diggers of tunnels, even working on V-1 ramps on the Channel coast.

Before she could react to this, he added quickly: 'That's why I'm here talking to you, because I have valuable information about all these new weapons that could save a lot of lives, might even hasten the end of the war.'

Helen sat back in her chair, startled, on her guard. She had no experience of warfare, had no training in espionage or grand strategy but instinctively thought she should remain sceptical. Didn't the enemy try all sorts of tricks? False leads, planting disinformation?

She looked at this man and decided he was completely genuine in the rejection of his former life. In that case, the obvious next step was to ask for the specifics of what he had to report.

And when he provided them, they scared the hell out of her.

Chapter Fourteen

The Germans were on the brink of launching their most deadly attack, she learned to her consternation, with the supersonic V-2 bombardment imminent.

This was confirmation of the warning Devereaux had given her at the Café Royal. Officially no one in Britain had heard about this, though rumours have been rife ever since Churchill went on the wireless last year to warn about Hitler's boasts of super weapons. Since June, however, most people assumed these new weapons were in fact the doodlebug. The buzz-bombs had been hitting London now for several weeks, causing havoc. They made a trademark phutting noise before plunging down and killing people by the dozen.

But this new thing Leo Beck was talking about was much more dangerous.

'I'm prepared to write a detailed report,' he told her earnestly, 'that you can send to London. Everything I know about the rockets which may give your people a chance.'

Helen was treading deep water. Was she to take this seriously? Could it be a trick to incriminate her? And even if genuine, there was an immediate flaw.

Friedrich Winter might regard her as his guest – all very amiable at a certain level of polite pretence – but in reality she was a prisoner in the house. How could she possibly get any report back to her people across the Channel?

———

A glimpse of light! Helen realised her position had improved. Maybe they needed her. Perhaps her position was not as perilous as it first appeared. In fact, she had something to bargain with – so the next session with Winter had to be a reveal-all moment.

'What was that meeting in the library all about?' she demanded of Winter, now she felt on much firmer ground. 'Time to be frank with me.'

He looked at her for some seconds before nodding. 'Yesterday,' he said in a slightly dramatic tone, 'you met members of the German Resistance.'

'Didn't know there was such a thing.'

He ignored this and began a long explanation of how his associates abhorred the National Socialist regime, how they guarded their security against infiltration by the Gestapo and the SD and how they planned to change the leadership.

A shrill inner voice sounded in Helen's head. Seriously dangerous stuff! A conspiracy against Hitler and the Nazi hierarchy? Should she be mixed up in this, just when she had glimpsed a way out? She sensed a cloud of doom hanging over these people if they were discovered. Perhaps that was why there were no women or children in the house. They had hidden their families away. Now she saw the real man behind the affable front; the risks he was taking, struggles with his conscience, the fear and the threat.

'Tell me,' she said.

'The meeting was to test you out.'

She shrugged.

'Our previous overtures have met with no success, so now we are looking for a personal messenger who can carry our message with true conviction, face to face, to the right people in the British establishment. To stress our serious intent at a personal level.' When he said these words he was looking directly at her. 'We think that with your reputation as one of the great aviators you will be listened to by the right people.'

She took a minute to get over this. Were they crazy, or was it a trick? First, she was let into the secret of the V-2 and now this! She didn't reply. Looked out of the window instead, considering her options. Reject or agree? The chaos caused by the V-1 was real enough. The prospect that this was a genuine approach was simply too serious to ignore.

Winter saw her hesitation and upped the stakes. 'Here's the deal,' he said, 'we get you back there...'

Her eyes went wide at this and she took a step back like a startled doe.

'Oh yes, we can arrange it, and when you get back to England you can describe this meeting and our serious intent to the right people and present them with this letter.'

An envelope appeared as if from nowhere and she could see the addressee written in a large florid hand: Mr Winston S. Churchill. 'With your name,' said Winter, 'you can do it, get it to the top, or at least find us the right people at the centre of government.'

What's more, he added, he would sweeten the pill by throwing in a long report on the V-2 from Leo Beck which, he said, 'will be of great interest to your people.'

She considered. How would the high-ups in Whitehall view this? Would they want proof beyond all doubt, hard evidence to weigh against the possibility of a fake, and a bonus to give it credibility?

Then it came to her. Of course, Leo himself could be the bonus. He could be the proof. It was at this moment that she had an inspired thought, deciding to test their credibility.

'Okay,' she said loudly, 'if you really can get me back to Britain then I'll take your message across – but I want something else besides.'

Winter stared at her with an expression that said he didn't expect her to issue conditions.

'I want Leo Beck as well,' she said. 'Never mind about his report. Him in person, much better than any report.'

Silence.

'I want Leo.'

Friedrich Winter was shaking his head.

'I want to take him back with me to London. The inside man, the man in the know, the rocket scientist who can provide all the answers. He can be my prize, my high-profile defector.'

Chapter Fifteen

She ignored the inevitable protests. If they wanted something that badly they would have to pay the price.

Back in the bedroom, she thought through her demand. It was cheeky. It was risky. She was putting her life in jeopardy by not doing as asked. She had a chance to get back home – so why take the risk? Where did all this bravery spring from?

It was time to ask herself the difficult questions: *who am I really? Do I have what it takes to go through with this?*

She thought about Leo. Could she do this to him? When he was talking she knew she was hearing the truth. He had some indefinable quality that made it impossible for him to be a plant. She could see it in his eyes, his expression, in the language he used. And back in London he would be precious gold. He'd answer all of their questions, the questions she could not ask because she did not have the science or the expertise. He needed to be face to face to give Britain's experts a fuller picture than any report could provide. He needed to answer specific questions that only a specialist expert could ask. Better in person, much more convincing.

However, did she have the right to demand this of him?

Making him a defector; placing his safety in the hands of an erstwhile enemy, taking a chance on him being accepted and being afforded reasonable treatment.

Never mind, she would protect him! Her vow quelled an inner voice that questioned her ability to back up such a promise.

Think positive, said the voice. *Silence all doubt. I will be his acolyte, his supporter, his guardian.*

'I'm sorry,' Winter said when they next met, 'I don't think we can allow this. Defecting to London? It's not in his best interest, it's asking too much of any man.'

'Then the deal's off.'

He looked at her, clearly disappointed. 'I don't think you're in a position to bargain, to set conditions.'

She stared out of a window.

'Internment for the rest of the war, some desolate camp in Axis territory, not a very enticing prospect.'

Silence.

'Maybe worse. Interrogation. Possibly by the Gestapo. No telling with them.'

No comment.

'Better to return to where you came from.'

She turned to face him. He and his conspiratorial pals wanted her co-operation and that gave her the edge. She was fed up with being a powerless pawn, now was the time to assert herself. *Don't be fobbed off with small fry,* the inner voice said. *Extract the maximum advantage.* Time to be bold, to live up to the promise she had made to her Hank and make her son proud. Make them pay the price. 'That's my deal. A defector in exchange for playing your messenger. I think Leo will agree.

And both of us will be an irresistible bait. The people in Whitehall won't be able to ignore your message if he and I arrive together.'

There was a long pause, then a mumbled statement about re-considering the matter; about asking such a lot of any man.

'And while you're at it,' she said, 'I want to know the answer to the next questions, the when and how of our exit. How are you going to manage it?'

Chapter Sixteen

Helen and Leo were escorted along a quay crowded with boats preparing to sail, halting by a small brick-built store containing all manner of tackle. Inside they were handed heavy knitted jumpers and sou'westers. Wordlessly, their rucksacks were taken from them.

A bulky figure unrecognisable in the dark took them aboard a tiny fishing boat. Helen noticed the name, *Valiant of Rozel,* painted above a bright orange rear coupled with a complex pattern of blues, reds, greens and yellows. The only shelter was a tiny wheelhouse. From gestures they understood they were to lie on the floor and keep out of sight.

Noises outside indicated the crew had arrived, lines were cast off, and the motion of the sea became distinct. It was uncomfortable, cramped and the helmsman clad in large yellow waders trod all over them to reach and work the wheel.

It was clear no one wanted to talk but Helen insisted on trying, ignoring all rebuffs. Eventually the helmsman conceded: 'You're not the first.' He had a bright red weatherbeaten face. 'Been a few before you, strictly on the QT, of course.'

'How?'

'Don't ask! Just be glad you're going.' He snorted. 'Next week you'll be dancing in Trafalgar Square.'

End of conversation. The tone was dismissive, derisive even, as if he thought such frivolity beneath his contempt, but she didn't care. In the cramped confines of the wheelhouse floor, she smiled. She was going home to a reunion with the son and family she thought had been lost for ever. She had a mental picture of the upcoming welcome, of Peter's wide smile, of joyful laughter at the big house, of familiarity, comfort, safety and normality. It gave her the strength to withstand the ordeal of the next few hours spent in the close company of this mono-syllabic man and his aura of fish and sweat. She could only surmise that Friedrich Winter had secret contacts among the fishermen and on the other side of the Channel, allowing him to facilitate escapers whenever it suited his purpose to do so.

Eventually the monotonous thudding of the engine reduced to a growl and they were allowed to stand. Dancing in Trafalgar Square? That reference produced another smile of recall: Charlie Jones, the king of swing at the Regal Ballroom, jitter-bugging, her blue suede dance shoes, the black dress, the glam-orous uniforms, the carefree laughter, the sheer pleasure of being with her dancing partner. A smile tinged with a tear.

A frisson of alarm broke the dream. She spotted the shape of another boat approaching. There followed hushed voices, furtive conversations at the rail, their rucksacks suddenly appearing on deck, the two of them urged forward and an awkward step across the gap between two heaving vessels.

No goodbyes, no ceremony, just passed across like the delivery of two parcels.

The next vessel was nothing like the fishing boat. Sleek, painted overall in grey with an atmosphere to match. Slick, precise, disciplined.

'Welcome aboard.' A well-modulated voice, a naval uniform

but no introductions. 'Go down the companionway and take station in the sickbay. And stay there.'

She met Leo Beck's questioning gaze with a reassuring smile. In her mind she was throwing a protective shield around the man she already regarded as an heroic collaborator. She believed in him implicitly; in his patent sincerity, enormous regret, bravery in travelling to what to him was an enemy country and his courage in rejecting what he'd belatedly realised was a monstrous project serving a monstrous regime. She liked his openness, a willingness to discuss any subject, about himself, his American childhood or his fractured parentage and above all, his obvious trust in her. She was attracted to his youth and his freshness, a man once conflicted but now determined.

The dawdling discomfort of the fishing boat was replaced by the relief of a bunk and the impression of great speed. It was in this manner and three hours later that Helen and Beck – she guarding her secret letter – climbed the ladder on to another quay, this time a friendly one: Falmouth Harbour.

Chapter Seventeen

F irst things first! She had to let them know at home that she
was back in the land of the living. Ignoring a tall army
officer dogging her footsteps, rebuffing his attempts to engage
her in conversation, she made haste for the harbourmaster's
office. They always had a telephone there.

'This is for official business only...' But the harbour chief's
protestations did not last long in face of her impassioned plea:
'I'm this minute back from the dead, I have to tell my mum;
she'll have been worried sick.'

But when he relented and the line connected to the Suffolk
farmhouse, the relief in her mother's voice did not persist.
'What on earth have you been doing? We've all been worried
sick, you being missing and us expecting the worst... all I can say
is, I hope you realise the damage you've done, given us all a bad
scare.'

'So sorry, Mum, really, it was just an accident...'

'Well, you've really gone and done it this time, so I hope it's
taught you a good lesson.'

'A lesson?'

'That you've had your fill of this flying nonsense once and for all. Just come home and be a proper mother.'

Helen could hardly hold the telephone receiver, the conversation ending on the verge of tears. Not the welcome she had been expecting. There could be few more wounding insults to fling at her than implying she was a poor mother. She had always thought of her work arrangement as a compromise necessary for the war; that her duties were of sufficient importance to justify being a weekend mother. In truth, however, she knew there was more to it than that.

When she emerged from the harbour office she was hardly in a fit state to face the man waiting outside, Lieutenant Jeremiah York announcing that he was head of the military police escort party taking her by train to London.

'So, you knew we were coming? You were sent...'

'We knew you were coming,' he echoed, and Helen forced herself to concentrate. This was Winter again. Not just his ability to disengage German harbour security when required, but also an obvious facility to communicate with persons he would normally have considered his enemy. She fingered the letter in her pocket and thought about her vow to protect Beck. She looked hastily around. 'Where is he?'

'We've got him.'

'Please, don't come the hard man on my guest. He's absolutely no threat.'

No response.

'Look, he's not going to do a bunk, he's co-operative and wants to help us, so please, don't spoil all my efforts and get hostile with him. That would wreck everything I've fought to achieve.'

After initial reluctance and much referring back by telephone, York's heavies eventually agreed to occupy the next compartment in the train, allowing Helen and Leo Beck to travel together as if they were normal unexceptionable people. All part of keeping up her charm offensive, even if members of the public were not allowed to intrude.

She tried to shrug off the wounding words of her mother and reassure Beck everything was going to plan, but he sensed she was not quite her earlier confident self. This was to be a journey of many surprises.

When the train stopped at Salisbury, the compartment door flew open and a tall figure with a mop of sandy brown hair stood there, raising a welcoming hand. A familiar face, a signature smile, but still a shock to her, albeit a welcome one.

Ashley Devereaux.

'What's this?' she said, wondering about the chances of their meeting being a coincidence. Then she noticed a small lapel badge, got up and advanced on him. 'Second Secretary,' she read aloud.

'I'm in on this little party,' he said.

She blinked. How many more hoops would she jump through this day? She didn't say any more, was too busy studying him, assessing him. His smile was a message beyond words. In one long lingering look a whole catalogue was written there. Their pasts, their complicated history. Highs and lows, hot moments and cool ones, great heat and icy coldness, intrigue and disappointments, light and dark.

'Listen,' he said, placing a hand on hers, 'you must be careful; don't go jumping in at the deep end.'

'Meaning?'

'I'm the advance guard for today's proceedings.'

She began to smile. Probably meant he'd joined the spooks. And it appeared that he had come to warn her of what to expect when they arrived at Paddington. A more discreet reception at the station, a quick visit to a hotel for a wash and brush-up, then both of them straight over to what he called the 'War House' for

73

a two o'clock briefing before some obscure committee, the name of which she instantly forgot.

War House?

Whitehall jargon, she was later to learn, both for her own elucidation and for the attentive Beck, referring to the government's War Office. An intimidating monster block of over a thousand rooms.

She put up a warning hand to Ashley. 'There's a limit to how long I'm ready to hang around in London. Okay, it's important, vital business, and I've got a big message to deliver... but still, I can't wait to get home to my boy.'

Those corridors, they were interminable. A different world up on the seventh floor. The people there inhabited a parallel universe to the rest of humanity. It was like a route march inside a carpeted tunnel. Two and a half miles of corridors, a Portland and York stone colossus at the corner of Whitehall and Horse Guards, this was the War House. They followed their leggy escort closely, fearing being lost in an unfathomable maze. The escort? A boy scout, one of dozens recruited specially to help visitors find their way around.

Helen was amused by him at first but soon began to worry about what she'd let Leo Beck in for. Surely, the authorities must give her defector the benefit of any doubt in favour of the solid gold information he had in his head.

Round yet another corner, dogging the boy's footsteps, and suddenly a figure stepped out of a doorway, blocking the way ahead. He cleared his throat. Sounded like the growl of a predatory beast.

His eyes fixed Helen's and didn't let go. 'Gascoigne,' he said. 'Security.'

She took in the brush moustache, the green bow tie and the Crombie overcoat. Inside the office?

'Mrs Fairfax? Before you go anywhere else, a word please.' Followed by a gesture toward a room the size of a broom cupboard. She noticed the number, 949A, which more than summed it up. No furnishings or frivolity, just a tiny table and two chairs.

She stepped in, and the queries that followed her initial exposition seemed concentrated entirely around her navigational error, over and over the same details and the reasons for her mistaken arrival in the Channel Islands until she felt the humiliation of evident disapproval, undisguised suspicion and even disbelief. Gascoigne made her feel dirty, as if her mistake had been deliberate. He stared at her, never breaking eye contact, took no notes but constantly clasped and unclasped his hands on the tiny table.

All this time Beck was left standing outside in the corridor in the company of their anonymous escort.

Eventually Gascoigne signalled toward the door and said: 'And now, him.'

Helen's patience had run its course. She'd had enough of this man's deadpan badgering and invoked her own protective instinct. 'When you talk to him, I want to sit in.'

'I think not.'

'Look,' she said, deciding it was time to turn co-operative into assertive, 'Leo should be treated with respect. What he's done has required considerable courage and self-sacrifice.'

When this elicited no response she got up to go, giving Gascoigne one of the special stares she reserved for the undeserving.

Beck had taken her place in Gascoigne's cupboard for several long minutes before a flustered official approached along the corridor, looking at his watch, indicating that she was urgently required to attend the conference room.

'Then get my guest out of there,' she said, pointing at 949A, and stood back to watch, with some degree of satisfaction, while officialdom went to work on itself, bureaucrat on bureaucrat.

Several minutes later they came upon a little cluster of people loitering outside a conference room and that's when she saw him again. Ashley blocked her lest she walk straight in. 'Before we go in...' he said, 'you just be careful in there, don't say more than you have to, play it cool.'

She gave him a puzzled look.

'It's a piranha bowl,' he said, 'they tear each other to pieces and you too if you're not careful.'

She gave him a wan smile. 'Don't try rattling me. I've just had a session with Security.'

'Bound to check you out.'

'So, how can this committee be any more frightening than...' and she nodded her head vaguely in a westerly direction. 'Like a grilling from the enemy.'

He ignored this. 'Just be wary, particularly of the tall fella with the grey hair and frigid face.'

'Who he?'

'Cherwell. Churchill's scientific adviser. The Prime Minister's man. He's out to destroy anyone who doesn't sing his tune.'

'Why should he want to attack me?' she queried, still refusing to be intimidated. 'For overshooting Weymouth?'

Ashley grinned. 'Well, it was some overshoot.'

Helen put an arm around Beck's shoulder, worried that her trophy scientist was alone and vulnerable, remembering again her vow of protection, giving him the warmth of another smile, beckoning him into the big room.

She stepped inside, faltering slightly, her confidence

momentarily paused by the grandeur of the surroundings: an elaborate marble fireplace, deep oak panelling, coats of arms, a magnificent candelabra and a sea of blank faces. She studied them. They sat, almost lounged, in bright red swing chairs around a vast oval table set out with napkins and notepads. She noted uniforms of khaki and blue, lots of gold braid, and others formally dressed in suit jackets.

She drew in a sharp breath; another room full of men to confront her.

She and Beck were shown to two facing chairs. A bland figure in the centre of the line was making some equally bland introductory remarks about taking evidence from witnesses appearing before the committee. She already knew a little of this. Ashley had briefed her on the history of Whitehall committees inquiring into German weapons. Had begun with a scientific committee, morphing into a fuel panel, then into a civil defence committee and now the 'rocket consequences committee'. She looked around quickly, noting that matching drapes were closed tight, as if they were frightened to let the daylight in.

Then she identified her likely bête noire. You couldn't miss him. A tall figure with a permanent snarl: Lord Cherwell. At the other end of the table she spotted a familiar face you saw every day in the newspapers. You couldn't miss him either – the big quiff and glasses. None other than the Home Secretary, Herbert Morrison.

Now she began to worry.

Chapter Eighteen

They were in no great hurry to hear their witnesses. Instead the tall figure was weighing up the probability that all the evidence of German secret weapon preparations was simply a deliberate plant of false evidence by the enemy designed to cause confusion.

'It is just that... it's all a big hoax.' Cherwell was wagging a finger. 'I tell you now, take it from me, there are no secret weapons.'

The slim man, referred to as Dr Jones, insisted: 'But all the evidence of vast installations is too extensive, too expensive and too elaborate to constitute a ruse.'

In the taut silence that followed the anonymous chairman called for more evidence. A small man, described as a Shell scientist, began to speak about his experiments with rockets burning high octane petrol and liquid oxygen.

'This is nonsense!' Cherwell butted in once more. 'These are the ravings of a third-rate engineer. Such views must be ignored. The rocket is a technical impossibility I tell you.'

Photographs were passed around of objects at an experimental station. These had given rise to sketches of a long-range rocket burning liquid fuel – this, she knew from Ashley Devereaux, was incendiary. Cherwell's insistent line was that only solid fuels were possible. The very concept of a rocket was still the subject of great doubt.

After viewing the sketches another speaker sheltering behind a pair of huge spectacles insisted that a rocket was 'therefore theoretically possible'. This, she discovered later, was Cripps, top lawyer and Minister for Aircraft Production.

Cherwell, exhibiting a fine skill for insulting people to their face, declared, 'Now we get even more nonsense, but then, what can you expect from a lawyer who eats nothing but nuts?'

Dark looks and murmurs of disapproval were heard from the other committee members.

Helen was mesmerised by these exchanges. So was this the government in action? Was this how the leaders of government and top civil servants behaved?

Then it was her turn. The chairman looked up, pointed a finger and invited her to give her 'evidence'.

She swallowed, licked her lips and realised all the lines she had so carefully rehearsed during their train journey from Weymouth had suddenly vanished from memory. She cleared her throat and looked at all the attentive faces. They stared back.

Her mind was still a blank.

Her mouth was as dry as a parched stick in the desert. 'Most unfortunately, er, due mainly to a navigational error...'

It was a stumbling start. She knew she wasn't making a good impression, but forced herself to continue and gradually she found firmer ground on her meeting with members of the German Resistance and talking to the rocket engineer – 'Dr Leo Beck, whom I'm pleased to introduce, sitting on my left, who wishes to help the British war effort.'

She had expected to be questioned about Friedrich Winter

and had been ready to elaborate on his strange set of associates, but no, it seemed they merited little interest. All was passed over in favour of Beck.

The rocket engineer had also been rehearsing his speech but did not get very far into his description of the technology before Cherwell was at him.

'Are you seriously contending that your colleagues–' and here he emitted a contemptuous growl '–that your colleagues in Germany have created a rocket powered by liquid oxygen?'

Beck agreed and began to describe the precise make-up of the V-2 rocket fuel when there was a further interruption.

'Why are you telling us this pack of lies? Liquid fuel? Quite impossible.' Cherwell's veins stood high in his neck. 'You must take us for fools. This is rubbish, a bogus story put out by the other side.'

Helen could not hold back. Her protective instinct led her to break into this exchange. 'There's no lying here. I brought this man over because I believe in him. I can tell a liar from an honest man.'

'You too could be a plant,' Cherwell said, glaring at her. 'It's rather too convenient to be stranded with the enemy, wouldn't you say?'

She swallowed, stunned. Was she being accused of working for the enemy? Surely he hadn't meant that? She was aware her mouth gaped. No words emerged. How could anyone accuse her of treachery? She was completely at a loss, never more insulted, never more wounded. Her lack of response fed into an embarrassing silence.

Into this void stepped the anonymous chairman. 'To sum up then,' he said, 'considering all the evidence before us today, we are of the collective opinion that there may be a rocket–'

'Sheer nonsensical ridiculous twaddle!' Cherwell was on his

feet, banging the table with his fist. 'I won't stay a moment longer to listen to this. I'm out!' And with this he stalked dramatically to the door and disappeared.

She and Devereaux were in the corridor, outside the committee room. He was sympathetic, calming, comforting. 'Don't take it to heart, it's just him.'

Helen was still smarting from her ordeal, appalled by Cherwell's rough handling. Did he deal with his family in like manner? Was he a bully at home as well as in Cabinet? She made a new resolution to teach Peter about proper standards of behaviour and never to conduct himself in such a hostile fashion, whatever the provocation.

Another member of the panel whom she hadn't noticed before approached and began to ask her about her Channel Island contact, Friedrich Winter.

'I'm Menzies,' he said – pronouncing it as 'Mingis' – as if this should be an instant reassurance. She looked at his thinning blond hair and tweed suit and sighed. Now seemed the right moment to produce her letter, the one addressed to Churchill.

'Are you in a position to promise that this will be delivered to the Prime Minister?'

'Certainly he will learn of it; beyond that I cannot say.' He smiled at her. 'However, I would like to read its contents and you may rest assured you have reached the right place to deliver it.'

She sighed. After her experience with Cherwell, she wasn't up for further resistance.

Menzies ripped open the envelope and scanned the contents. He didn't react. Indeed, he didn't seem at all impressed. 'Yes, well, you see, we know all about this, a rather long story, and to be frank, we really don't want to encourage them.' He shrugged. 'Much the best for the awful Adolf to carry on losing their war. Much better than having a new lot in charge in Berlin who might actually know what they're doing.'

She thought about the sincerity of Winter, of the risks he was running, of the danger to his little group from the Gestapo, and of her role in the endeavour to broker a deal with Britain. Was this how peace overtures were snuffed out, as if Whitehall wanted the war to go on, for the slaughter to continue? She felt deflated and let down. It seemed as if her mission had not only been traduced by Cherwell but now dismissed by this new man.

He smiled at her and patted her arm. 'Leave it with me – but we do want to hear a lot more from your little defector fellow.'

———

In the absence of Cherwell, Leo Beck was given his head at the second session, saying that just one in five of the V-2 rockets would have a wireless facility. So most of the rockets would not be able to report back on where the missile fell.

Radio direction for guiding the weapon on to a specific target had been rejected by the Germans because they knew British scientists would bend the beams.

The missile was, he said, simply a scatter weapon designed to spread terror. Therefore, those controlling the V-2s would be unable to tell how accurate their aim was in four cases out of five.

This, Beck asserted, was their Achilles heel. It gave Britain the ability to feed disinformation into the world's spying networks about where the missiles were falling, creating the

For the Children

potential for fooling the rocket men about the accuracy of their targeting.

The man with the big quiff broke into Beck's briefing. Attention switched to the ruddy face and the London accent of Herbert Morrison. 'How are these things guided towards our city?' he wanted to know.

'Everything depends on the gyroscopes and the vanes, or fins,' Beck replied. 'These fins are at the base of the rocket. What you should be looking for is – have they made any improvements? When I left, the system was so poor they could only manage a scatter-gun of strikes across a very large area.'

He went on to refute Cherwell's accusation that he was a plant. 'If so, would I be pointing out the defects of the weapon, of how to limit its effects? These are not the actions of a plant, or double agent.'

The chairman responded in a neutral tone. 'We are making a careful note of what you say.'

Then Morrison spoke again. It was an authoritative voice, one of decision. 'We are dealing here with a potential menace of great gravity,' he said, completely contradicting the Cherwell line. 'I am apprehensive of what might happen if long-range rockets are used. I have a high degree of faith in the Londoners' courage and spirit, but there is a limit, and the limit will come.'

Elaborate plans were then revealed for a mass evacuation of London's population in the hope of preventing panic flight. More than one and a half million had already left the city because of the V-1. Now eighty-seven selected routes were planned for people to walk to assembly points, such as cinemas, where they would, as before, board buses to take them out of danger.

Even so, there were fears for the aged and infirm. Morrison ended his remarks on a gloomy emphasis: 'An extensive use of this weapon will make the city uninhabitable. It will be impossible for the government to stay.'

Helen and the others filed out of the conference room in a kind of daze.

'Such a depressing scenario,' commented Devereaux. 'Enough almost to make you want to come to terms with Hitler on the spot.'

Chapter Nineteen

A homecoming should not be like this. A joyous occasion overlaid with high levels of stress. However, as Helen walked into the big farmhouse kitchen in Suffolk, everything appeared normal, just as she had last left it: the table, the sinks, the big old coke stove in the corner.

'Welcome home, wanderer!' Her mother's smile was broad, the strength of her greeting seemingly undiminished. They looked at each other, smiling, and some of Helen's tension drained away. Everything seemed as usual, nothing had changed. She peered at her mother closely; a comely woman who looked after herself. She'd put on a touch of lipstick.

'How are you, Helen? All in one piece?'

'All in one piece.'

'No injuries, wounds, bits missing?'

She shook her head, asking in a plaintive voice. 'Where is he?'

'At school.'

'Oh, of course.'

But they were still laughing, smiling, no sign of resentment, no lingering after-taste from their earlier disagreement.

'First things first – tea and cake. That marzipan one you liked so much. Saved it special. For you.'

There were two large bowls on the table: one full of rosy red apples, most likely from the farmyard orchard, the other bowl containing potatoes.

'Here, let me!' Helen took a knife from the drawer and started to peel. Joining in, it felt normal, yes definitely normal.

'That's one thing we have in plenty,' her mother said. 'Short of most things, but we'll never run out of our staple. In season, of course.'

Helen was casting a fresh eye over the old place. 'Hmm,' she said, scanning the kitchen, shaking her head, 'these big old Butler sinks... after the war we need to get you something more modern.'

'Oh I don't know, we've managed all these years. Why change now?'

'Get you up to date, Mother.'

'Well now, time to tell, what happened to you?' An abrupt change of tone. 'How come you vanished? Was it bad? Did it hurt?'

'Just an accident, Mum, no pain, just tired... very tired.' This was the moment to deflect direct questions. 'Can't really say much more, sworn to secrecy and all that, but I can tell you one thing.'

An arched eyebrow. 'Oh?'

'I got my toes wet.'

But this much anticipated joke did not go down well, being met with a stony silence.

'So, how is everyone back here? Dad, the boys...'

'Thomas and Nat, they're doing their bit.' A little twist to the mouth. 'Don't you want to know about Peter?'

'Course I do.'

'He'll be overjoyed. You'll be wanting to meet him down at the school gate. With all the other mums.' A long stare. 'Poor little mite. Always asking after you. "When's my mummy coming home?" Sits by that window, willing you to come round the corner.'

'Here now,' Helen said.

'But you put yourself in danger.' Now it was coming; the expected eruption. 'We all thought you was dead. Gave us a terrible turn.'

'Sorry, Mum.'

'And what about Peter? He hasn't got a dad – and you very nearly robbed him of his mother as well. Not fair on the little lad, you must see that.'

Helen went early. It was only a five-minute walk to the school but she set out a good twenty minutes before the bell, determined to find a prominent place by the school gate so her face would be the first one Peter saw when he shot out of the classroom door.

She smiled in eager anticipation of the moment. Of course, she knew about the danger of over-compensating, of pampering and spoiling, but she put that thought to one side. This was about making it up to him for all her long absences. Despite the anticipated pleasure of seeing her son, her mind was in turmoil over her mother's responses. So many emotions. Guilt, a defensive reflex, uncertainty.

Turning the corner, she realised she wasn't the first to arrive. A little knot of mothers had already congregated around the gate. She had known most of them since childhood and it was the big social occasion of their day.

'Hello, stranger!' It was Margot, Jason's mum, who worked

in the town dental surgery. A rictus spasm of welcome. 'Word was, you went missing.'

A shake of the head. 'Just out of touch for a bit.'

'Must be strange to have both your feet on the ground.' This from Abigail, Aimee's mother. She worked in the tanning mill down by the river. Enough to make anyone a bit sour, Helen decided, fielding the inevitable and barely disguised resentments of the town's stay-at-homes, noting the baleful look from Sybil Quare, who'd made a career out of pregnancy. Present score: six and still counting.

'Glad to see you're in the pink.' A different tone this time. A genuine smile of welcome. 'Back from the abyss. Was it awful?' Her friend Emma had always been supportive.

'Difficult,' Helen conceded. 'And scary.'

'You always did go head-first into things. Still, better than sticking around here all your life. One of my big regrets.'

'Plenty of important jobs out there,' Helen said. 'Do you want me to put a word in at the right place?'

'Thanks for the offer – but not just now.' Emma looked around at the others, lowering her voice. 'Just don't get wounded by some of the things this lot say.'

'I won't.'

All talk was silenced by the clanging of the school bell and the entire focus of the group became centred on the big blue door across the other side of the playground. Silence, tension, then suddenly a metallic grinding as the door was dragged open and finally, the flood. The heady release of juvenile joy.

They poured into the playground, all smiles, caps askew, loose ties, unrestrained shirts and flailing satchels in a frantic rush for the gate to freedom.

'Mummy, Mummy, Mummy!'

Helen only had eyes for Peter, sweeping him up into her

arms in a moment of supreme ecstasy. Cuddles, nuzzling, laughter.

Then, as they made their way home, waving to Emma and the others, he was all questions. 'Are you home now? Are you going to stay?'

'I don't know, darling, we'll have to see.'

'You were away such a long time. And you missed my birthday party.'

'I know, I know, but I'm here now. Did you save me any cake?'

'We ate it all. What did you do? Did you fly aeroplanes again?'

'Mmm, most of the time.'

'How high did you go?'

'Oh, way up, very high, above the clouds, up near the sun.'

'Will you take me too?'

'Maybe, one day.'

'Will you teach me?'

All inquiries about progress at school were met with impatience. She had better luck with what happened after school. Her father had given Peter wood and nails to fashion a toy aeroplane; they were going out next week to look for conkers; last week he fell out of a tree but no harm done; on Fridays they went to the stream to jump across the stepping stones, but best of all was the spinney where someone had fixed up a rope swing from a tall tree that you could whizz around in a wide circle rather than just swing in a straight line.

Helen had a complaint. 'Grandpa's been telling me,' she said, 'about you climbing on the roofs of all of his sheds and jumping across the gaps.'

'Only little gaps.'

'And unscrewing the knobs on the tops of the brass bedstead?'

Here a knowing grin. 'If you do it slowly, ever so slowly, he can't hear it squeak,' followed by a fit of giggles.

News of her return from the land of the missing had clearly spread around the district. Neighbours dropped in to greet her bringing small gifts – a couple of scones and a precious jar of marmalade and then, much to Helen's surprise, her two brothers arrived, home on leave from the forces. Finally, the full family in one room; even Dad, extracted from one of his many sheds, hammer still in hand, grinning at her. 'Knew you'd be back. Can't keep a good daughter down.'

Her mother, of course, could not maintain the jollity. Had to get in a dig about a weekend mother.

'Leave her alone, Mum, she's doing great.' This from Nat. 'It's what she was built for, what she's meant to be doing.' This comment reflected years of youthful challenges, dares and adventures that had made her the woman she was. 'She's all right! We can see to Peter.'

'You?' Their mother was incredulous. 'You? So you can take him to school and sing him to sleep at night, yes, while sitting in a tent in the desert...' Turning to Thomas. 'Or you, in the middle of the Atlantic, yes? I tell you, he misses her. *When's my mum coming home?*'

'You're clucking like an old hen, Mum, he'll be fine, plenty of kids like him. It's the war.'

'It's Peter I'm thinking about.'

'Mum.' It was Helen, leaning in, looking her mother in the eye. 'Listen.' This was the discussion they were always meant to have. 'You need to understand. I have this ability. This is my special gift.'

'Your special gift is your son.'

'Listen, I don't want to sound bombastic, but it's true, I've got something special to offer, better than most of the flyers. My level of skill means I can really help the war effort. A crying shame not to use it. The country needs it. It's not peacetime, it's war.'

'Plenty of men around to fly.'

'What's the use of giving it all up? Would you attack doctors or scientists for letting others do the child-minding?'

'You're exaggerating again.'

The conversation petered out, unresolved, the fracture between them still raw. The country needed her, she repeated defiantly to herself... but then she had to admit there was more to it than that.

Back in her old room, lying on the quilt fully dressed, an old image came to her, the same one that tormented her on many a sleepless night. That awful moment. The rapping at the front door. The telegraph boy standing on the doorstep, a message in his hand. The messenger of doom. Hating herself for reaching out to take it. A clash of deadly cymbals as the words unfolded before her eyes on that tatty stuttering type sheet glued to the message pad.

Deeply regret to advise you stop Believed to have lost his life in air operations stop Profound sympathy stop

How could she equate her lovely smiling Hank with that awful coffin? The black-clad pall bearers. The drab and dreadful scene on a day of squalls and showers. The old church, the icy coldness, the pit, the earth...

She couldn't accept it. Couldn't do nothing.

She swallowed and sat up. No, she would not give in. To tamely surrender now would be to let him down. She owed him more, much more; she owed him due vengeance. Payback to the enemy for their crimes.

It was her role and duty to carry on the fight.

Chapter Twenty

In the morning Thomas and Nat unearthed Helen's old bicycle from one of the many ramshackle sheds in the yard. The brothers, determined to keep an upbeat tenor to their leaves, stirred the whole farmyard into a frenzy of activity. The dogs, sensing some serious fun lay just ahead, were barking and prancing around the yard as three cycles were retrieved from cobwebs and dust, primed, oiled and tyres inflated.

'Last one to The Mill buys the pints,' Thomas insisted.

'And that includes you!' Nat wasn't letting Helen off the hook.

So off they went, laughing and pedalling manically like they were back in their teens, back in the days when they were serious cross-country bikers, the canines in full pursuit. Bessie, a collie-Labrador cross, always a Helen favourite, trailed faithfully by her side. It was impossible to be downhearted in this company. The race was on. The race was serious.

This, she told herself, was where the daredevil spirit came from. Pushing the boundaries always took you to another level. It was exciting and challenging and persisted long after the first flush of youth. She remembered the parachute jump with

Thomas and Nat as teenagers. Now that was a challenge. *But I'm not reckless*, she told herself, *I weigh the risks, I listen to reason...*

She grimaced, acknowledging a slight fault in the logic. Well, most of the time.

It was a dead heat at The Mill and the rounds were shared.

It was home time again at the school gate and Peter, on the way back to the farm, was in one of his inquisitive moods. She knew what was coming: the 'why?' game. They played it often. Today it went like this:

'Mummy, why is there a war?'

'Because another country is trying to bully us.'

'Why?'

'Because the people there listened to a very bad man who told them to do it.'

'Why?'

'Because they always do what they're told.'

'Why?'

'Because he has a very loud voice.'

'Why?'

'Because he's a very bad man.'

'Why?'

At this point Helen hesitated and her knowing and canny six-year-old thought he had finally stumped her for an answer. She could have told him that this bad man's father hit him too much and his mother loved him too much but decided this version of the truth was unsuitable for her child, so she said, 'His mummy didn't teach him better ways because she wasn't feeling very well as she'd caught a cold in the rain.'

'Oh.' At this point, faced with such a prosaic if questionable explanation, the questions dried up, proving that she wasn't after all cornered without an answer and the game was declared a draw.

Later she smiled at the memory, acknowledging that she had enjoyed a happy and privileged upbringing plus the great gift of a son, good fortune that had been denied to others. She reflected on the conversation in the flight hut at Hatfield with a Polish pilot while they waited for their ferry 'chits'.

Stung by a series of complaints about life in wartime Britain, she'd asked: 'Then why are you here, Dominika? Why fly for the RAF?'

'To get back at those bastards trampling all over my country.' The woman's bitterness was full on. 'Do you know, they even kidnap children?'

Helen's scepticism vanished in the face of the ensuing traumatic story. Dominika and her husband had got out of Poland just in time – but not before their young daughter had been stolen from her school playground by the Lebensborn squads, ready to send her and hundreds of other kidnapped children to German families for forcible adoption. In a desperate action Dominika had bought the girl back for 40 Reichsmarks from a corrupt official at the railway station.

'There's no depths to which they won't sink – evil, murder, venality, you name it.'

There were other worries swimming around Helen's head, notably, the fate of Leo Beck. Just what was happening at the War Office? How was her protege faring at Farnborough? His was priceless information on the V-2, precious gold in intelligence terms, but some doubts about the attitude of the escort, Lieutenant York, caused her to wonder if everyone on the team was fully aware of the fragility of the source.

Poor Leo! He wasn't a robust man. They'd had a long conversation on the train up from Weymouth on the subject of his conflicted parental background. Bullying father, bovine mother. Eventually the poor woman, transported unwillingly like an item of livestock to a Germany she didn't like, couldn't handle the ordeal. All her powers of forbearance and her sense of duty failed her and finally she had fled.

'I took her to the station,' Leo said, 'and put her on a train for Vienna. She had friends there. Hopefully, they helped her cross the border. She wanted back to the States.'

'Did she make it?'

'No idea. Brought down on my head huge trouble from Father.'

'How awful. You must be suffering a terrible sense of loss, of divided loyalties.'

'Not very divided. He's so dogmatic, won't compromise, full of nationalist fervour. Actually, I'm really worried about my mother... whether she's still stuck inside the Reich...'

Helen's sympathy swelled; a man estranged from his father and worried for the wellbeing of his mother; again, she counted her blessings.

Fears for Leo's proper treatment at the hands of the British authorities sent her scurrying to the telephone. It was located in the hallway next to the front door and a tiny window of leaded glass. At the third attempt she located Ashley Devereaux.

'Is Leo being treated well?' she wanted to know. 'With sympathy and consideration?'

But Devereaux had heard nothing and his even manner annoyed her. In her mind's eye she saw threats everywhere in the hostile attitudes of Gascoigne and Mingis, the latter being some kind of top spook, it had been hinted.

'Can't you press? I want to make sure Leo's okay. They could be doing anything to him, thumb screws, the lot.'

'Don't be ridiculous.'

'I gave him my word. That I'd protect him.'

'Brave of you.'

'Look, Dev, I can't sit here doing nothing. You're being ridiculously complacent – so if you won't do anything, I will. Make a big fuss. Anything. Lobby Churchill if necessary.'

There were deep sighs from the other end of the line. 'Now look, Helen, don't be silly, you won't get near the Prime Minister or No. 10.'

'Your father. He's an influential person, he could intercede on our behalf...'

'I told you before, I won't talk to him.'

But Helen was past caring about the Devereaux family squabbles. This was too important. 'If you won't do it I'll gate-crash his office and speak to him myself.'

'For goodness' sake!'

'And I'll tell him you sent me.'

She could hear several exasperated noises down the line before he finally said, 'All right, you win. You are a little blue-bottle at times.'

'I only want what's right.'

A deep sigh, then: 'I'll do something.'

'By ten tomorrow morning,' she said, 'or I will. You know I will. I mean it.'

Chapter Twenty-One

The phone rang at 9.30 the next morning and ten minutes later Helen had her hat and coat on and a bag packed.

'Back to that place?' Tight-lipped disapproval greeted her when she announced she was heading back to London and into the danger zone, a city under siege. 'You're getting too involved,' her mother said. 'Let someone else take it on.'

'I am involved,' Helen replied. 'Can't explain but it's about what you always taught me as a child. Keeping your promises. Loyalty to your friends.'

The train journey was slow, delayed, crowded and dirty. Normally, after a ferry run when it was necessary to return to base by rail, she would sit on her parachute in the corridor if all seats were occupied. Now, however, it was straight standing, all her gear having been lost at sea and none re-issued.

She distracted herself by thinking ruefully about her threat to gatecrash Devereaux Senior's office and make a scene. It had been an impromptu gesture to spark the son into action – but would she really have done it? She blushed at the thought. She would have hated someone doing that to her. It was all bluster, she reassured herself – yes, pure bluff.

At London Devereaux had sent a car for her, whisking rapidly down rubble-strewn but traffic-free streets, away from the gloom of a bomb-blasted Liverpool Street, back to the hub of operations which was the War House.

He was chuckling quietly to himself when they met in reception. She gave him a quizzical look wondering at his change of attitude as he ushered her into a corner away from official ears.

'Seems Herbie took a shine to you.'

'Who?'

'Morrison, the Home Secretary. Thought you were a plucky little blighter.'

She snorted.

'Mind you, it helped when I whispered in certain ears that Winnie was on the case.'

'Really?' Her face lit up. 'Is he really?'

'Course not... but it does tend to concentrate minds.'

Helen's look turned sour. Ashley never used to lie, but now it seemed the civil service had turned him into an arch manipulator. But then, perhaps he wasn't one of them after all. Perhaps his various references to the Air Ministry or Foreign Office meant something else.

'You should be pleased,' he said with a big smile. 'All in the cause of furthering the interests of women.'

Another puzzle – still not solved when he announced that she was seeing someone important to plead her case; a 10.30 appointment, not at the War Office but the Ministry of Home Security. Morrison's ministry.

It seemed as if she were now fighting a war in corridors and committee rooms. She sat fidgeting on a seat in reception rehearsing what she was about to say – but to whom? All this wartime security; no names on the stations and now no name on her appointment card. Had she over-reached herself? Was she heading into a hornet's nest?

Finally, she was called, escorted to a door and spied a slim label with letters that were barely discernible.

They read: E. Wilkinson.

The penny dropped. She was being seen by Ellen Wilkinson, one of only three women members of the wartime coalition government, a minister of state reporting directly to Morrison.

Impressed, yes, she was definitely impressed.

The minister was a short woman with a mop of bright ginger hair. Her dress was a maze of bright colours – reds, yellows, greens. Not what you expected from a Minister of the Crown.

Wilkinson smiled, called, 'Come on in,' and strode round her desk to shake hands.

'Thanks so much for seeing me,' Helen said, and was waved to a seat. 'This is a real surprise and pleasure. I've always followed your career with great interest...'

'Not everyone approves of my politics,' cut in Wilkinson.

'But you're sticking up for the poor and for women, that's what's really important – I heartily approve. It's really encouraging that you're one of several women in the government–'

Helen realised she was gushing when the other woman cut in. 'What can I do for you?'

'I need help to protect the man I brought back from Jersey.'

'Ah yes, you were the one who...'

'Flew over and sailed back.'

They both laughed.

'The thing is, I have given my promise, my solemn promise, that I will protect him. He's Leo Beck, by the way.'

'The defector?'

Helen nodded. 'That's him. He's giving us vital information on the V-2 rocket, but I'm fearful that the security services are bullying him. They're hiding him away and I suspect they're giving him a hard time because of his nationality. You see, I personally persuaded him to come over on the basis of reasonable treatment and I'd really like to see him to make sure he's okay.'

Wilkinson was whisking through the pages of a diary. 'Let's see, the committee is meeting next week and will probably need to take more evidence from this man. Seems an eminently sensible arrangement. Whatever plans the security people have, they must produce him then.'

Helen made a face. 'Next week is an awfully long time... if they're playing nasty.'

'Never fear. We'll flag it up and then they'll know they have to produce him in an acceptable condition.'

'An acceptable condition...' Helen echoed doubtfully, wondering what devilment might be concealed in those words and sceptical that a mere civilian, even one of ministerial rank, could give orders to the military. 'Can you do this?'

'Never fear, I'll drop a word in Herbie's ear. Don't worry, Herb and I are close.'

'Told you I'd fix it,' said a smiling Devereaux out in the corridor.

'But can she really do it?'

'Course she can. They're lovers.'

Helen was shocked. How could Ashley know that?

'Morrison's a major cabinet minister. What he says goes – very powerful man – and she's his fancy bit and after the war... who knows? He'll probably stab Atlee in the back and take over the party. That's the word among the politicos, anyhow.'

She still had a worried brow and Devereaux wasn't finished. 'It's fine to be getting your man out, very well done! But don't be getting too close to Wilkinson. Don't be too much of a fan. A lot of people have got it in for her. Dodgy links in the past. Communist background and all that. You don't want any of her problems rubbing off on you.'

She waved a dismissive hand. Helen *was* a fan and had made it her business to read up on all Wilkinson's long and varied history, her political associations and her many campaigns. She began to wonder about a lone woman in politics, about working and surviving in this rarefied environment. How did she cope fighting her corner over such a long time in this world of men? What did it do to normal female instincts? Later, much later, knowledge of Wilkinson's background would prove to be extremely useful.

'Look,' Dev said, giving her a long earnest gaze, 'no need to rush back. Jerry's taken a break. Hasn't been a single doodlebug over in the last forty-eight hours. Well, maybe less, maybe twenty-four hours. Anyway, the café has a more than adequate shelter.'

'But you don't have time to get to the shelter.'

The Café Royal, Ashley's favourite watering hole. She knew that right enough. The 'in' set needed their relaxation after the tension of constant and long periods of intense duty. 'A chance to forget the bloody war for an hour or two' was how they'd describe it. And it was where Helen had 'accidentally' bumped into him before her fateful flight.

Should she agree?

Her eyelids flickered in confusion. A bout of emotional turmoil. She was still grieving for the hero of her life; for the man who had crossed the Atlantic to tread in valedictory shoes and take her to the heights of pleasure; a man she owed, a man who had given her Peter as a permanent reminder of her debt.

Yet she still felt the draw of an old friendship, sought its warmth, sought to rekindle what had once been there.

What had once been there...

———

It had begun as an accident. They were from different worlds – Devereaux an upper middle class figure, the son of a prominent aircraft manufacturer, she from local farming stock, meeting at a cricket match in which her brothers were boisterous participants. Her job had been the scoreboard, female players being a rarity. Next, an invitation to a dance, then a discussion about animals, mainly dogs and horses, and finally the discovery of a common obsession: flying.

But that wasn't all. Devereaux was a lame duck. His withered right arm made him a liability both as a flyer and as an active scion of his pioneer aeronautical family. The result was a transference; he projected all his fascination, insight, skill and ambition on to her. In a sense, he became her. Her support, planner, organiser, backer and propagandist. He was her and she was dependent on him. He even contributed the aircraft, a Gipsy Moth, that took her across oceans and deserts and made her one of an elite band of long-distance pioneers.

Then, the split. During Helen's long and lonely record-busting flight to Peking, Ashley Devereaux gave in to the entreaties of his family and married a member of his own class: Lady Olga Cavendish, the moneyed owner of a string of superb show horses.

Helen's reaction to this abandonment was to submerge her hurt and work to keep the partnership on a business footing, to pretend to herself that she no longer had feelings for this man.

And then joy; into her life strode the man from Missouri. Marriage and a beautiful son.

That was then.

This was now.

'No, Dev, sorry,' Helen told him, 'you have to live this life under the Blitz but I don't, I'm getting back to the family and Peter.'

He looked disappointed but walked her back to the Tube, anxious to talk, clearly needing someone with whom to share the latest stark figures. 'Looks like Hitler really means to level this place. The figures the intelligence boys have come up with are terrifying. Talking about rockets that carry ten tons of high explosive. That's four times bigger than anything they've dropped so far.'

'You're scaring me,' she said, quickening her pace to the station.

But he wasn't finished. Talking about it was his way of coping. 'Apparently, the Germans are making thousands of these things. Plan to send one over every hour round the clock... we're talking 10,000 dead and 20,000 seriously injured. Civil defence will be overwhelmed, won't be able to cope.'

At the station she put a hand on his arm and said, 'I feel terrible getting away while you have to stay. Surely, they'll evacuate the city?'

'On the cards... if the intelligence proves to be correct.'

Part of her was still attracted to him; the other part saw the very thought of a re-engagement as a massive betrayal of her husband's memory.

'Best of luck, Dev,' she said, 'look after yourself.'

Chapter Twenty-Two

It all kicked off a week later; the urgent summons, the car provided, a fast-striding escort smoothing her way through the endless corridors to conference room 641 with not a sign of the dreadful Gascoigne to waylay her. Devereaux, Leo Beck, that fellow Menzies you pronounced as Mingis and a man she didn't recognise appeared to be waiting for her outside the door.

As she was waved through, Devereaux moved close and whispered, 'Someone's dropped out, so you're in.'

She was already inside the room before she could express her puzzlement at this remark.

Instead she smiled a big welcome at Beck, glad to see that he appeared to be in good shape, though it was obvious he was agitated and wanted to speak privately. What he did manage to say to her in a low voice was: 'Something important to tell you.' This was followed by a stricken grimace. 'But I don't know if I've done the right thing...'

Her attention was drawn away by a familiar if unwelcome voice. 'Sign here!'

So Gascoigne, her old adversary from 949A, had made an appearance after all, thrusting a pen into her hand and when she looked down she saw the document was the Official Secrets Act.

This is all moving much too fast, she thought. After all the talk with Devereaux about the V-2 she had an instant premonition; that before whatever was about to happen in this room a dreadful explosion would occur and destroy them all. In her mind's eye she lived the terror of a rocket strike: the overwhelming noise, the ceiling caving in, enormous steel girders crashing to the basement, a rain of falling bricks and plaster, the crater, a dust bowl, the wails of the trapped, the numbing silence of the buried...

'Thank you for coming in,' said a voice, breaking into her nightmare. She made an effort to concentrate and stared about her. Curtains closed as before, another set of strange faces. It seemed as if the very walls of the room were holding their breath. In the routine circumstances of a formal interview she might have been intimidated and reacted with shyness, but this was not a normal occasion. Who were these people who never announced themselves, never explained, never gave names?

She noted the absentees: no Morrison, no Cherwell, no prime ministerial advisers, nor politicians. She had enough about her to know she was now dealing with the secret world and this was how the spooks behaved. All normal civility was off the menu, so why should she pay them deference or respect?

Scared and intimidated – but her blood was up.

It was the young, good-looking one who made the running. Smiled a lot, smart suit, red bow tie, an obvious charmer and therefore all the more dangerous.

'We've brought you in because we're very impressed with

your reactions to the difficult situation you found yourself in at the Channel Islands,' he said.

She sighed inwardly. This was a change from all the earlier suspicions and smears produced by Gascoigne and Cherwell.

'How you conducted yourself when stranded in Jersey was highly inventive and resourceful,' the voice said. 'In the face of a thoroughly unfamiliar situation you acted with commendable aplomb. Confident, creative, decisive, commanding. All the qualities we are interested in.'

Helen said nothing, aware this change of tone was leading somewhere, wary in fact, about where this conversation might eventually land.

'We know you have a grasp of the broad picture of the German secret weapons programme and the imperative need to find evidence and detail of its existence.'

She said nothing.

'And we'd like to put you more fully in the picture.'

The words *Why me?* were screaming in her head, but she merely raised a querulous eyebrow and said: 'And this is because...?'

Red Bow Tie stared back at her and merely said: 'This is because we now need to resolve a certain situation.'

A tall figure with strands of thinning ginger hair spanning a bald pate had been standing silently at the back of the room next to a large, covered board. It was now that he moved into action, removing the covers to reveal a large map of northern Europe.

He looked at Helen directly and announced, 'This is what we need to explain.'

It was a history lesson, an elaborate briefing that took in the discovery of the German base for developing both the V-1 and V-2 weapons, a tiny speck on the map called Peenemünde, on the German Baltic coast, which had been bombed and damaged by the Allied air forces just months before.

Now the Germans had moved their production facilities to a secret location – no one knew where – and at the same time set up a new base for test firings in Poland, at a place called Blizna.

At this Helen's brow knitted. It was all getting hugely involved. How did this affect her? Again, the unspoken, unanswered question: *why me?*

He was tapping the map and telling her that debris from the test firings was falling all over Poland; that the Germans were racing about trying to recover the debris to prevent V-2 secrets from leaking out, but that Polish underground fighters were often beating them to it and scooping up the remains.

She felt like shrugging but didn't.

'You'll know from other conversations that getting our hands on this debris is vital so that our experts can work out how this thing functions and then how to destroy it. Right?' He looked at her questioningly, forcing her to nod, as if she were in some tutorial.

'Well, the other day, a complete and undamaged test rocket landed in the mud of the River Bug. Normally, these things disintegrate on hitting the ground. There's no explosive in them. The nose cone's filled with sand but the impact still wrecks the rest of the rocket – but this one is different. Solid gold! A complete rocket intact in the oozy mud of the river.'

He looked hard at her. 'The Poles hid it in the mud, saw off the Germans and have now transported it secretly to one of their barns.'

At this point the smoothie with the red bow tie took over the briefing. He put his hands on his hips and smiled at her. 'So you see, we simply have to get hold of this thing. A complete undamaged rocket. Amazing good fortune. And we must have it.

Transport it back here to the UK so the Farnborough boffins can get to work on it.'

He paused and looked at her intently. 'The problem is, how to get it back from Poland.' A long breath. 'And that's where you come in.'

Chapter Twenty-Three

Helen scowled, mystified, and her attention was caught by a movement behind.

It was Leo, swallowing, making a face, mouthing a silent word. *Sorry.*

'What we have planned,' Bow Tie said, 'is to send in a Dakota – our trusty transport plane – to bring back the vitals of this rocket. It has to be a twin-engine job because of the weight of all that metal. It's going to take off from our forward base in Italy – that's the nearest point to Poland for our chaps. Then fly across Axis territory and land at a deserted aerodrome behind Jerry's back, pick up the goodies and fly home again.'

He shrugged. 'Simple really; nothing to it.'

There was laughter from the other side of the room but she wasn't joining in. He was being ridiculous. *No, no, no!* The negatives were screaming in Helen's head. Dozens of daring crewmen were vying for dangerous missions, anxious to prove themselves, any one of them could be detailed for the mission.

'You'll be aware of how vital it is to have expertise on the spot when this thing is examined.' The briefing was relentless.

'We're not relying entirely on our friends the Poles for technical expertise and analysis. When we fly in our Dakota we're also sending in our own expert.' And here he pointed. 'Your very own friend, Mr Beck.'

Helen switched her gaze back to Leo, who seemed to be shrinking into himself with regret and embarrassment, still mouthing that word. *Sorry.* She looked back at the briefer.

'And that's the thing, you see, Mrs Fairfax, our Mr Beck will only agree to make the journey on one condition.' Pause. 'He'll only go if you go too.'

Helen was trying to take in all the implications of this prospect, conflicting emotions racing through her head, barely conscious that an argument was taking place among the anonymous members of the panel.

Well, not entirely anonymous. Gascoigne was leading the charge. 'I still say it's too big a risk. We only have their word on the veracity of all this. It could still be a German con. A plant. Beck could still turn on us when he's back on the ground, back in German territory, and betray the whole operation.'

'I must say I find that extremely unlikely.' It was Bow Tie again. 'The Farnborough team have given him a clean bill of health. Say he's completely genuine, he wants to help us all the way, no chance that he's part of any trick.'

'Still a risk!'

A slight cough and all eyes turned to Menzies. 'This is my assessment of the situation,' he said. 'The prize is so big that almost any risk is worth running.'

This seemed to settle the argument, a final judgement from a man she guessed was at the top of the Intelligence tree.

Bow Tie turned his attention back to Helen. 'So you see, you and Beck appear to be our team. With his unique expertise and your proven resourcefulness and flying experience, we very much hope you'll volunteer for this mission.'

Chapter Twenty-Four

Devereaux was sitting on a corridor seat and shaking his head in astonishment. 'Good God, Helen, do you have to put your neck on the line every time? It's like you're some sort of danger junkie!'

She snorted. 'Really? After all the stuff we got up to in the Moth. Wasn't that a bit of a risk? Tehran and Calcutta...'

'A measured risk. We knew what we were doing back then, taking all the necessary precautions, but this... this is crazy. Flying a Dak across enemy territory? You'll never make it. They'll shoot you down.'

She looked away. 'Not according to them in there.' She pointed at the committee room door, although her tone sounded somewhere short of conviction. 'Apparently, the Germans are in a bad way. Retreating so fast the Ruskies can't keep up. And their air units are in disarray.'

He snorted. 'Easy for them to say. Sitting nice and comfortable in the War House. And a Dakota. Have you flown it before?'

'No prob. Do you doubt me?'

'Of course not, but it has no armament, can't defend itself, it's slow, it's vulnerable, you'll be dead meat if you meet Fritz over Vienna or the Tatra mountains.' A taut silence then. He broke it with another protest. 'Look, I had nothing to do with this thing. I had no idea what they were going to spring on you. Apparently the bloke they had pencilled in for the job walked away. I think this is a very bad idea. Leave it to someone else...'

'Leo. He'll only go if I go.'

A dismissive snort. 'Ignore him.'

'I can't. I brought him over, remember, I did a big sell job on him, persuaded him to defect, and that takes courage. He only agreed because he trusts me. Trust. Protection. And a promise. These words mean something to him and they mean something to me.'

'You're making yourself a martyr. You've done your bit. Think of your son.'

'I am thinking of my son.'

Devereaux looked away and gazed out of a small slit window, high up in the wall, without making further comment. She sat grim-faced staring at the floor, but felt the imperative need to answer. 'This is what Peter will expect of me – when he grows up,' she said. 'This is my opportunity. To do something significant.'

'But why?'

'You know why.' Her eyelashes flickered. 'I have to do this. For him. For Hank.'

Another long silence, then Devereaux said, 'Forgive me for straying into your private life, for saying this, for being so very blunt... but avenging a dead husband is all very well but the son is the living embodiment of the man.'

When she didn't reply, he said, 'I would suggest a first priority would be to foster the interests of the man's son, to protect and to advance...'

'No!'

He stopped.

The flame of anger over Hank's going flickered white hot. In Helen's mind, it would not be doused by this kind of cosy philosophy, a rationale, she told herself, for doing nothing and accepting the injustice of his death at the hand of an oppressive, cruel and bestial enemy.

'There is evil out there,' she said, 'I have to do this.'

Chapter Twenty-Five

They offered Helen twenty-four hours to consider her answer but she'd already made her decision. She would not pass up the chance to fulfil the vow she made the day she fled the V-1 in London. At the end of that awful day of destruction and panic, she had promised vengeance to the perpetrators of terror.

'My decision,' she said, 'is *Yes* but with one important proviso.' She took a deep breath. 'I won't consider this project without power of command. Having limited authority would be a recipe for disaster.'

There was a long silence at this and she thought back to the moment in the Channel Islands when she realised she had the whip hand over Friedrich Winter. This was another of those moments. 'If I'm to fly this aircraft, it will be as captain of the ship, but I also want overall authority for the mission. That is my condition.'

The shark in the bow tie coughed and found his voice. 'I think the committee would not normally look favourably upon such an ultimatum.' Another pause, then a slight quizzical shrug of the shoulder as he added, 'I rather think we had someone else pencilled in for this role.'

Helen shook her head, indicating a complete rejection of such an idea. This was the moment, she knew, when she had to take the toughest of stances, a time to be as assertive as never before. There would be difficult decisions to make and it would be impossible if someone else were making them. Besides, it was all a question of justice, of doing the right thing. By Leo. And by Hank. And by Peter.

She faced her inquisitor. 'No good at all unless I'm Number One,' she said. 'Any woman taking on this job has to have ultimate command – otherwise, she'd be trampled to death by the male ego. My presence then would be worse than useless, just window dressing.' There was a firm set to her jawline, then she changed her tone to one of sweet reason. 'Look, I'm different from your normal run of officers. I'm not out of the form book. I'm used to dealing with totally unfamiliar situations, making tough decisions, getting out of awkward jams.' She had in mind the half dozen forced landings, smashed props and overturned aircraft that had been her pioneering experience. She said, 'I know the man, I know the subject and I know the aircraft.'

She also knew they'd seen her log book with all her flights in Blenheims, Oxfords and Dakotas. They'd also trawled her record, including the pioneering thirties. She held her breath. They were in a bind. They needed the expertise of Leo Beck, the man who built V-2s, to be on the ground when the remains of the test rocket were dismantled. He also came with a condition attached.

'So my stipulation remains. I'll consider myself highly privileged to be part of this project – but only if I'm leading it.' She used The Stare, the one her brothers always remarked upon, to gaze back at the assembled spooks, projecting what she hoped was an impressive air of confident command.

Nevertheless she had to quell the cold chill of apprehension as she awaited their decision.

———

Outside, as they sat on uncomfortable hard chairs in the corridor, Devereaux chuckled and shook his head all at the same time. 'I have to give it to you,' he told her, 'it'll be all around the War House about you. For sheer balls, that was a royal command performance you gave in there, even though I still say you're off your silly head.'

'I want this job,' she said shortly.

'And how!' He rolled his eyes. 'And you've set them a bit of a conundrum. Putting an Attagirl in charge.'

'I'm not going to be bossed around by a bunch of air force cowboys.'

She let him prattle on as the realisation began to seep into her consciousness that this time she had jumped straight in at the deep end. As the boss of Operation Skyhawk – that's what they were calling it – she would not be operating alone but as a member of a team. And she had never been a team player. As a lone aviator all those years back she had merely been supported by the young and pliable version of Devereaux himself. That was then.

Now, if chosen, she would have to do what she had never done before: prove herself in command.

It took less than twenty minutes. The door to Room 641 eased open and she was summoned back in to be wrapped in Bow Tie's beatific smile and learn the all-important verdict, proving that he and his nameless acolytes on the secret committee were capable of quite radical decisions when faced with the challenge of arranging the impossible.

Chapter Twenty-Six

The aircraft shook like a beast struggling to free itself from a mantrap. This was a visceral experience, the roaring vibration entering every fibre of the being, the noise of the engines throwing a deadening blanket over eardrums, speech all but impossible.

Helen, wearing a tight expression of acute concentration, gripped the half-moon control column, eyes switching between instruments and the rushing runway disappearing below. This was her territory; despite that, she doubted if anyone really felt comfortable with a level of noise that seemed to invade every corner and millimetre of the brain space. You could only dream about the concept of the perfect silence. Finally, at full throttle, the bucking beast freed itself from the grip of gravity and lifted into the air.

This was the Dakota, workhorse of the Western military and beloved of its pilots for its rugged nature and welcome habit of always coming home. To her right, at the co-pilot controls, was Flying Officer Rozhkov, half Australian, half Russian, veteran of the RAF's transport flight. Behind was her flight engineer and navigator Roly Lucas and further back Jack Silvers, the radio operator.

Lucas was already checking for drift and correcting their course towards an obscure corner of a remote region of Poland – Axis territory and more than 1,000 miles across enemy air space. They all knew the risks; this was a flight without a single defensive armament. Their only hope: guile and disguise.

She looked down briefly at the name tag on her new air force overalls; *Fairfax,* it said, *flight captain.* Her mouth relaxed into the hint of a smile, recalling the words of the chairman back in the War House: 'Commendable ingenuity and foresight in Jersey... a commanding presence at interview... for a highly unusual mission a unique and extraordinary leader.'

A gratifying personal endorsement and instant promotion to a three-striper, but this was no longer the rarefied atmosphere of the War House in London. This was Italy, or that portion of the country denied to the Germans and now used at Brindisi by a sizeable chunk of the Allied Mediterranean air force.

She turned to look back at her 'cargo' in the bleak interior of the Dakota; a collection of desperados, Polish Home Army volunteers flying in as resistance fighters. Their perch, on bucket seats along the sides of the craft, was even more uncomfortable, vibrations going straight into their backs from the single skin airframe. It must surely appear to them that the aircraft was nothing more than a collection of fragile tinny boxes bolted together.

However, the most valuable cargo, as far as she was concerned, was Leo Beck. It was his technical expertise in the search for the secrets of the V-2 that was at the heart of this journey. She reminded herself once again of her promise to protect him from the expected, if understandable, animosity of the Poles.

Out on the wings, two Pratt and Witney Wasp radials were

doing their best to assault everyone's eardrums. Gone were the RAF roundels; in their place some large black letters imitating the style of the Luftwaffe's equivalent transport plane, the Iron Annie. And below, a nondescript grey paint was picked out with a dark blue lining which they hoped would make them invisible from the ground.

She recalled the urgent preliminaries to the flight: the tests, the briefings, the loading and the introduction to the crew. 'You'll be dealing with some very rough trade on the other side.' This was Quarmby, another spokesman, another source of instruction. 'That's why your co-pilot is practically a native. Speaks the lingo, understands the people and their psychology.'

He didn't say it, but she suspected that Rozhkov was the man pencilled in as leader before being stood down to make way for her.

Arriving in Brindisi, she had told herself this was the moment to sharpen her resolve, to quell lingering doubts or trembles. Time to banish bad habits like shyness and a tendency to give way to stronger personalities. Time to be as assertive as never before. No more charm, no more smiles, no easy-does it. It was one thing to talk tough to a set of London spooks. Now she had to do it for real.

She glanced at the dour-faced man to her right, presenting another test she could not fail. She'd already had one run-in. 'Flown one of these beauties before?' he demanded, slapping the cockpit frontage when she first took her place.

'Naturally.' She tapped the blue bible of the ferry pilot, a compendium of notes of how to fly a thousand different planes.

'Well, you need to know a couple of things about this one,' he said, 'you'll need a boot full of rudder to take her into a turn, and she's a tail dragger.'

She didn't like his condescending tone but countered with an even one. 'My little book has all sorts of useful things to look out for, quirks and tricks. For instance...' She opened a page. 'The tail wheel lock is under the throttle, and not as marked next to the oil controls.' She smiled. 'Useful or what?'

'Of course I knew that,' he said, staring away from her out of the window.

It was going to be a battle to assert her authority, she knew, as she maintained a sharp look out on the horizon. The Dak was no match for a fighter, defenceless against cannon fire, but so far they were lucky. No hostiles had made an appearance and she peered back over her shoulder and used the voice pipe to attract the attention of Lucas. 'Present course and position?'

He came forward with his chart, hollering like a town crier above the din, tracing once again their planned routing; eastwards across the Adriatic to the tip of the Albanian coast at Scutari then turning northwards to cross Hungary to reach the Danube. She looked at the markings below their flight path: Sarajevo, Budapest, Slovakia, Krakow.

'At 1800 hours we should climb to ceiling,' Lucas said, and she knew this was to cross over the Carpathian mountain range into Poland.

She thanked him and thought back over the last frantic forty-eight hours spent briefing and getting to know the crew. She had immediately taken to Sergeant Lucas, an older man, calm, phlegmatic and, she predicted, cool in a crisis. Just the sort she needed for the job. They'd even exchanged notes about their children.

'Even as parents, we have to put ourselves in danger,' he said, throwing a ring of reassurance around them both. 'It's part of our duty in this war. No reason why it shouldn't apply to everyone in the service.'

He was past the age when he could have been selected for the infantry or the guns and could easily have opted for a quiet number in a supply depot, seeing out the war as a sedentary soldier. Instead, he had volunteered for the air force and then again for this particular flight. In her mind, that made them equals – or, as Devereaux would doubtless have put it, had he been present, 'equally bonkers'.

She was lifting the nose of the aircraft preparatory to perform the climb manoeuvre necessary on the approach to the Tatra mountains, still scanning the sky and finding it empty of the enemy. Would their luck hold all the way? And back again?

Like Lucas, her thoughts turned easily to family. What was Peter doing at this minute as his mother piloted her way into the great unknown? Sitting on one of her father's old tractors no doubt, turning the wheel and pretending to drive; perhaps playing snap with his granny – he was mad about the game. Very soon it would be time for another chapter of the adventurous *Just William* and his lisping nemesis, Violet Elizabeth Bott, the annoying girl next door, read to him as he squatted on a cushion by the fire. Lucas's son, she learned, wore a shirt proclaiming loyalty to Tranmere Rovers. Peter's was for Bury Town.

'What's that?' Rozhkov's voice cut into her thoughts like a slap to the face, bringing her sharply back to the present. 'See it? A black dot, over to starboard?'

She looked, nodded and said nothing.

'It's them,' Rozhkov said, a slight lift to the timbre of the voice. 'Best pull away before they spot us.'

Helen shook her head. 'If we've seen them, they've seen us.'

'All the more reason...'

'Quiet, please,' she said. She could feel Rozhkov simmering in a sweat of anger and panic but she resisted the instinct to flee. She knew this was to be her moment of trial. Guile and good old-fashioned impudence would get them out of trouble. Her jaw jutted and her fingers seemed glued to the stick.

Very soon the black dot enlarged and they could see quite

clearly the newcomer was a Messerschmitt Bf109, perhaps the fiercest of the world's fighter aeroplanes, not that they had any chance against even the weakest cannon. The newcomer was travelling at least 100 miles an hour faster than the Dak and overhauling them at an astonishing rate.

'You've wasted our chance to get away,' Rozhkov said bitterly.

She held her breath and stared at the approaching adversary. She held the lives of all these people in her hands but had no doubts. Hers was the right tactic. There would be no wilting. And for some unfathomable reason she thought of Peter and his obsession with playing snap. She wasn't a card player, yet she said: 'When you're playing the weakest of hands, a ruse is the best option.'

Rozhkov made a dismissive gesture.

She said: 'Get ready to wave.'

'You don't know what you're doing...'

'Wave now, faster, more vigorous than that and smile, smile...'

She was flying straight and level but performing a sedate waggle of the wings.

'You're mad, let me have control.'

'Shut up and wave.'

The 109 pilot cut his speed and came alongside, clearly mystified, and Helen pushed open the sliding pilot's window, braving the airflow, and waved like a visiting royal. She could see the helmeted figure indicating his wireless mike. Answering, she pointed above, then made a cutting gesture.

The 109 pilot flew alongside for another long minute, confused and uncertain. His aircraft looked sleek and evil and she knew the wings contained hundreds of rounds of lethal cannon shells. She could see him quite clearly inside his Perspex cockpit cover.

But would he fall for it?

There was a hole in her stomach as she thought about his finger on the button and the patter of bullets which would tear through the thin skin of the Dak, killing them all. But crazy things happened in war and in the chaos of the German retreat the man might just accept that this aerial stranger was in fact a friend.

She waved again, examining the enemy plane at close quarters, something she did not expect to do; a strange and bizarre colour combination, she noted, one part a dusty violet purple, another grey-green, the underside an ash grey. The big black cross was there, of course, but just below the cockpit window was a name produced in a handwritten style.

Ingeborg.

On seeing that, Helen waved even harder.

Inside the belly of the aircraft the mood was grim. The man with the livid scar running from his temple to his chin peered from a porthole window at the 109 flying alongside.

He was still clutching the stock of a British-issue Lee Enfield rifle. How useless this weapon now seemed, along with all the other paraphernalia of rebellion, the Sten guns and the grenades.

It was a bitter moment. He and his fellow fighters had come to raise an insurrection against the German occupier of their native Poland. Instead, they were looking at instant obliteration in the air before ever reaching the homeland.

He looked in despair at the next man, a gaunt forty-one-year-old with permanent seven o'clock shadow, sucking matchsticks because of the no-smoking rule.

'Meet you on the other side of hell.'

They'd both endured much to get this far: escape from the battlefield of Europe, a long trek to Britain, then harsh training for the return. Now on the cusp of their hoped-for uprising they faced ignominious extinction. Some minutes before they had stopped listening to the voluble man Rozhkov and his tedious complaints. Their one slim hope lay with the 'girl pilot' whose reputation he appeared determined to traduce.

In this vein they peered from the portholes and awaited their fate.

Chapter Twenty-Seven

The pilot of the 109 clearly had better things to do than fuss with a strange and cumbersome transport plane chock full of wildly waving passengers. Maybe the female face did it.

Whatever it was, Helen saw him shrug and pull away.

Rozhkov couldn't speak.

Lucas gave her the thumbs up but shouted, 'Surely he should have recognised a Dakota.'

'Lots of captured aircraft on both sides,' she answered, feeling the tension drain rapidly away. She was coming down from a high and became almost incredulous at her own actions, asking herself: *where did I get the sheer gall for that?* Was it the adrenalin of action, rising to the occasion, the ego of command? No, she told herself, she wasn't attracted to danger like a moth to a flame, as Devereaux had claimed. She had normal reactions to fear, but the appearance of the fighter was precisely the moment to live up to her son's expectations. He expected courage and she could never have faced him, or even looked herself in the mirror, had she turned tail and run.

There was a movement in the seat opposite. Rozhkov looked

as if he were about to be sick. When he did look up his expression was bleak. 'That was a really crazy thing to do back there. You could have got us all killed.'

'Oh, don't thank me for saving your precious neck.'

'There was enough distance, enough time. You should have veered away, turned back.'

'And done a runner? Don't be stupid. You could see the difference in speeds, he had all the advantage. To have run would have been a signal to him... Here was his enemy.'

'Nonsense.' Rozhkov glowered and then looked away, refusing to make eye contact, his face a froth of fury. Suddenly, without another word, he disengaged the straps, stood and climbed out of his seat, headed for the belly of the plane. It was usual for crew movements to be sanctioned by the pilot; a co-pilot was not expected to abandon his position without authority. Should she have pulled him up about it? She knew this was another test, but she was reluctant to rush into a confrontation.

The flight continued without further conversation as if all was normal, except that the seat on the right remained empty.

Then Helen was conscious of another presence, a person behind, perhaps waiting for her attention. She turned.

Leo Beck gave her a diffident little smile and lifted the ear flap of her helmet. 'Thought you should know...' he shouted, but the rest of his words were drowned out by the noise of the engines.

'Speak up, Leo.'

'The other pilot... well, he's not speaking well of you.'

'You can tell?'

'Enough Polish to know it's not good.'

'Go on.'

'He's conspiring against you, trying to whip up feelings, talking about bad women, bad flying, that sort of thing, fermenting a rebellion, trying to get them on his side...'

'Out of my way!' A gruff order from Rozhkov who had unexpectedly reappeared, shoving and pulling Beck behind him so that he could regain his seat. 'Who let this little Kraut turn-coat on board? Why is he here at all?'

'I'd be obliged if you treat all passengers and crew with respect,' she said sharply as Beck retreated.

Rozhkov ignored this and turned to stare at her. He was using the intercom, pointing an accusing finger. 'It has become painfully obvious to me and anyone with any common sense that we have a problem.'

'What problem?'

'You! You're the problem. Not competent to do this job, just a girl, they must have been mad to appoint you... over me.'

'Ah! So now we have it. The man passed over, the bruised feelings, the personal pique.' She drew herself up. This was the moment she knew would come – albeit earlier than she hoped. 'Let me tell you something. I won't have my orders questioned. This is not a matter for debate–'

'You're not up to the job!' It was a shout, a protest, a demand all in one. 'I think you had better hand over this mission to me, to someone who knows what he's doing. I'm an established flyer, lots of experience while you... You're completely out of your depth.'

She pressed the autopilot button and leaned closer, as near as the straps would allow so that she could get up close to that mottled angry face.

'I am in charge of this aircraft and this mission... and you are not. Do you hear? NOT. I know you've been trying to stir things up back there–' She pointed to the rear of the aircraft. 'But that does not impress me. Shades of mutiny. We will deal with that later. In the meantime, I have no intention of relinquishing my position, so you had better decide, right here and now. Are you with me, or are you against me?'

Chapter Twenty-Eight

Rozhkov was snorting and shaking his head all at the same time, as if someone had just made an absurd jest, foolishly challenging a determined and masterful aviator about to pull the irons from a disastrous fire.

He looked at Helen. 'Am I with you?' Another snort. 'Certainly not.'

Her straps flew free at an angry flick of the button and she was towering towards him, leaning over the large control pedestal that separated the two pilot positions. A range of levers with coloured knobs kept them from touching: two whites for prop speed, two blacks for throttles, two reds for mixtures. Careful to raise her arm to clear the levers, she jabbed a finger at her antagonist.

'Then get out of that chair. If you won't obey orders, you no longer have any authority, or any role on this flight. You are no longer a member of this crew, so get to the rear.'

Her reaction seemed to take him by surprise. It looked as if he hadn't expected defiance. Traces of shock and incredulity were evident as he said, 'You can't sack me, I'm the co-pilot. This is my–'

'I don't need a co-pilot,' she thundered. 'I've flown aircraft like this plenty of times on my own or with just an engineer, so get to the rear.' Her arm was outstretched in the direction she wanted him to go.

He swallowed. Perhaps he thought she would crumple and surrender. 'I'm not falling for this bluster,' he said, then regaining some of his earlier confidence, said, 'Told you before, this job's too much for you. Just step aside and I'll take it from here.'

'Sergeant.' A quieter tone from her now.

'Yes, skip,' Lucas answered without pause, demonstrating his close attention and making plain his allegiance.

'Do you have the key to the box?'

A rattle and the sound of a lid being opened. The captain's box contained several items, usually secret material, but it also included a pistol.

Rozhkov's tense gaze followed her every move, saw where her attention lay. He said, 'You must be mad. A firearm in an aircraft, would wreck us, shows how much you know—'

'Open the window!' She was sliding open hers.

'What?'

'Open your window!'

'Crazy woman! She's going to kill us all.'

But she wasn't handling the gun. Open windows were not a device to deaden a firearms blast but a ruse to scare him. What came out of the box was a pair of handcuffs. 'Silvers.' The radio man appeared, bunching up in the confined space, surrounding and pinning the now astonished co-pilot to his seat.

'You and Lucas do the necessary, please.'

It was a struggle: the confined space, unwilling wrists, the twisting resisting body, a stiff mechanism making the job difficult. Grunting, sweating, swearing, twisting, struggling, the co-pilot was a puffing, wriggling monster, opposition Lucas and Silvers were determined to defeat. It looked like mission impossible but these two were not to be thwarted and finally the deed was done.

Rozhkov was spluttering: 'There's a whole planeload of tough fighters back there with weaponry...'

'Who cannot themselves fly a plane,' she said, 'and who will not fancy a crash landing, a return to Italy or making themselves a martyr for you. All they want is to get to Poland.'

After much pulling and hauling, Rozhkov was lifted from his seat and deposited unceremoniously in the body of the aircraft and fastened to a stanchion before an array of astonished faces.

'The captain says,' Lucas announced, 'that no one is to talk to him – or to pay any attention to what he says.'

Back in the cockpit Helen resumed control, scanning the sky in a resolute but sullen silence, angry that she had been forced into such drastic action. It had wrecked her hope, revealed now to be a naive one, of leading a happy, focused and co-operative crew.

Lucas's head came level with her eyeline. He was studying her face. 'Why so down?' he asked. 'You did absolutely the right thing. You had no choice.'

She nodded, not wanting to speak.

Had that been her voice commanding Rozhkov to get to the rear? She hadn't liked the sound or the tone of it. Was that what this job had made her, the harsh wielder of authority? But Lucas was right; she could not have met such aggression with passivity. Alone on those early pioneering odysseys across desert and tundra there had been an element of self-containment about her; perhaps also a shade of the romantic. No longer.

She knew now she would have a fight on her hands when – and if – they managed to put down in Poland. Rozhkov was a voluble and mutinous problem and Leo would be hated as a German national. Doubtless Rozhkov intended to lead a group of troublemakers, stirring up the locals to an understandable resentment, but whatever else happened she had to protect Leo.

Her steel was being tested at the very outset of the mission. For everyone's sake she must hold her own or lose respect of the crew and the ability to command. It was her operation; she would not relinquish it.

She fell back on her personal credo: *remember who I am and why I am doing this.* She was doing this for them – for Peter and for Hank and for Leo.

She called for a navigational check and was reassured they were still on course. She did her best to put these troubles out of her mind, her attention taken by changes of course due to drift and wind, then by the big climb and finally by the search for their destination. This was a grass airstrip used until two days previously by the Luftwaffe. Since then, the anonymous briefers back at Brindisi had assured her, the German airmen had retreated westwards. She scanned the horizon for any sign of further aerial contact; once on the ground they would be twice as vulnerable.

Stiff and crinkly Air Ministry charts were being held by both Lucas and Silvers who peered anxiously forwards for the landmarks they memorised: four sheds, a line of trees, a small river and tracks in the shape of an L.

The strip was situated in a vast rolling green countryside shorn of urban development and they had already spotted and then discarded one 'probable' sighting.

She could hear Rozhkov talking non-stop at the back of the

aircraft, doubtless pouring poison into any listening ear. Other flights, she knew, had the benefit of sophisticated navigational systems, a ground beacon in some cases, but such equipment was not possible in occupied territory. Instead, they had to search the target area systematically in wide sweeps.

As well as locating the place she was tensed for a fast turn-around; once landed they needed a rapid disembarkation of passengers and the new cargo loaded for take-off. She couldn't afford any delays. The crew were coached for a streamlined operation: identify the new cargo, discover the weight of the heaviest item and place in correct position. It had to be slick. Every minute on the ground was a peril.

Still they circled, expecting signs from the ground; bonfires had been promised. Such a long way to come to fail now.

At last a second sighting looked promising; they were down low, visibility was good and all the elements, sheds and the river, appeared to be in place. They completed two circuits in wary preparation but without the necessary confirmation.

Something vital was missing.

People. The place was deserted.

Chapter Twenty-Nine

Helen scanned the ground, but nothing stirred and the sheds remained closed tight.

Suddenly, a transformation. A lamp flicked out the recognition signal and small figures – it seemed like hundreds of them – appeared as if from nowhere; in fact, from hedges, bushes and sheds. Bonfires were lit and Roly Lucas gave the thumbs up sign. Sighs of relief. Now to get the Dak down.

Helen swallowed. No need to feel nervous, she'd done this a thousand times.

Back in the belly of the aircraft they'd sensed the tension of the moment. Rozhkov was at his most jeering, screaming out insults so loud it was impossible to miss them even above the cacophony of the engines.

'Getting windy, Fairfax? All of a dither! Admit it, you know you're no good.'

She clenched her jaw and circled around once more to check the strip for obstacles or traps left behind by the enemy. That job was supposed to have been done by the partisans, but you never knew. Two Fieseler Storch aircraft had been in residence just forty-eight hours before but the place appeared to be clear of hidden perils.

The voice again: 'Going to make a mess of it, are you?'

She could see a lot of surface water and knew a waterlogged strip might prove problematic for their take-off. Despite this she made the decision: she would land. In truth, she was always going to risk it, the importance of the mission militating against caution in favour of the calculated risk.

But hadn't she told herself that once before?

'Stuck in a funk?' The voice from the back was unremitting. 'Just give me the job. Give the job to a proper professional.'

She brought the Dak round on the final approach. *Don't let him win*, she told herself, *don't let prejudice get to you.*

But when the wheels made contact with the surface a great shower of spray flew into the air, enveloping the aircraft, blotting out all vision, turning the final moments of arrival into haze. The surface water acted as an emergency brake and the Dak bulldozed to a sudden stop, slewing slightly to starboard as it did so.

Bodies surged, straps strained, breathing held.

Then many gentle sighs of relief.

The voice continued: 'Told you! You're a lousy pilot. Mucked it up again.'

'I'm going to gag that bloody man,' Lucas said.

Turning the aircraft around for the anticipated fast getaway proved a cumbersome manoeuvre due to the water. The place was swimming, but eventually the aircraft was taxied close to the largest of the sheds. This, she guessed, was where the cargo would be hidden. She kept the props turning.

'Okay, Roly, get out there with the clipboard, all officious like, and do your stuff. No messing, no delay.'

Then she turned to Jack Silvers. 'You know what to do. This lot have to be out quicker than–'

'Don't worry, they're on their way. All except him.'

She ignored the problem of the hollering Rozhkov, who had been handcuffed to a stanchion next to his seat, turned away and opened the pilot's sliding window. She peered down at what was happening below, unimpressed by the speed of reaction on the ground. She could see now that most of the crowd were children, many of them shoeless, milling around purposelessly, enjoying the spectacle and no help at all in the operation. In their midst a huge figure approached at a sedate pace; bronzed, broad-shouldered, shiny bald head and a huge black beard that looked like a bush. He had on a ragged grey overcoat with a rifle slung over the shoulder.

She'd been warned to expect him. This had to be him. The Bull.

'An incredible man,' Devereaux had said back in the briefing room at Brindisi. 'The man's as bold as brass. He's no secretive figure, with that head and beard he stands out a mile. His photo's been all over the German wanted posters for years but still they can't get him.'

She shrugged. 'How? What's his secret?'

'Four long years and he's managed to stay alive, surviving in the forests. They've sent out hunting parties and patrols without success, that's the measure of the man. An expert survivor, top explosives expert. Used to run a quarry before the war. Wreaks chaos on their lines of communication.'

'And this is my contact?'

'This is your contact. The name's Kaminski – Jerzy Kaminski – but everyone calls him the Bull.'

She was still peering down from the cockpit window, looking at the meeting between Lucas and the Bull, but it didn't seem to be progressing well. None of the instant spark of action she was expecting. Instead Lucas was looking back up at her, shaking his head and shrugging his shoulders.

'Dammit, what now?'

She disengaged from the straps and hauled herself out of the cockpit, back to the door, coming smartly down the three steps and walking quickly to where the two men stood.

'Problem,' announced Lucas. 'They're not ready.'

'What?' She was outraged. They had been assured this was to be an efficient operation, the cargo and escort ready and waiting. 'We were promised,' she said loudly. 'This was an integral part of the plan. Not ready! Why ever not?'

She was vaguely aware that this was the second time in the day she had lost her temper, that her hands were on her hips and that the Bull was staring at the badge on her overalls.

'Captain Fairfix.' His gravelly voice slowly spelled out the details of name and rank, if slightly in error. Then he looked up and demanded: 'Why do they send me a girl to do a man's job?'

She didn't hold back. 'Because I'm the best man for the job.'

He looked back at her with an unblinking gaze and slowly the deep furrows around the eyes relaxed and he began to laugh. Deep bellows of mirth. 'And that's telling you,' he said, pointing at Lucas.

'We can't hang about here in the open,' she said, angry with this man and fuming that all their efforts were now being set at nought. He might have been written up as an unrivalled resistance leader but to her he was now a dismal disappointment. 'We're absolutely vulnerable to attack here, we'll just have to go back without the goods.' She stamped a foot. 'What a fiasco!'

Lucas, who had been looking behind them, coughed and

asked: 'Over there, behind that shed... those horses... they're being led this way, but this doesn't look like a farm.'

The Bull grinned broadly. 'The horses, my friends, are for you.'

Flexible. You had to be flexible on military operations, that's what she'd been told. No grand plan ever survived the first shot. And now it seemed this pithy aphorism applied to her.

The Bull, it appeared, was not the dilatory figure she took him for. He had a fall-back plan. The Germans, he said, had moved unexpectedly into the area after the landing arrangements for the Dakota had been made and too late to effect a change. The result was that the partisans could not move their great prize – the complete undamaged V-2 test rocket recovered from the oozy mud of the River Bug. It was still at the secret location being dismantled and examined.

'They're all over us,' the Bull said. 'We can't move in daylight or at night; patrols and a constant presence. We have to stay locked down and invisible and hope they don't stumble on the barn.'

She looked around at the ragged partisans and the unabashed young spectators staring at them and at the plane. 'Not here then?' she queried.

'Not here,' he confirmed. 'Twenty kilometres east to the barn and all our test locations. We have to wait.' He shrugged massive shoulders. 'The Germans, they won't stay long, they'll move soon enough, the war's going against them, they're under pressure from the Soviets.'

Helen was shaking her head, exasperated. 'This is a disaster. We can't stick around waiting: we'll be picked off by the next passing enemy aircraft or infantry unit.' She saw, in her mind's eye, the scene back in London on receiving the news that they had been destroyed on the ground and the disappointed expressions of Devereaux, Quarmby and the effervescent Bow Tie.

She said, 'We're too visible sitting on this airstrip, like one big target waiting for a hit.'

But the Bull was smiling, pointing, indicating the approach of a grinning figure leading a team of four horses. 'Here's Milosh,' he said, 'so you can turn off the engines now.'

Those massive legs, big hooves, powerful muscles; the incredible strength of the drays who could drag many times their own body weight. She'd seen plenty of shire horses back in Suffolk. It was famous for them. And this set, she had to admit, were as strong as any, hitched up to the tailwheel of the Dak and hauling it backwards towards a line of trees.

'You can't expect to hide an aeroplane under some trees,' she objected, her voice incredulous, 'and expect to fool everyone.'

'Just watch,' he said.

Lucas shrugged and said in a quietly hopeful tone: 'He is a man of the forest.'

They followed doubtfully as the majestic giants plodded through the puddles and across a wide strip of grass, hauling the aircraft backwards to a gap in the green curtain. They were open-mouthed as the canopy gradually enveloped it above and to the sides. This was followed by an avalanche of children carrying branches and greenery to camouflage the entry point.

'We've got some military camouflage netting to make a complete job of it,' the Bull assured them. 'Never fear!'

She shook her head, still doubtful. Lucas and Silvers were by her side.

'Will it work?' wondered the sergeant.

'Better than going back empty-handed, I suppose,' she said.

'There is still one big problem,' Lucas said.

'Don't I know it.'

Rozhkov was still chuntering. You could hear him through the trees.

———

She squeezed her way through the new camouflage wall and climbed the stairs back into the aircraft, stepping to the rear. Rozhkov was curled up into a distorted and painful position, still locked to his seat. They faced each other with mutual distaste.

'I'm going to give you a second chance,' she said eventually, recognising that she couldn't keep him locked up any longer. The delay, after all, was open-ended. 'By rights I should take you back to Brindisi in cuffs to face the music... but there are bigger things at stake here than your petty resentments and silly prejudices.'

The prospect of release had rendered Rozhkov temporarily silent.

'First, I want your promise to obey orders and conduct yourself as an officer should. To assist in our mission at a very difficult time.'

His mouth twisted in an ugly scowl, then he managed a slow and reluctant nod.

However, the minute Lucas produced the key to release him Rozhkov was straight out of the door, hobbling painfully and stretching cramped arms, seeking out the Bull and initiating a rapid protest monologue in Polish.

The Bull pointed a finger and replied in English, apparently for the benefit of Helen and her crew. 'Polish–Soviet operation? What are you talking about? Aren't you an officer of the British? Didn't you come here to help? Where is your loyalty?'

There was more from Rozhkov. Angry urging, and a mime of handcuffs around wrists.

'I have promised my co-operation to the British,' the Bull said flatly and turned away.

Rozhkov slunk into the shadows before there could be any further confrontation.

Why? Helen asked herself. Why such a poisonous trouble-maker? Was it simply angst at being passed over for command of the mission, or was there more to it, another motive, some hidden factor that was driving this man to extremes?

———

They were sitting in a group close to the business end of the Bull's camp, set in a forest glade where a roasting fire took centre stage. There were also hot coals for frying and a boiling pot. The place had an air of confident permanence about it. The lean-tos and the fern-covered shelters were testimony to that.

Helen sat with her crewmen on mossy grass despite the dampness of a recent rainfall, the evening having faded away, and she prepared herself for the next task: convincing the Bull of the necessity to use Leo Beck, a delicate task that would require great tact.

She looked around, awaiting her opportunity. The place stank of kerosene, over-cooked meat and the embers of the fading fire. The charred remains of a meal, probably a pigeon or a rabbit, were strewn about and weapons were casually propped against adjoining trees. She saw a ragged cast of desperate men, some missing limbs, hollow eyes, tangled hair and the scrawny look of those suffering permanent bouts of indigestion. She recognised one, Aleksy, who'd already been introduced and he gave her a grin. The others seemed to regard her with a mix of curiosity and reserve.

'Let me introduce you,' the Bull boomed. 'You've already met Aleksy, he's a musician by the way, though you might not guess it, but now he plays a more deadly tune. Over there, Igor, once upon a time our leading headcase at the Warsaw University and then Natanael, a biologist...'

'Why such...?' she exclaimed, before stopping, fearing she was being set up for a joke.

'Simple. We have the brains here, though right now they may not look it. The Germans hate all Poles but they especially hate intellectuals. So, if you have any claims to professional status and want to avoid the shootings you quickly find yourself a job sweeping the street or working in the market and if that doesn't work...' He boomed his laugh again. 'You end up here.' There followed a roll call of peacetime talent: Daniel, Henryk, Olaf and Tobasz, doubtless adopted names for the sake of security, representing doctors, teachers, scientists and a smattering of businessmen. 'And we have some very interesting talks in the evenings,' the Bull said.

'Well that's just fine,' Helen responded, 'because I have some interesting things to discuss with you.'

Rozhkov had already been at work to poison minds on the subject of Leo Beck's presence. The Bull took Helen aside and mentioned this. 'He's been calling him "This bloody Kraut turncoat, untrustworthy, probably a plant, maybe a saboteur..." And he's been asking my men why they would countenance an enemy agent.'

Helen knew she had a job on. The Poles were naturally brim-full of antagonism for anything or anyone German.

'Why bring him?' echoed the Bull. 'We have all the experts we need. Specialists, professors in technical subjects, working busily away as we sit here tonight, taking the rocket to pieces to penetrate all its secrets.'

'Because he's unique!' she countered, giving him the details of Beck's close association with rocket manufacture and his strong personal motive to neuter its effective use. 'It's not about nationality, it's about how many thousands of people can we save from being killed by these appalling bombs.' She gave the Bull her most earnest look. 'This is why we're here. Because we need every possible help we can get.'

He still looked unhappy. 'But what is this man to do that our people haven't already done?'

'An immediate check to make sure everything is what we think it is.' She lifted a palm to stem an immediate protest. 'He knows more than anyone here. There are many different types of rocket. Some launched from planes, others at ships. We have to know we're looking at a V-2 and not any of these others.'

She decided it was best not to mention the internecine war going on among the scientists back home, of the need to settle their arguments, or the need to make sure the Nazis had not managed to make any telling and deadly improvements to their original designs.

'Leo's a brave man who has volunteered despite great personal risk to give us his all,' she said. Studying the Bull's expression, she thought she was convincing him.

The moment was spoiled, however, by a shriek and a cry that rent the silence of the night.

Chapter Thirty

Helen sprang up, panicked by that cry. There was something primeval about it, even something vaguely familiar.

Then it rang out again. And this time she recognised it. She recognised her name. 'It's Leo,' she said, scrambling to her feet. 'Where is he?'

'In the aircraft, sheltering from all the unpleasantness and hostility.'

She started to run. 'Someone's got to him, he's calling for me.'

Lucas was also on his feet.

'Got your sidearm?' she shouted over her shoulder, heading immediately for the forest hide, Silvers trailing behind.

They were all on the run, very soon crashing through the branches, heedless of the camouflage that had been so carefully placed to protect the Dak.

That cry, that voice, it was an SOS. Some local nasty with vengeance in his heart was threatening retribution on the person she regarded as the least responsible for all the harm perpetrated by the war.

Sharp twigs snatched at her face and hair and branches flicked to one side as she plunged into the depths of the wood to reach the hidden aircraft, heedless, almost unfeeling, of tiny pricks of pain.

She arrived, seconds before a panting Lucas, wrenching open the door, shouting the name. 'Leo! Is that you? Are you there?'

A volume of quick-fire male angst greeted her. Polish, or Russian, she knew not which.

She flew up the steps. The cockpit was empty. She strode to the rear. Beck was cowering in a corner seat, his eyes focused on a standing figure a couple of feet away. A tall man with staring eyes whom she recognised as one of the Bull's assistants jiggled a machete up and down as if in an involuntary spasm.

She looked again at Beck. There didn't seem to be any blood. Then back at the man and at the top of the seat next to him, split and splintered into pieces. He'd obviously been chopping away at the fittings – whether to create terror or to practise for the act of assassination she did not know.

The voice was still in full volume, uninterrupted by her entrance, highly strung and hectoring in an unending diatribe, but she thought she could read in it more pain and anguish than aggression. She made calming motions with her hands and asked him softly to put the weapon away.

At that moment there was a presence behind her – Lucas.

But there was also another: the Bull had clearly followed the headlong chase and his booming voice brought the would-be assailant's monologue to a close.

After several sharp exchanges, the man dropped the machete, which clattered noisily to the floor, and he walked dejectedly out of the fuselage.

'Sorry,' Beck gulped, slumping back in his seat, making a visible effort to take a hold of himself. 'I apologise for shrieking, but I thought he was...' He indicated the splintered seat. 'I wouldn't have stood much chance, I kept telling him I'm here to help...'

'Are you hurt?'

He shook his head. 'We kind of conversed, a rough and ready exchange. My bit of Polish and his smattering of German. Said they didn't want my help and now he had the chance to get his own back on people like me. At least, I think that's what he said.'

She took his arm. 'From now on, you stay close to us.'

He looked up at her. 'What's happened? There's blood all over your forehead and face.'

She put her hand up and it came away smeared with red.

Lucas stepped forward and handed her a handkerchief. 'That's the result of running like a mad thing through those trees,' he said. 'It's scratched you to hell.'

Back by the brazier someone produced a glass of something alcoholic to steady shredded nerves all round. Beck swallowed and said, 'He was dangerous, yes, but beyond all that shouting I didn't think he really wanted any harm. He was hurting, he was grieving, he wanted to get it all out. Something bad happened. I don't think he really understood himself.'

Just then the Bull reappeared and said: 'I apologise for my deputy's actions. He's slightly crazed about Germans. You see, he doesn't know where his people are.'

Helen nodded. 'We understand. We guessed he'd lost control of himself. Terrible things happen. Everyone is touched by this dreadful war.' She drew in a long breath and added: 'Like that man, I myself suffered a loss and have made a promise of vengeance.'

They were all staring at her, Lucas, Silvers, Beck and the Bull, curious to know if she would explain.

'This, just being here, doing this... this is my vengeance,' she said.

The Bull coughed. 'I've given the order,' he said. 'There will be no more attacks on your man.'

Chapter Thirty-One

It was an uncomfortable night. Helen and the crew were not equipped for camping out in a cold and damp Polish forest. They had their flying overalls and that was all. As a gesture of goodwill they were afforded places in a shelter. This had a low log and fern cover placed over a deep dug-out. 'Tomorrow I teach you how to live like a native of the woods,' the Bull said.

Igor, a small, scarred man with a ragged beard, approached to extend the hand of friendship. He grinned at them a gap-toothed smile. 'Don't think badly of us over this unfortunate business,' he said. 'I know what you're going through.'

This took Helen aback... until she discovered some time later that Igor had once been a professor of psychology. English, it seemed, was becoming the camp's second language.

They were quickly found items of bedding: ragged bits of sheeting, a torn tent flap and some threadbare blankets. 'Pack it with moss, it will keep you warm,' said the big man, enjoying his role of forest host.

'This delay...' Helen was shaking her head, still frustrated at being grounded. She didn't want to become an expert at living in the forest. She wanted to be gone. 'We must find a way of getting this V-2 material back tomorrow,' she told him.

'Tomorrow I fear will be too soon.'

Reluctantly, they turned in.

'I didn't expect this,' Lucas said.

Silvers added, 'Me neither!'

She knew they were worried about their safety. They'd be thinking of their families and Helen sympathised. Stranded in an enemy forest? It wasn't what they'd bargained for. Of course they wanted to fly straight back. It was the obvious option and even she had thought of Peter and been tempted – but they were all volunteers charged with an important mission.

'Look,' she said, when they were settled and alone, 'I know this was not in the plan. It's a real bad turn-up – but this job was never going to be straight forward.' She was talking while trawling around, looking for extra covering. 'One thing my history has taught me: when flying into the unknown you have to be ultra flexible.' This produced an ironic laugh from Silvers. She weighed some fern-like material in her hand, deciding if it would provide extra insulation. 'We're expected to deliver,' she said, looking back at her crew. 'To bring back the goodies... and one way or the other that's what we're going to do.'

There was an urge to talk, to draw them and Leo Beck together for reassurance, though her frustration and anxiety were palpable. They would have ice on their beards in the morning and she needed to nip in the bud any tendency to complain.

The memory of all those barefoot children, crowding around the Dakota, helping to build the hide and then disappearing to order, was another factor making her feel uneasy. So much had gone wrong! A quick succession of shocks had plagued this perilous journey from the beginning, and she thought back to the strangely muted attitude adopted by

Devereaux at their departure from Brindisi. He clearly possessed some unstated oversight role attached to the launch party but she'd been too preoccupied with her own preparations to pay much attention, merely glimpsing him conversing with a number of people she did not recognise.

Worse, their farewell had been utterly matter-of-fact just like, she recalled, any of those other departures in her early days. It was assumed then, of course, that she would always return.

Now she would have liked from him just a little more emotion.

And those horses! When she expressed disbelief at their use the Bull had filled in some intriguing gaps in the story of the rocket's recovery. She knew the Poles had deliberately buried the fallen missile in the mud to hide it from the Germans – but what then?

'That's when Milosh came to our rescue,' the Bull said. 'It took three pairs of his beauties one night to pull the rocket out of the mud, load it onto a trailer and trundle it all the way to the barn. It's heavy and it's big.'

How big she was to discover later.

Her eyelids flickered but she was too much on edge to sleep and she dozed fitfully and inevitably began to think of home and Peter. She felt the pain of separation and conflict over her choices which had led her to this dire place and predicament. She had tried making peace with her mother just before leaving for Brindisi, phoning home to put the best possible gloss on her continued absence, saying this was 'Just one more job that shouldn't take too long'.

'I've heard that before,' was the unforgiving reply.

She'd even managed a few words over the phone with Peter whose principal concern at that moment had been for his pet rabbit Josh, a present from his grandpa.

After the call she vowed to make it up to her boy promising herself that when she returned she would be an even more attentive mother; safeguarding and caring to be sure, but also to give more of her own personality. More instructive walks, more reading, crosswords, multiplication tables and later, when older, teaching him how lucky he was to live in a land of plenty.

Eventually, she must have dropped off because soon she was having the Peter dream. A recurring dream in which her child would grow and mature into manhood. What would she wish for him? What might he become? Tradesman, craftsman, professional... yes, an architect! He would design lovely new houses for all the people who'd been bombed out; homes for heroes, as the slogan had it, and for all the evacuated children from London who'd lost homes and for the poor people in the awful crowded tenements in Bury's back streets. Here was the gleaming vision of the future, the boy Peter now a grown man, qualifying as an architect with a big gleaming brass plaque outside his office. She swelled with pride at the glorious wording spelling out PETER FAIRFAX BA (HONS), RIBA and ARB.

Half awake, half asleep, this was her dream-cum-daydream under a blanket of moss and cardboard lying silently in a Polish forest until she became fully conscious and alarmed at quiet voices nearby. It was still dark, dawn had not yet broken, the scene just visible in a low hostile haze. Through sleep-heavy eyes she peered about, saw the shape of two people squatting in a talkative huddle and listened to their whispers.

Instinct told her to investigate; her body told her to stay put. She was stiff from the makeshift bed, rough to any patch of exposed skin, and she thought she'd probably been lying on several different tree roots, all with excruciating sharp shapes trying to rearrange her torso. She was surprised she had slept at all.

When she began to peel back the sheeting that served as a

blanket the sharp sting of morning cold attacked her and she retreated in a shivering reflex back into the warmth of her uncomfortable cocoon. Eventually, by sheer willpower, she forced herself into the chill hostility of the new day.

A familiar sound came from the whispering couple, then a chuckle. A familiar sound. One of them was the Bull.

More movement suggested some kind of a development – perhaps the Germans had moved away, or worse, even closer. Either way, she wanted to be the first to know.

They met as he heated over a tiny stove some black and treacly substance he claimed was coffee.

'News?'

'An informant. We have a network. We know what goes on quicker than the Germans, even with all their radios and telephones.'

'Well?'

'A man from two villages away.' He looked at her carefully, gauging her reaction. 'Some more of your rockets have fallen from the sky. More bits of metal for us to find.'

'Let me come.' Her reaction was instinctive. It was out before she could think it through.

'It will be safer for you to stay here, under cover, away from dangerous eyes.'

'I don't want to be safe; I want to be active. That's why I came, not to sit on my backside under a mossy blanket. Let's bring in the new rocket.'

It was something positive to do, some material to find, a tangible gain instead of the vague promise of material in inaccessible places. This new find might be the only 'cargo' they would get. Perhaps the only remnants they could get back home.

'We will see.'

She roused the rest of her party while listening to whispered huddles across the clearing. Others were stirring and she could hear voices, louder now. The place was becoming alive, strange meals were being cooked, weapons checked, a buzz of excited voices.

Then another voice, a much less welcome one. 'You have to be mad. Taking her on patrol?'

Of course, nothing would go smoothly with Rozhkov on the loose. This time he spoke English, intending for her to hear. 'She'll get you arrested. Put her away somewhere safe. Out of harm's way. Cut her out of it. Dump the Brits.'

She would deal with him later.

The Bull was back, shaking his head. 'Hunting rocket remnants is a dangerous business. The Germans don't want us to get our hands on their secret material. Sometimes we meet their search parties. Sometimes shots are fired.'

She was up for it – then caught the eye of Roly Lucas, who'd been listening in, and his expression caused her pause. Why risk herself when she was vital to the mission, and to the chances of the crew returning home? Why risk stranding Leo Beck in a hostile land? Why risk not returning home to Peter?

A mental picture of her son's face, his cheeky grin and his remorseless questioning came to mind, so how could she justify joining this expedition? In such a quiz, honesty with Peter would have been required and he'd soon have boxed her into a corner.

Her gung-ho moment was rapidly undone. Eyes flickered but she held back a sudden impulse to blub. It wouldn't do to be openly emotional in this place. Devereaux's accusation came to mind and she repeated to herself a silent denial: *I'm not a danger junkie.*

Then she nodded a resigned if guilty acceptance to the Bull and contented herself with taking on board the details of the partisans' operation, giving a rueful glance to the ancient Polski

Fiat pick-up truck when it sped out of camp crammed full of fighters.

Later in the day, after an uneventful but fretful morning, the Fiat returned with the fruits of the search. Helen and Beck were staring at a heavy blackened metal object that looked like a giant cooking pot. 'Surely, never part of a rocket,' she said. Its vaguely domestic appearance seemed to defy the image of a sleek vehicle of the sky.

It was in a bad shape, split wide open, the force of its landing exposing the innards of strange channels and pipework. She peered closely and decided that it actually resembled a cross between a mushroom and a bell. A jagged hole gaped at the bottom.

Beck pointed. 'The nozzle, where the exhaust gases escape to force the missile into space. What we have here is the combustion chamber.'

She and her party had been examining the giant chamber in a clearing some way off the main camp, dispersal being one of their forest tactics, and the others had left as she continued making copious notes which she expected she would have to present at a later stage to Quarmby, Devereaux and Bow Tie, possibly even to the dreadful Cherwell. Finally, she put away her pen and walked the few hundred yards back to the main camp.

It was then that she experienced a sudden chill.

What she expected was missing. She anticipated greetings from familiar faces; she expected a bubbling cooking pot over a fire; she expected people lounging, talking while cleaning equipment; in particular she expected Sergeants Lucas and Silvers to be present.

But there were none of these. Instead the place was deserted. Totally abandoned. No trace of the fire or recent habitation. The huts were empty; the silence scary. No voices, no birdsong, just a whisper of wind through the leaves on the trees.

She swallowed and fought to control her fear. Suddenly she felt abandoned and alone in the forest, friendless and defenceless in the heart of enemy territory. Disowned and vulnerable.

Chapter Thirty-Two

Helen turned and caught herself. A figure was approaching from the way she'd come and it was with some relief but much confusion that she recognised Aleksy.

'Deserted,' she said, gesturing at the empty clearing.

He too stopped and studied the space with a strained expression. Then slowly the worry lines on the face disappeared and he grinned, pointing at the base of an old oak.

A hand was beckoning to them, the rest of its owner hidden among luxuriant foliage.

'An alert,' he said. 'A precaution. Maybe a patrol is nearby.'

They strode across the clearing to be ushered into a narrow pathway where the situation was explained. The Germans were in the area. 'We've stirred them up bagging their latest chunk of wreckage,' said the man, 'so now they're out hunting us and we have to be careful.'

Helen was shortly reunited with her party and advised to climb a tree – much the safest place in the event of a search. 'You can, if you like,' Lucas said, looking up with some trepidation at the height required, 'but I'm staying on the ground.'

'No problem,' she said, recalling many a childhood romp in

the woods behind the family farm, but stayed down to be at one with her crew. She had the sense from all the messages that a German incursion into the forest was unlikely. Much traffic had been spotted on the nearest road but usually the Germans didn't like forests where they were likely to be ambushed and picked off by hidden marksmen.

As time went on tension relaxed. She told herself to calm down and this was when she became aware of new faces among the trees and the undergrowth. Young faces, bedraggled faces with forlorn expressions, mere children turned refugees fleeing the crackdowns. One, despite the dirt and the rags, was undeniably female. Helen schooled herself not to recoil at the damp odour. There were no bathing facilities in the forest. A gentle smile was all that was needed. The waif, tiny and thin and no more than seven or eight, moved shyly closer and closer until they were side by side, an arm reaching out for reassuring human contact.

'You've made a friend there,' Lucas said.

Soft words, despite the language barrier, seemed to forge a closer link. Soon Helen was the centre of attention for the other youngsters and wished she had toys or crayons or cards or some musical instrument to keep them occupied. Nursery rhymes, even in a foreign tongue, seemed the best she could do. *Baa baa black sheep, Little Jack Horner, Hickory dickory dock, Hey diddle diddle*; the meaning of the words didn't seem to matter.

She looked at the sores, the filthy faces, the ragged and malnourished members of her little group. What kind of a future did these kids have, even if they made it through the war? They only knew this forest life: jungle cats, undomesticated, wild. Some of them even kept their distance from her and she saw in their expressions the tough, the rough and the hostile.

Helen thought back in contrast to her own childhood. What fun it had been to be a small child – the freedom to roam, hopscotch, hitching a ride on the back of a horse cart by hanging on the tailgate, and trees. She'd loved climbing trees. She looked again at her audience and saw only a bleak future for them as wrecked personalities; always on the outside of the civilised world, condemned to be pariahs, unfit for normal society.

She sighed and looked down at her adopted waif – by dint of signs in the sandy soil she discovered the name was Marta – and wondered at her own reactions. Was she compensating in some indefinable way for her absence from home? Certainly, when cleaned up, there would be physical similarities to a certain person: the pert nose, the engaging smile, the alert eyes. How sad that this little one would have none of Peter's advantages in life, comfort, safety and the prospect of a bright future. She thought about all the ambitions she had for her son, then looked again at this adoring face and such concerns seemed irrelevant. Just at that moment it was enough to live for the day. To cuddle and be close to this perfect tiny being. How nice it would be to have a daughter, a contrast to all that boy stuff back at home.

She approached the Bull once again. 'Something I've been wanting to ask... about all these children. What are they doing in such ragged clothing and poor condition, stuck out here in the wilderness?'

'Keeping out of harm's way.'

'In this cold, with no shoes or proper clothing?'

'You obviously have no idea of what it is like to live under the occupation.'

'But children?' It was a voice of incredulity.

'They're vulnerable,' he said. 'Easy meat. The ones with blue eyes and blond hair the Germans take away and try to turn into little Nazis. The others who look strong and healthy, they turn into slave labourers.'

Helen recalled with horror her colleague Dominika's story

of buying back her daughter for 40 Reichsmarks. Worse, she sensed there was a third category of victimised children. 'And the others?'

'Starvation, death, lethal injections.'

At this all three sat in shocked silence, each with their own thoughts. About a regime that used kidnap, slavery and the murder of children as a state policy; about doctors who administered death doses to weakened little bodies; about strutting men in fancy uniforms who sanctioned and ordered such behaviour; about a war fought with such bestiality.

'And in the midst of all this,' she said with another touch of incredulity, 'you find time to help us.'

He nodded. 'In return, we hope you'll help us – by winning this war and ridding us of this plague of beasts in human form.'

Chapter Thirty-Three

I t was the ideal day for it: damp, drizzly and misty. They began by winding around their shoes strips of old rags taken from clothing discarded by the forest fugitives – filthy, ragged material that Helen regarded with distaste and flinched when it touched her.

The Bull caught her reaction and said: 'Tread lightly; these are your ballet shoes.'

They set off, pulses leaping, following the big man's instructions, being tutored in the art of stealth, following a zigzag pattern through elusive footpaths they would never again be able to recognise or negotiate without guidance. They went Indian file: the big man first, then Helen with Beck bringing up the rear.

Droplets of rain brushed her face, damp briars snatched at her clothing and despite earnest attempts at a silent routine the noise of their progress through grass and undergrowth seemed to pose an affront to the silence of the forest. Every hundred yards or so they would stop for the Bull to listen, happily to hear only the sounds of nature.

At one brief stop she turned to smile encouragement at the

engineer. She needed to keep his spirits up. She'd been hammering away at the Bull and finally he had agreed to this expedition, with Beck allowed access to the barn. She urgently needed to get her prime asset into the secret workshop so he could assess the progress the Polish scientists were making in uncovering the inner workings of the rocket.

It was no small distance and her legs began to ache with all the deliberate plodding care until she became aware of another presence. An indistinct figure was conversing with the Bull. She reproached herself for having been taken by surprise. It emphasised their status as amateurs of the forest.

They were being beckoned forward, the shadowy figure evidently a silent sentinel who had given the all-clear. A low building came into view, creepers entwined around blackened windows, moss covering the roof, the whole edifice abandoned and derelict. A door which looked never to have been opened in a hundred years suddenly gaped wide enough for them to enter single file.

Helen had no preconception of what she might find but once inside she stumbled and almost fell, plunged as she was into semi-darkness. Gradually, however, eyes that had been accustomed to daylight were adjusted to the gloom. Flickering candle flames were the only source of light. A massive metal object the length of a line of three double-decker buses lay prone in the straw and the dirt, its innards laid bare and disassembled like the autopsy of some mammoth crime victim. Spectral shadows were cast into dark corners, hinting at mysterious things in recesses not reached by the candlelight.

She took a deep breath and held it. Her first view of the monster. Here at last was the V-2, being systematically gutted like some giant body in a mechanical post-mortem.

She turned to urge Beck forward but he was already kneeling to examine the entrails of his own creation. Muffled sounds of metal on metal and the intermittent whine of a drill were the only noises to be heard, even though she could see several hunched figures working at benches alongside the walls. Her nose was assaulted by a strange mix of oil, kerosene, charcoal and sweat. A hint also of old cooking. These men, it became obvious, lived, worked, ate and slept in this hideous place.

She turned her attention to a tall man with a pronounced stoop and foppish brown hair whose urgent tones in conversation with the Bull did not augur well. She had anticipated antipathy to the presence of Beck and had her arguments ready.

'This is Borys,' the Bull said. 'I've explained but he still wishes to query why...'

She gave Borys her best smile and touched the RAF badge on her overalls. 'Can you translate? Tell him this...' The roll call of her reasons: the unique insight of a man who worked at Peenemünde, the necessity of establishing the exact nature of the weapon, the need to provide firm evidence to resolve scientific disagreements back in London... and the fact that she wouldn't have flown into dangerous territory unless utterly convinced of the man's sincerity.

'But he could be a plant, a saboteur...'

She shook her head. 'I give you my word, as I have given him my pledge of protection.'

Later Beck himself filled in the details of how his reception had progressed. First, he had to explain that many wrecks were not the principal threat but ship or air launched variants of secondary interest to the Allies. Still they assailed him on the question of loyalty and trust. Could they trust someone who'd renounced his country? Someone who had been hugely disloyal. A betrayer was always questionable, the tall man said.

'Think about it!' Beck repeated his answers. 'Loyalty to who? To what? A criminal regime conducting a war expecting to kill half the world to build an empire of the bully and the brute? How can you be loyal to that? It's our great dilemma; do I wish my country to be defeated to end its repellent ideology?'

The clincher was the 'my country right or wrong' argument put to the man Borys: 'If it were your country, would you follow it to the very end, despite all brutality, all horror?'

Finally, the technical details of his examination emerged: the wreckage being dismantled was indeed a V-2. It burnt liquid fuel at the rate of nearly 3,000lbs per second and propelled itself to the edge of space. The flame temperature was higher than the melting point of the steel in the bowl-shaped combustion chamber she had just seen dredged up from the river bed. To overcome this problem, alcohol was forced between the inner and outer walls of the chamber as a cooling mechanism.

More vital facts about the rocket were coming to light: it could fly for 200 miles and was controlled by graphite control vanes in the exhaust which deflected the gas stream, plus small aerodynamic controls on the four large, fixed stabilising fins.

'These controls are its Achilles heel,' Beck said.

Contrary to what the Poles thought, the V-2 had no radio beams directing it to its target. The design team led by Werner von Braun had deliberately dispensed with these because they knew from experience that British scientists would 'bend the beams' to nullify the system.

'As the result of this, the vanes and the fins are a crude method of guidance,' he announced, 'and makes it a scatter weapon, rather than an accurate one.'

Beck's expertise had seemingly won over Borys, though others turned their backs on him, but it was necessary for Beck to have an extended period to examine the workings. Travelling in and out of the barn each day posed a risk. He should stay, sleeping over with the others, joining their sparse meals, a person protected from the instinctive rejection of fellow workers. Helen emphasised his importance, that she had given her personal pledge of protection.

She still worried about Leo Beck, feared for him stuck in this dark and dismal dungeon with distinctly unfriendly company. She had grown closer to him and now regarded him as a friend, acknowledging his bravery and dedication in volunteering to fly to Poland and place himself under great stress in the barn. She saw him as a great fighter for justice. She knew the security people back home were suspicious – he was still a shadow in their world – but if Operation Skyhawk returned successfully to base she would not abandon him. She would support him and champion his cause. Did she even dare to glimpse a continuing friendship after this dreadful war?

'Don't worry,' the Bull said, seeing her frown of concern, 'you may see us as an irregular force but we maintain a strict discipline. Besides, these are not rough men; they are his kind.'

Back in camp, the Bull was becoming gloomily reflective after a meal of pierogi dumplings. Had she ever stopped to think, he demanded, how the best ingenuity of man was directed to the science of killing; that the most notable advances of science were for mass murder.

'What's the cost of your man's wish to go to the moon? First, hell on earth, thousands dead. What kind of madness is that?'

Her mood did not improve with the appearance after a sustained absence of her rogue crewman Rozhkov. Before she could seek an explanation he demanded to know 'Where have you hidden that little turncoat?' Swiftly followed by: 'Not run off with all the evidence, has he, to hide it away and deny its existence? You've been had. You know that, don't you?'

Helen drew a deep breath and prepared for the inevitable

confrontation – but before she could reply Rozhkov retreated into the shadows and she was left wondering once again about this strange mixed-up man and the significance, if any, of his continual antagonism.

Silvers sighed and said, 'Someone was telling me they saw him way back in the forest, talking to some strange people.'

'Who? What people'

He shrugged. 'No idea.'

Helen was wary. Rozhkov represented trouble and she was weighing up her options for the return flight: drag him back to Brindisi to face a court martial – or simply abandon him to the forest.

The latter might be the kindest, she thought; he seemed thoroughly at home among the people of the Resistance.

Chapter Thirty-Four

The cooking pots were in a terrible condition: encrusted, blackened, battered and burnt with continual use. Helen had spent an hour attacking the least obnoxious utensil she could find, scraping, brushing and washing until it resembled a pale imitation of its original self. Then she set to, taking her turn as cook, trying her hand at scrambled egg with some kind of nameless fish caught in a forest stream. It stank – but no one complained.

There were eager recipients for her meagre fare. She looked at their calloused hands and into their pasty unshaven faces, heard their wheezy coughs and harsh breathing and tried not to pay attention to the ugly skin growths, cuts, wounds and burns – the price they all paid for forest living. Aleksy had even tried to engage her over his painful feet. 'Sorry, I'm not a doctor, nor a nurse,' she'd told him and Lucas had quietly brought out the Dakota first-aid kit to do what he could for some gigantic blisters.

And then, again, there were the children. The orphans and the strays. Pathetic, hungry and skinny frames; large sad eyes that carried a heartbreaking appeal. She didn't want to represent their lost mothers, but feared that she probably did. She blinked away a tear and thanked the heavens that her Peter lived in a land of relative plenty.

She knew it was wrong but she still managed a slightly larger portion for Marta who had been at her side, armed with a tiny, improvised scraper, anxious as always to be close and eager to join the clean-up. 'For the cook's assistant,' she said, forcing a faint smile.

But Helen didn't feel good, couldn't repress her frustration at the way things were going. Too much sitting about! Too much awaiting events. It wasn't good enough, she decided, and it was up to her to spark this mission into life. She refused a mug of tea from Lucas and suddenly erupted in an angry outburst at their stalled progress.

'Do you know what really bugs me?' she demanded of her two crewmen sitting close by, but didn't wait for a reaction. 'Back home they're still disputing the very existence of the rocket.'

She was seething, remembering the rough-house treatment she'd received at the hand of Lord Cherwell and frustrated that the London scientists were still at war over the fundamental question of whether the rocket was a reality. She had seen the evidence laid out before her, but the key to convincing people like Cherwell was the question of fuel. Actual physical proof of the existence of a liquid fuel powering the V-2 would surely defeat all the sceptics and she knew that a Polish chemist had been sent fuel samples from the downed V-2 to analyse.

Her jawline tightened as she stomped through the camp until she found the Bull with some of his supporters. He was sharpening a bayonet, his feet close by the fire, while spooning mouthfuls of beetroot soup.

She gave him The Stare. Sometimes this worked better than any words; in the absence of the need for a verbal response, the object of The Stare did not have to defend himself. Instead, her unspoken message was all the more powerful, better than if it had been delivered by megaphone.

'You look troubled today,' he said.

'By our lack of progress. We must get our hands on the fuel tests. That's going to be vitally important.'

He shrugged. 'Professor Nowotny. He's conducting a proper chemical analysis.'

This was her incontrovertible evidence. 'Well?'

'He's had it for some time, the test results are probably ready but we can't get them.' He pointed out towards the big city and she understood: the Germans had stopped retreating. Now their security blanket covered the countryside. No courier could get near the city to collect the fuel phials and the test results. The occupier had the place locked down and the Bull's star witness was effectively bottled up 200 miles away.

That's when she made up her mind. Another tricky decision. Ramping up the risk once again – but this time, she insisted to herself, it was an operational necessity.

She spotted him in the gloom of the next morning. A small black-haired man, hunched, crumpled, smelly and shifty, shy to the point of being painful to watch. He shuffled into the camp staring relentlessly at the floor, as if afraid of meeting anyone's eye, and it was a wonder he didn't fall.

The Bull acted as interpreter. 'Here's your man,' he said.

'Are you vouching for him? There can't be any leaks.'

'Used him before. Believe me, he wouldn't be here if there was any doubt.'

'Background?'

'Ran the town photo shop – when there was one. Now he lives in a cellar with the tools of his trade.'

She looked down and registered the case clutched protectively to the man's side.

'First,' the Bull said, 'he wants the necessary details. Height, eye colour, scars and weight.'

'We'll have to convert from the imperial,' she said, turning the pages of a thumbnail manual issued by the Air Ministry. 'Five foot six, hazel, no scars and eight stone.'

'Now the picture,' he said. 'You'll have to get rid of that RAF overall.'

At a nod, the small man was opening his case and Helen knew a little of how the press operated from her days as a young pilot flying around the globe, courting publicity and funds to continue her exploits. She recognised the top-rank equipment of the day: a Kodak Retina, the pioneer 35mm camera. She could see quizzical expressions from her crewmen as she discarded overalls in favour of a plain blouse in washed-out blue and a nondescript scarf around her head.

A tent flap served as an interior background as the little man got to work, coming out of his shell sufficiently to issue instructions about where she should stand. At this moment his timidity was transformed into a sudden and unexpected loquacity about the many dangers they faced on the path they were about to tread. Relayed almost verbatim it, was almost a rant: 'Your details must be 100 per cent accurate, they must be exact and precise in every respect, they will either save your life or lose it, I am only as good as the material I'm given, if you think I'm being pedantic you haven't met the enemy whose love for bureaucracy goes beyond all common sense, but then their system is based on it and thrives on it, is endlessly changeable and adaptable and that's what makes it so powerful and dangerous, and if we use out-of-date documents to copy from they will have changed some tiny particular and you will be exposed... and dead.'

Helen sighed. 'Has he finished?'

The little fellow put down his camera, looked at the floor and nodded.

'He'll deliver tomorrow,' the Bull said.

'He looks as if he could do with a good meal.'

'He's been paid. Potatoes and carrots.'

At this the man looked up and held her gaze. He was delivering a heartfelt and desperate final message. 'This is how we exist. Tell your armies to hurry up, will you, please?'

———

'Well?' said Lucas, 'Are you going to let us in on it? What was all that about?'

She sighed. They would have to be told. She needed them to play their part.

Silvers demanded: 'Who was that strange bod with the camera?'

'A forger.'

'And what is he forging exactly?'

'My travel pass, work permit and health card.'

They were giving her the sort of strained stares adopted by parents stricken into silence by the antics of a hyperactive teenager. In fact, there was an element to her behaviour which enjoyed shocking them. *Stop playing the brat*, a silent voice warned, so she adopted her most reasonable tone. 'Look, you know as well as I, we can't let this thing drag on any longer. Got to do something to sort it.' She drew in a deep breath and ploughed on. 'The professor with the fuel tests has them in his clinic but we can't get to him. His place is right away from the forest, in Krakow. All roads are blocked. The men here can't get through to collect his tests.'

'So how did they expect to get through?'

'By bike. But German checkpoints make it impossible. You have to have the right permits, and anyway they nab everyone for their slave labour camps. They're desperate for manpower.' She paused before delivering her punchline. 'But that doesn't apply to women. They only see women as skivvies and I'm posing as a vital war worker. Not only that. I can ride a bike. I'm good at it. It's my thing.'

Lucas was shaking his head. It was a reversal of normal roles. No longer the underling, he was adopting an altogether fatherly demeanour. 'That's ridiculous. You don't need to risk yourself or your family. One of us could do it.'

She snorted. 'Don't be daft, you're male, you'd be picked up and sent off to some labour camp. Or that other kind of camp. Maybe just shot on the spot.' After a pause, she added, 'I'm the one, the only woman, I can do it, I have the best chance.'

Lucas was still shaking his head. 'The risks,' he said, 'think of that and your little boy, and anyway, just how far is it?'

'Two hundred.'

'Ks?'

'Miles.'

'Crazy, you'll never make it.' He was still outraged. 'You can't possibly know if this professor has done his tests or whether he's being watched. You might not be able to get near him.'

Lucas turned for moral support to Silvers. But Silvers hadn't said a word and didn't look likely to put his name forward to volunteer for such a job. His expression said he didn't sign up in this man's army for crazy antics risking arrest by the Gestapo or being shot as a spy.

Chapter Thirty-Five

At first Helen recoiled in distaste when they gave her the dress, wondering what kind of person would donate such a dowdy garment full of holes and smelling of the farmyard.

But then she stopped herself. This was a country ravaged by poverty imposed by a monstrous occupier with the explicit intention of working its people to death – and then destroying them. She was lucky. It must have been difficult to locate anyone with a spare garment, let alone the white blouse, embroidered vest and lace-up boots of the peacetime peasant.

The Bull read her reaction. 'You have to look the part... and live it. The smellier you are the less trouble you'll get.'

She did her best to look pleased. During long conversations in the hut she'd learned the facts of the Polish predicament; the middle and upper classes were destined for enslavement or destruction; only workers and peasants were tolerated at the barest level of subsistence for the use of their labour.

She did her best to be optimistic. The clogs felt as if lumps of lead were weighing her feet and the cycle, when it arrived, was so worn it would have been junked back home. These were to be the tools of her new trade.

Her crew continued to object. 'You don't know the country,' Lucas pointed out, 'and you don't know the language.'

'I can read a map. Most Germans don't speak Polish anyway, so I can mug up on a couple of Polish phrases – hello, good day, on my way to work, this is my bike...'

'How are you going to hide the fuel samples... if you get them?'

'I'll find a way. Look, biking is my passion. Did a lot of it. Races, time trials, some of those steep pull-ups in the Lakes.'

They were all against it – even Beck. 'This is terribly risky,' he said, his worry evident in a wide-eyed concern. 'You're making yourself vulnerable. What happens to the operation if you're caught?'

She didn't answer and knew his unspoken fear. He felt vulnerable and exposed without her protective presence and didn't expect to last five minutes if she vanished from the scene.

The forger's documents, when they arrived, put a dent in her confidence. The sheer comprehensiveness of them was a shock. She picked up the *Kennkarte* identity card, printed on oil cloth and with her picture secured with riveted eyelets. Red stamps known as the *Gummistempel* covered the edges of the forger's dead-eyed photo of her. Two fingerprints were there, so were all the details of her supposed life: date and place of birth, date of issue and expiry and her occupation (clothing worker), counter-signed by some official in the 'General Government of Poland'.

'Study and remember,' the Bull advised, then gave her another – a foreigner's work card. She looked with some distaste at the cover, all in black with the Nazi eagle and the prominent words *Arbeitsbuch fur Auslander*. More fake detail of her previous employment with a plethora of stamps, dates and signatures.

But two documents were not enough; this was her introduction into the byzantine world of German pass bureaucracy. She had a certificate allowing travel to work; another for ownership of the cycle. And also, the health card.

There was another problem to solve before leaving. She ordered Lucas and Silvers not to turn on the aircraft radio while she was away. 'To save the battery' was how she put it, but the crew weren't fooled and knew the real reason; she wished to turn a Nelsonian blind eye to any order from the Air Ministry for an immediate return flight. 'I'm the one on the ground and I make the decisions, not some chair-born warrior in London,' she said. 'They signed me up because I'm different, so I'm going to be different.'

It was a convincing performance, but outward appearance masked internal doubt. Her action was necessary, she insisted to herself, because she was the leader. The mission was imperative; it was up to her to deliver. The success of the operation was all down to her. She saw her brothers' faces. What would they have done? Backed off?

At the end of the day they would all approve and applaud her success; they, in her mind's eye, were Hank, her brothers and her young son.

———————

She set off at dawn pedalling hard against a facing wind. It seemed as if a gale was pitched against her across the flat open countryside of the Polish plain. It was natural, of course, to find it hard going at first. She'd over-estimated her level of fitness; had spent too long in a pilot's seat. *Keep going!* That was the imperative. She'd soon get back her rhythm, she told herself; soon slot effortlessly into the leg-pumping routine that had seen her make short work of rides across the English countryside.

Only it didn't work. When there was no let-up in the force

of the wind and she found her stamina fading, it was time to be realistic. Her plan would fail at the first hurdle if she persisted in battling on and knocked herself out. Once, some years before, she had struggled doggedly for too long and put herself in a hospital bed with glandular fever. Common sense now told her to be sensible and conserve her strength for the long journey ahead.

She spotted a sheltered dell created by a circle of trees, rode in and dismounted, breathing heavily. Her sight was temporarily impaired by the contrasting movement from daylight into deep shadow. All at once a dark shape loomed at her from the darkness.

She stepped back, glimpsing a male figure, jerky of movement, a shifting gaze, lips working constantly. She heard a voice but did not pick up a word. However, she understood. His voice, gruff and rough, spoke of desperation. Perhaps he hadn't slept or eaten for days, perhaps on the run, perhaps evading the round-ups, the forced labour battalions or the concentration camp sweeps. She saw a toothless mouth, a ragged coat, no buttons and odd shoes.

She tried talking in a soothing tone, hoping to calm him, make him a friend. These were the people who lived in gutters and ruins, slums and cellars, a shifting transient almost invisible band of desperate fugitives determined to stay out of the reach of the occupier.

He moved closer. The voice was loud and harsh. Her tactics weren't working. She put up a defensive hand but he grabbed at her, knocking her over, the bike spilling in an untidy heap. The parcel she had wrapped so carefully fell from the basket and rolled into the dust. The man instantly switched attention to it. Lacking in co-ordination but nimble just the same, he scooped it up and vanished into the trees.

'Hey! Come back!'

175

But it was useless. He was gone. She gasped. It was all over in an instant. She had failed to react. He'd been too fast for her, dealing a serious blow to her chances of success. Gone with him were her precious supplies meant to keep her going for a ride of many miles. Borys, the camp cook who performed miracles over the camp fire, had prepared her his speciality; three potato pancakes and some precious bread and a tiny pinch of cheese. This was meant to see her all the way to Krakow and back.

Now she had none, and was facing several days without sustenance.

She sat in a heap, massaging her bruises as well as her pride. A comprehensive defeat – almost before she'd got started. Others would throw in the towel, she told herself.

But not me!

Nevertheless, it was naive to think she only had to look out for the Germans, that all the locals were friendly. This proved there were perils aplenty and not just those dressed in field grey. She should have heeded the hints given round the camp fire, of elements of the Home Army attacking each other.

'What ridiculous behaviour!' She said it out loud in exasperation. How could they expect to succeed like that?

She looked outside the shelter. The wind was still blasting. Best wait, on her guard, for a let-up in the weather. Time, in fact, to dwell on the wisdom of taking on this job.

Despite her earlier certainty, what would her Hank have made of it? *Never give in... get up and go... fight the good fight!* She could hear his voice, his sheer good-humoured resolution; she could see his bright smile, the tall physique; could feel the undimmed optimism, the enormous confidence, the utter certainty of victory. 'There's no way this guy Hitler can win, we're simply too good for him.'

Time, in fact, for her to live up to his ideal and his words. However, this comforting exhortation had been tarnished by hurtful remarks made by Devereaux back in London. 'You're putting your man on an impossible pedestal,' he'd said to her in one brutal bout of home truth telling. By which he meant a false pedestal. Once her husband had been flesh and blood with all the joys and flaws of a normal mortal, he said, but in death she had sanctified the image through a fine mist of haloed heroics.

'Shut up, Dev,' she said out loud, as if her sceptic were sitting beside her. As she still saw it, the man from the new world had come with majesty and valour to mend the ills of the old.

Chapter Thirty-Six

It was the shriek carried on the wind that alerted her. A disturbing sound, a wail of agony, a human cry of distress.

She stopped cycling, dismounted, and stood still to listen. And there it was again, a high-pitched siren of agony, no doubting it.

Helen had resumed her journey when the gale dropped to a low intensity, relieved that the old machine was still in working order and advancing up a by-road into a sprawling village. Now she spotted in the distance several vehicles parked in the sort of chaotic manner that indicated a rushed arrival.

Keeping to the shadows, she pushed the bike closer, anxious to keep out of trouble but drawn nevertheless by the sounds of turmoil. A hubbub of conflicting voices, male and female. The first, stentorian, the latter protesting. Then she recognised the uniforms and the caps and shrank back, still studying the scene. She saw a row of stone houses and struggling figures in a dusty road. Someone carried a tiny shrieking form away from a house. They were followed by a woman. Her cries of anguish pierced the air. She clutched and flailed at the figure in grey, but another uniformed figure blocked her path, beating her back with a baton and throwing her to the ground.

Helen recoiled, almost choking at this display of brutality, but there was more. A chorus of high-pitched female voices erupted and a man in shirt sleeves darted forward towards the child. Immediately he was blocked by more grey figures, this time shoving pistols into his midriff.

Out in the wide street the wriggling child was being shoved into a prison-like vehicle with bars at the windows.

Almost immediately engines started up, doors slammed, exhaust fumes plumed into the air. More women appeared, banging on the sides of the van but to no avail. It reversed rapidly and sped away.

Helen knew what she had just witnessed. The Bull had warned her. These were the Nazi kidnappers at work, the Lebensborn squads, raiding a village, filling places allocated for Polish children deemed fit for 'Germanisation', torn from their mothers' arms, never to be seen again.

She swallowed, mentally allying herself with the stricken mothers. It was almost certain there were other victims in a crowd that now milled about in a chaotic but impotent tableau of grief. Instinctively she wanted to express her sorrow, to move out of the shadows and commiserate with the victims, but she was still a realist and she had a mission to protect. The squads may have left in haste but the Nazis had doubtless posted more brutes nearby to quell any tendency to rebellion. It would be suicidal to expose herself to scrutiny.

Helen held back but a big woman in a stained blue overall was staggering toward her hiding place in a state of great distress, clutching and twisting her hair, muttering under her breath, tottering and unheeding where she went.

When close Helen stepped out, arms outstretched and gave her a huge hug. She said, 'I saw.'

The woman stared back, surprised. 'English?'

'I am.' Helen swallowed, overcome by the emotion of the moment. She felt tears prickle her eyes and said, 'I'm a mother too. I'm also a fighter. After the war I'll try and get him back for you.'

The woman was still distraught. 'Why?' She spread her hands in disbelief. 'Why they take my Thomasz?'

'For foster parents in Germany.'

'He no need German parents. He has parent. Me. He mine. I want back.'

Helen kept the close contact. 'The Third Reich will be beaten and there will be consequences after the war,' she said. 'Maybe we can locate him.' There, she had said it again. Later she admonished herself for a fatuous irrational response made in the heat of an emotional moment; a desperate desire to offer hope as well as solace. Given the present chaos and the complete unpredictability of the war's end, it was a daft thing to say.

The woman snorted, pushing Helen violently away. 'After war? No good. I want my Thomasz back now.' And with a dismissive wave she staggered back to her group of distraught mothers, yelling frantically for the return of her son.

Helen felt wounded. She choked back the insult but admitted the point: what good was she in this situation? She felt completely helpless. And for one terrible moment she imagined that it was her Peter who'd been wrenched from her grasp and carried away.

For the next few minutes she entered a nightmare of transferred sympathy. In her mind she became one of these stricken mothers, pleading for the child's return, battered by brutes in field grey, calling on local menfolk to get the children back. She was, for that traumatic moment, a victim; life as the mother of Peter would then have had no meaning. The child had been a piece of her; she'd fought to raise him through all the tribulations of early childhood only to have him snatched away. She felt emptied out, depersonalised, a shell. An involuntary cry came from within her, which she quickly stifled and backed further into the shadows to avoid detection.

It was time to move away and continue her journey, leaving behind this awful scene. The image would not leave her and she could envisage the unendurable nights of sleepless agony these women faced, torturing themselves over what was happening to their sons and daughters.

They would never get to know what had become of the lost children; whether they survived, how they were treated, whether in satisfactory conditions or not, whether miserable or happy. It would be a lifelong sentence of silent despair.

As Helen continued her journey she thought about the future of the children sent to Germany to new sets of parents, and little lost Thomasz in particular. Of course, there would be precious little chance of locating them after the war. And besides, what was best for Thomasz? If the years rolled by and he survived, fully assimilated into his new background, what would be the gain in dragging him back to a forgotten past?

Helen would not forget this day. She made another promise, similar to her earlier vow. Somehow, in some as yet uncharted manner, she would find a way to thwart this loathsome inhumanity.

Sly, deceitful, dishonest.

Three words she would have used to excoriate a petty thief, but now she had to apply them to herself. Helen had been afflicted by a crisis of conscience from the moment she'd spotted the man on the yellow bicycle.

It had been quite clear for several painful miles that her own machine wasn't up to the job. The saddle was the most uncomfortable she'd experienced, nothing like the latest Raleigh she had at home, a comfy ladies bicycle with basket and pannier. In fact it was nothing like cycling down the captivating, twisty lanes of the Suffolk countryside. This was flat, plain, straight country. Still, she conceded, all the better to detect perils ahead. She'd carefully prepared the old boneshaker with hiding places – under the saddle and inside the handlebars – filling them with decoy confiscation goods; a tiny sack of coffee, some bread, anything that might please a thieving cop at a road block.

Despite all this, it was still a boneshaker and now there was a persistent slow puncture. She was quite capable of mending a puncture, but the repair kit provided contained only one weary patch which refused to adhere to an even wearier inner tube.

She tried to push such worries to one side by diverting her attention to an acute observation of the villages she passed. Stark block-like houses, fancy gables and vast sloping roofs under a leaden sky which cast dark shadows on the cobbles.

What did for the machine in the end was a giant pothole which she failed to negotiate because of her architectural obsession. The front wheel buckled, the tyre ripped, a disaster for a 200-mile trekker.

Where to find another machine in a land where motor vehicles were unobtainable and the cycle was both treasure trove to the locals and a desirable item on the occupier's confiscation list?

That's when she spotted the yellow bicycle.

It was simply ripping down the road. It had gears, grace and a rider who was unusually energetic. She watched in awe and envy as this well-oiled apparition zinged past a row of houses. Her interest piqued when the rider stopped, left his machine against a hedge, failed to secure it and hurried into a doorway.

Presumably there was some rapid chore to be performed before resuming his ride. Perhaps a visit to the bathroom? He'd be out again in a moment.

Helen monitored this episode with close attention, slyly ensuring that no one was watching her, conscience stilled by necessity. When the man didn't show she made her move, acting swiftly to substitute her bike for his and riding rapidly away to observe proceedings from nearby cover.

It had to be done, she told herself once hidden from view, but she still suffered self-disgust. This was strictly against her moral code, the one she had been insistent on teaching her young son.

She looked back as the energetic cyclist emerged from the doorway to discover the switch. This sparked a furious reaction: shouting, waving his arms, looking up and down the road for the culprit, so angry in fact that he threw the old bike on the floor, kicking out in disgust.

She felt like the lowest kind of heel, was tempted to return the yellow bike with apologies, but held back in view of the urgency of her mission. She consoled herself: he was a clever fellow; he would mend the old bike. Through self-loathing, she echoed silently the words *for the greater good* and *an operational necessity* without feeling any better. She would compensate a Polish person for her crime on another occasion – not this person, of course, but another.

She was back on the road, pedalling with renewed power and vigour toward her goal. This was the office of Professor Nowotny, the man with the task of carrying out the scientific analysis of the V-2 rocket fuel. She had the address and the greeting codeword; what further hurdles would she encounter?

So far there were no patrols or checkpoints and she had a top-rank bike – but no food. Cafés and bakeries were non-existent and smallholders protected home-grown produce like family heirlooms. All she could do was pedal on.

She was on a long straight track below a ridge. The surface was poor, requiring constant attention to avoid the ruts, but when she did manage to look up she saw in the far distance a windmill atop of a small hill. The huge blades were turning in the wind and gave her an idea.

She turned off the track and approached the mill cautiously in case the military were present. No vehicles or signals of danger were evident and she came up close to read a notice. Ordinarily the jumble of Ss and Zs would have meant nothing, but the Bull had primed her; the mills were usually allowed to dispense flour to the local populace only on a Sunday between the hours of seven and nine. She recognised the day and the numerals.

It was mid-week, so there was no queue. All was quiet, save for the creaks and groans of the turning sails above. She rapped on the door, rehearsing her practised phrases and fingering the passes in her pocket in case confronted by someone in uniform.

Instead the door was opened by an aged stooping figure with a round face, huge eyes and a squashed nose, putting her in mind of an owl. He was wagging a finger and shaking his head.

Helen gave him her widest grin and said: 'English.'

That gave him pause, then he carefully scanned the area around the mill and beckoned her in.

The place was a turmoil of ropes and pots. She'd never seen the inside of a mill before and indicated by hand signals that she was hungry. Perhaps this was the old man's revenge on an occupier who demanded ninety-five per cent of his business; perhaps it was because he was alone and solitary and welcomed the company of a young woman; or perhaps it was because she made a fuss of his rather silly spaniel who first circled and barked at her, then became her slavish new friend.

Whatever the reason, she was soon the recipient of a vast tankard of fresh water, an enormous hunk of bread, a cosy bed of sacks and blankets in the corner of this friendly jumbled chaos and a fresh supply of bread and cheese for the morning.

Next day she set off in good spirits, giving her generous host the thumbs up for Poland. He responded with a grin and the Churchill victory sign.

Her route took her away from known hotspots and areas of hostile concentration, but eventually she had to enter the town, timing her arrival for the late afternoon. This was a place you didn't loiter. She had an address, an apartment with a tiny shop window showing a strange assortment of objects, watches, clocks, medals and crockery, which would classify it back home as a junk shop, only here it was a pawnbroker where every article had significant exchangeable value. The bell tinkled as she pushed open the door and she was met by a tiny female figure wearing a turban, long coat down to her ankles and a knitted shawl.

'The crown has three emeralds,' Helen managed in her clumsy attempt at Polish.

It didn't register, and the old lady merely blinked at her from behind a pair of enormous spectacles.

Helen had to say it all again, plus an assigned name, 'Maria from Skopje,' before the old woman sighed, nodded and pointed outside to the street.

She retreated, standing on the cobbles reluctant and confused until a side door opened and the magnificent yellow bicycle was dragged into a narrow alleyway leading to a yard cluttered with boxes and parcels, detritus of the pawnbroker's trade. This had to be. The bike was too visible in the town and too valuable; she'd already been robbed once. From now on she'd have to blend in with the crowd. And what a crowd!

Krakow was clearly a city in flux; a dumping ground for refugees from all the other places Poles had been excluded: Silesia and the eastern provinces annexed by Russia. She'd been pumped full of street tactics by Aleksy; warned to keep her mouth shut, avoid police and watch out for the first sign of any smart, well-burnished open-top trucks.

On two wheels she had grown in confidence and felt a degree of safety but now, taking the first tentative steps as a pedestrian, she felt conspicuous and vulnerable; almost naked, as if everyone could see right through her disguise. She adjusted the headscarf, allowing just enough hair to show at her forehead, clutched her big bag and felt the Ausweiss in her pocket, praying that the identity, travel and work cards were as good as the little forger had promised. She had memorised her route and felt one degree better when after several hundred yards no one peered or pointed, then almost jumped when a loud voice boomed out across the street.

She swallowed, looked behind and finally remembered. The voice came from a loudspeaker attached to a lamp post, one of the propaganda broadcasts made twice a day in every street, dismissed by the locals as 'the yap': German victories, ever more restrictions and a list of names of those sentenced and executed for flouting regulations.

At Grzegorzi Street a disconsolate and ragged crowd waited by a tram stop. Across the road a group of men in rags scrubbed at white daubs of paint on a concrete wall, watched by a slouching figure in field grey, and she knew what this had been: the PW sign declaring Poland's patriotic defiance. As she waited, Aleksy's warning about dangerous vehicles seemed unnecessary; there were precious few motor vehicles, the wide streets used mostly by horse carts, bicycles and walkers, spread like thin gruel across a vast acreage of cobbles.

A shaven-headed boy hailed her. He was a newspaper seller and she bought a copy as a way of establishing an aura of normality. While she waited for change she glanced at people in the street and decided this was a city divided in two: one part was represented by the group of well-dressed, well-scrubbed women standing chatting nearby. They had lace collars, fashionable coats and clean boots and their briefcases were the trademark of the occupier and his extended family. The other half of the city were across the street, a ragged crowd done up in shapeless overcoats, clutching parcels and waiting for a bus.

The tram, when it arrived, consisted of two shabby blue cars coupled together. The first appeared to be almost empty, the second crammed full of people jammed to the doors, and she understood when she saw the detested uniform of the solitary passenger at the front. The jolting, grinding journey to the city centre gave her another window on life under occupation: urchins selling cigarettes, long queues outside bakeries, the penurious misery of the flea market, huge swastika flags draped across civic buildings and grinning military bandsmen with pistols at their belts.

The tram went through a tiny gate in the city wall, through the Jewish area of Kazimierz, now cleared, across the Vistula River, past the liquidated but still walled ghetto at Podgorze and into the industrial zone of Zablocie. Here she alighted, slipping seamlessly into the crowded street, an unremarkable and dowdy figure in a headscarf lost among a throng of people moving to and from the factories. This was the one place where you were unlikely to be troubled by police.

A little knot of people traded sought-after items, others exchanged news and gossip. Just the place for her stake-out.

There had been no time or opportunity to fix a rendezvous; she simply had to clock her quarry leaving his workplace, the stark three-storey concrete block opposite, occupied by the Central Government Laboratory.

She kept her gaze fixed on the glass entrance, worrying that a tall man in a black coat might be him, then another in a grey fedora. Fretful minutes ticked away while she considered the three things she knew about Professor Nowotny: following the closure of his university he now worked at the lab performing tasks for the occupier; in secret he carried out missions for the Home Army Resistance and lastly he was an eccentric dresser.

But was he still a reliable contact? Could he be under heavy surveillance? Might he have 'gone over'?

Her life would depend on the answers.

Just after seven a strange figure emerged, walking hurriedly away towards the town. She noted the details: plus-fours, a black suede jacket over a patterned jersey, dark bow tie and cream fedora. In his left hand a buckled brown leather briefcase. Clearly this was someone harking back to an earlier age; someone clinging to the remnants of a former life.

But was it him? Surely, dressed like that, it had to be Professor Nowotny? Didn't it?

The figure with the big briefcase took the tunnel under the railway tracks and crossed a busy square choked with trams and crowds. After a moment's hesitation she followed, closing the gap between them when he waited to cross the road under a street lamp. She was desperate to get a better look at him, consulting the photograph she'd been supplied for comparison, but still wasn't sure. Probably the older version of the young face in the picture. Perhaps, maybe!

She continued to follow, fearful of appearing furtive, because she had not been schooled in the techniques of a police detective or surveillance operative. She'd never been to spy school and a loitering woman would surely attract attention. She couldn't peer in at shop windows, the one trick she'd read about, because as they entered an increasingly dowdy district there were no shop windows at all. If stopped and questioned about her destination, what could she say? What excuse would convince?

Her eyes were everywhere; eyes looking for other eyes that might be following, fearful at the same time that she might lose her quarry in the approaching gloom. Eventually she arrived at a crumbling courtyard with the name Tomasza painted into the stone. It seemed to sum up the rest of this tired district. Sections of decorative facia had fallen from the houses into the road, revealing ancient spalling brickwork blackened by age. She passed an old lamp along the narrow footway. There was a post-box built into a corner, and red geraniums past their best filled stone troughs in a cobbled yard. She was just in time to spot a heavy door closing.

She gave it ten minutes, then swallowed, gathered her courage and knocked. Gentle taps, not the hammering signature of a police squad, still worrying if it was really Nowotny she'd been following.

The face, close up when the door opened, gave her another chill of doubt. It was older and more lined than seemed likely.

'Professor Nowotny?'

The reply was in Polish, so she went to Stage Two of her routine. 'The crown has three emeralds' and 'Maria from

Skopje' were intended to identify her as a representative of the Resistance.

For several seconds the figure in front of her looked stunned and she began to fear she had made a wrong identification. Then he looked over her shoulder, both ways along the street, grabbed her by the collar and pulled her roughly into a seedy hallway, slamming the door behind him.

'Jesus Christ, don't they teach you people to get a proper grasp of the language?' he growled, glaring at her from close quarters.

She breathed out in relief. These were two more facts she knew about Professor Nowotny: he was a fluent English speaker. And before the war he'd been a Rhodes scholar at Oxford.

Chapter Thirty-Seven

He took her into a small apartment which revealed itself to be almost as meagre inside as out, owing to the fact that he'd been kicked out of his comfortable pre-war villa by the Germans and deposited in this run-down place.

However, he could still count himself lucky to have a home of his own, secure employment, a wage and the ability to maintain some small symbol of status for a once prominent scientist. None of his furniture had survived the change – that had been confiscated – but there were country scenes on the walls, framed photographs of himself and former students, professional certification, books on chemistry and a family portrait featuring a middle-aged woman wearing a strikingly beautiful white cotton pinafore dress, the first time she'd seen anyone wearing such a garment in this country. It spoke of a different period, a more exuberant, carefree time.

Helen looked discreetly around, concluding he lived alone and didn't ask questions for fear of re-opening wounds on whatever misfortune had befallen the woman in the picture. A rickety desk, a chair built up with cushions and a gramophone completed his stock of luxuries. No radio, of course; ownership strictly illegal and punishable by death.

When he turned to face her Nowotny was still twitchy. 'Establish your bone fides,' he demanded. 'Describe to me the likely make-up of the material in question.'

She shrugged. 'I'm not a scientist, I'm a pilot.'

'A pilot?'

'How d'you think I got here?'

'Then tell me how much you know.'

Helen paused, wondering how much to reveal of the rumpus back in Whitehall. 'Well, I've listened to all the discussions about the various possibilities with regard to the fuel.'

'Ridiculous. There's only one possibility. Don't they know I've got liquid fuel samples.'

'That's what Professor Jones has told Lord Cherwell.'

'Cherwell?'

'Professor Lindemann, I believe, before he was elevated.'

'Huh! Jones and Lindemann, I should have known it.'

'You know them?'

'Of course I know them, contemporaries at Oxford. You better take back a message for these gentlemen.'

She grinned in anticipation.

'They're idiots if they think it's solid fuel. Cordite? Quite impossible. No, there's no doubt about it at all. It's A-Stoff, which is the key. Liquid oxygen. The other's alcohol.'

She repeated his message, not daring to write it down. 'So are you ready with your analysis?'

'Ready?' He glared. 'Ready? I've been ready and waiting for weeks. You're late! I've been expecting someone to contact me for ages...'

'But not someone like me?' She finished his sentence for him, expecting a smile, but he didn't lighten up.

'Never mind,' he said. 'I'm glad you're here, a godsend in fact.'

'Oh?'

'You understand, I haven't been able to communicate before today. I'm watched all the time. Almost twenty-four-hour surveillance. You were lucky to make it here without being intercepted. They make it almost impossible to get word out to the Resistance.'

Helen had a bad feeling about all these caveats. Or were they excuses? 'What are you getting at?'

'You must warn your people urgently. A dreadful thing is about to happen. You've heard about all these children being kidnapped?'

Helen stiffened. 'Tell me!'

'The Lebensborn programme, turning little blue-eyed and blond Polish children into Germans? Taking them away to foster parents in the Reich, eliminating the language, extinguishing their nationality, banishing their parents...'

'I saw it happening on the way over.'

'And those children who fail the test... slavery or the victims of medical experiments.'

'I know, it's terrible. What about it?'

But the professor would not be hurried. He wanted to justify and talk about his difficult life. 'Dealing with these dreadful people and pretending to be a willing collaborator, it's a cross I have to bear.' He shrugged. 'But I do have one advantage. I hear things. I get to learn what's going on, I'm a tolerated insider... and something terrible has just seeped out...'

'Tell me!' She repeated her demand more insistently.

'I heard a couple of days ago. There's going to be a Lebensborn swoop next week. Down by the area of the forest run by your man Kaminsky.'

It was like a smack in the face. Kaminsky – the Bull. The camp now concealing her RAF crew, Leo Beck and the Dakota. More specifically, the nearby village containing dozens of endangered children.

Chapter Thirty-Eight

The yellow bicycle was no more.

When she pedalled out of town at the hour when watchers are said to be at their least watchful – four in the morning – the cycle was coloured an unremarkable black. Her contacts at the pawnbrokers had been busy with a paint brush. She felt fatigued but optimistic, envisaging a rapid return flight to Britain carrying home the relevant rocket secrets, a difficult mission finally accomplished.

The dark cloud on the horizon, however, was the imminent raid by the Lebensborn squads. She was still angry and motivated to fight it. What did the recipients of these poor, damaged children think they were getting, she asked herself. They couldn't profess innocence of the crime, given the amount of compulsion required: the children would be punished for speaking Polish or talking about their true parentage. The new foster parents would have to enforce these brutal diktats; that made them complicit.

Later, at the war's end, there would be a difficult period of accounting. Should these children be reclaimed and returned home – or left to their new lives? An agonising inquest for all parties.

Helen skirted a pothole at the side of the road and thought about the day ahead. Back to Blighty! That old motto and a more cheerful thought. She smiled away the raindrops of a drizzly early morning. Back home with Beck and the crew; back home with the highly prized secrets; back home to Peter. What a story she had to tell, albeit a highly censored one. She felt quietly satisfied. She had made her significant contribution after all, her sense of mission justified and complete. The boy could be proud of his mother. She had fulfilled the pledge she made to validate her husband's sacrifice and memory. In her own way, she had lived up to his example of courage and commitment. It only now remained to deliver the final act: a warning to the village to clear out before the Nazi kidnappers arrived to drag the children away.

She thought again of the professor and their conversation that morning: he'd been almost psychotic about getting her away from the apartment without being seen. When they were finally certain the streets were clear of watchers, she left with a fat envelope containing Nowotny's scientific conclusions and two precious containers of what the Germans called A-Stoff and B-Stoff. Later she would follow his advice and carefully secrete them inside the tubing of her bicycle frame.

'Take care,' he warned. 'The A-Stoff is dangerous.'

In a new mood of euphoria she pedalled hard to return to the forest, grateful to freewheel down a gentle slope, admiring a lush green meadow fringed by the inevitable woody horizon of pine, larch and spruce. She passed large timber country houses resplendent with shiny new paint, others dowdy like cow byres. Buoyed by a great sense of freedom and optimism, she neglected to exercise her usual caution on the approach to the next village. As she rounded a sharp corner a figure stepped into her path, right hand raised. Behind him a chequered pole marked a new barrier.

Instantly, she took in the uniform, the collar decor and the accursed coal scuttle helmet.

For a second she was tempted to mow him down and cycle rapidly around the barrier. Then her peripheral vision caught other figures similarly clothed and carrying weapons.

She slowed, inwardly cursing, trying to remember the drill of wide-eyed innocence she had rehearsed for such an eventuality. With a sick feeling in her stomach she brought the cycle to a stop. Just as she thought she was breaking free!

She swallowed, then got a grip of herself. *Remember who you are; what you're about; remember you have to save the children; remember Peter – do it for him.*

The guard was small of stature. His helmet was too big for his head. There was acne, a nasty rash of ugly spots, and a humming odour of wet serge uniform.

She'd been warned: the young ones are the worst, filled with ten years of vile classroom propaganda and poisonous Nazi 'education' on the subject of the *untermensch*, the sub-humans. Try for the older ones, they'd said, but she didn't have the opportunity. Did this one view her as a sub-human?

'Papers!'

She gave him just a hint of a rictus grin before delving into her bag to produce her ID.

He looked at her glassy-eyed, much as you might examine a tadpole when you thought you'd caught a fish. And when he touched the woven fabric of the *Kennkarte* she noticed a slight tremor of the hand. Maybe this was his first day on checkpoint. He appeared to be mouthing to himself the details as filled in by the Bull's master forger: expiry date, birthplace, profession. Perhaps he was as nervous as she?

He said something in a scratchy tone that sounded as if his

voice had only just broken. She didn't respond and he repeated more sharply: '*Arbeitsbuch!*'

She nodded, recognising the word for the work pass and he proceeded to draw his index finger slowly down all the entries once again. She watched, mesmerised. His finger reached halfway down.

Then it stopped.

He turned.

He called to someone behind and her heart sank.

Some little detail was clearly amiss. Perhaps the Bull's forger was not so masterful after all.

She stood stock-still, not daring to move, lest she betray her inner turmoil. So they were going to investigate her pass; match serial numbers and query the validity of the fictional officials who had authorised her document. Had the forger used fake or real stamps as authentication? Would all the lists match up? What she did know was that forgery was a major crime. The end game would be terminal.

It had, she silently acknowledged, been foolish to place herself in such danger. She'd thought she could get away with it, that luck and pluck would see her through, but this job should have been allocated to a single person without family responsibilities. Lucas had said as much and she hadn't listened.

Instead of that earlier optimism, she was cast down by the image of her son.

Peter, the orphan.

Not a brave mummy but a dead mummy.

The tension was making her rigid but slowly she became aware of noises – shouts, engines, stamping feet – behind her. Guardedly, imperceptibly, she turned her head and glanced round. Opposite was a shiny open-topped truck, like the one Aleksy had warned her about. It was loaded with riflemen, clearly all set for a round-up. There were staccato orders and the counting of heads.

An acid taste came to her mouth. What did these people think they were doing? Helmets, rifles, dashing about as if they were on a battlefield – and all to bully old men and boys, hands up against the wall, hitting, thrashing, kidnapping and sending off to the Reich for a slave labour. She stopped shivering and regarded them with contempt.

A three-striper approached and took the offending pass. Her mind was racing. How to throw him off the scent; persuade him to forget her dubious documents, still less the bike, with its hidden treasures?

She wriggled her shoulder as if she had an itch and shifted the shoulder strap of her bag. This was her unstated invitation: *inspect this, you booby, there's more interesting stuff in here.* She had to play to his predictable responses. To get him to react to her smile and its false promise of friendship and approval.

He looked at her, grinned, then reached for the bag, emptying it out on to the top of an inspection platform: lipstick, handkerchief, diary, the photograph of a random male, a lighter with an unknown inscription and, hopefully, the most tempting lure of all, the almost full packet of Morvitan cigarettes.

This was the package of items designed specifically to appeal to his prejudices: a clutch of feminine items to allay his suspicions and confirm his assumption that women were harmless and represented no danger at all.

More shouts came from behind and she pretended not to see his fingers at work. She was lucky. They had a timetable. They were about to launch another street swoop. They were German. They had to keep exactly to time.

He handed back her passes, waving her away under the illusion that she hadn't seen him squirrelling away the lighter and cigarettes.

Not just a bully and a kidnapper, she thought, *but a petty pilferer to boot.*

Chapter Thirty-Nine

The rain clouds rolled in, blotting out a weak morning sun, casting fields and hills into a miserable gloom, threatening to squeeze the life out of the day.

Poland, the professor had said, was being crushed between two malevolent giants. On one side Nazi Germany terrorised, oppressed and stole territory; on the other an avaricious Russia stood ready, waiting to pick up the spoils and cast the country back into oppression. And Polish society itself was riven by conflict between the many different patriotic groups, from the nationalist, militarist and religious conservatives of the pre-war regime to rebellious workers and those who backed the Soviet partisans.

The pedals turned, the wheels hummed, sweat poured from her brow as Helen rode eastwards in an immediate dash for the forest camp. The enormous relief at beating the road block turned her a little crazy. She laughed out loud, shouted nonsensically and waggled her bike all over the road like a trick cyclist, putting on a turn of speed that took her zooming past a farmer's horse and cart, grinning at his expression of surprise.

She felt like singing and cheering and such was her uplift of spirit that the overcast day simply could not dampen her elation. The road ahead became a golden avenue of escape; she loved all the wayside madonnas, the haystacks, the hills, the churches. The experience had a purging effect. She felt free of all previous constraints. Now she had an overwhelming purpose in mind: get back to the airfield and prepare for the return flight – but first, warn the villagers!

A farm dog dashed into the road just behind her and set off a paroxysm of barking that sent her even faster on her way and momentarily changed her mood, her mind ranging over strictures the professor had issued – care over the volatility of his samples and warnings about dealing with the Red Army... 'they're no friends of Poland'. This strange interview had concluded with a request for a letter of recommendation so his daughter might study in Britain after the war, which Helen had happily supplied. How could she refuse?

Out in the depths of the countryside no motor vehicle intruded into rural life and well before reaching the forest camp she was immediately wary when spotting a truck in the distance. Then caution turned to smiles. It was the old Fiat pick-up. The Bull had sent out a search party to look for her and she was overjoyed to greet Lucas and Silvers and the familiar faces of Milosh, Borys, Igor, and Aleksy.

'You okay?' Lucas wanted to know. 'We were worried...' He began to tell her about developments back at camp but she cut him off. Her passionate urgency over the looming threat to the local children had them all diverted immediately to the endangered village.

When they arrived the place looked deserted. She knocked on several doors without success, surveying the lane and the straggly layout of the village. The houses were mostly of wood. One was dwarfed by an enormous red tiled roof which seemed to smother the walls and tiny windows. Another had a well in the garden with a mechanical device for raising the bucket. A third was so shabby with farm implements and a mosaic of tools left outside that she wasn't sure if it was a house or a barn.

'Probably taking shelter in the woods,' Aleksy suggested when there was no response to their knocking. 'They think we're them.'

'So they've heard?'

'Everybody's heard... in a general sense, but you bring specific information that the nasties are coming this way. These people have to move.'

More door knocking until someone opened, and the effect on the household was shocking. Fright and panic. Small children shrank into a corner while the mother, dressed in a shapeless floral smock, went to pieces, rushing from room to room, opening cupboards and shutting them again without deciding anything, running round the house like a headless chicken, picking up objects and putting them down again. 'Must take this!' An old photo frame, an ancient group, a family heirloom. Then the family Bible – she held it aloft; later a jazzily painted coffee pot. Finally, she sagged, distraught, her hair dishevelled, clutching her head in her hands and began to weep.

By contrast a gawky teenager with a widow's peak, gangly arms and an ungainly gait demonstrated considerably greater control. She looked stoically about her, then asked questions, clearly thinking through the implications. 'When will they come?' she wanted to know, and 'Will we get a warning?'

The necessary promises were given but Helen was shocked and dismayed by the devastating effect on these families. She couldn't leave them in this state of disarray and panic, simply ringing alarm bells and walking away. The best she could do was to offer them urgent and sound advice. 'You must leave the danger area. At the very least, get the children away to relatives. Don't send them to the forest. The little ones will never survive the rigours, they'll die of the cold and starvation. You must get them inside somewhere.'

Aleksy coughed. 'Apparently the relatives are poor and reluctant.'

She was momentarily annoyed that they did not heed her words – but then she relented, trying to imagine what it would be like if they had changed places. How would she cope?

'Send them to your relatives with something to offer,' she suggested. 'Exchange valuables for money. Promise supplies.' Then she had what she considered an inspiration. 'My mother always hid her jewellery... so sew yours into the hem of their dresses or trousers. It may keep them alive.'

This produced blank looks.

Lucas said: 'They don't look like people with sparklers to spare.'

Helen fought against these apathetic responses. She wanted to infuse them with the energy to survive the coming onslaught. 'Don't stay,' she told the teenager, who looked much the most likely to organise an escape. 'Take the whole family. Everyone should go. And don't leave anything of value for those awful people to plunder.'

Another figure appeared, a woman with a sharply wizened face peeking out from an all-encompassing ankle-length black coat, perhaps alerted from next door. A small child clung to the folds of her garment and Helen was struck – despite the dire circumstances and the uncomfortable evidence of poverty and its effects – by just how appealing a picture this little human being presented. She was perfection in miniature: the beautiful face, the snub nose, the appealing eyes. *Cute* was the word to came to mind.

She hesitated in mid-message and lost focus. This child had stirred something deep inside her, perhaps a submerged wish, some thought for her own future?

She looked away and forced herself to listen to the translation. The woman was asking what to take on such a long journey and would they ever see their homes again.

Helen shut out the vision of the distracting child and her dishevelled mother and strived to return to her thoughts on how best to flee imminent danger. 'My advice,' she said, more gently than before, 'is to take your warmest coat and your best boots.'

As the conversation continued other young children ventured forward, staring silently at Helen, and all her earlier resolve to brook no delays to a 'next steps' operational plan began to falter. Instead, these young faces prompted a wave of longing in her and a flashback to the days of babyhood of her precious son. She looked at all these children and thought what a shame it was that Peter had no brothers or sisters.

When it was time to depart a third adult appeared as if from the woodwork, shy, wheedling, appealing. 'She's asking,' said Aleksy, pointing at the children, 'can you take them?'

Helen stopped stock-still, shocked at the very idea of becoming a substitute mother to a vast collection of children, then slowly shook her head. 'Not possible, I'm afraid, head for as far away as you can.'

All this had a profoundly disturbing effect. She felt the pain of these women. Beyond outrage at the great injustice about to be perpetrated on the village, their plight awakened in her a strange regret – not of loss but of missing out on the normal expectations of life. She felt herself incomplete.

Then she put this thought aside; she was a widow and a mother. What was she thinking?

Back in the truck she exclaimed at the complete absence of menfolk.

'Either dead, grabbed for forced labour or hiding in the forest,' Aleksy said. 'All you'll find here are women, children and the very old.'

Lucas looked her in the eye. 'You've started something now, going there, talking to those people.' He shrugged. There was a certain set to his expression. 'But the thing is, can you finish it?'

On the journey back to camp she vowed no more delays, no more crises. Just get to the airfield and prepare for the return flight! Mentally, she began to calm herself, ready for the challenge of flying the Dakota back to Brindisi. She also decided this was the moment to reassert her authority, asking: 'What's all that booming?'

'Russians coming this way. Not here yet, but close.'

Lucas looked at her earnestly, asked if she were ready for his update and said: 'Their partisan groups have already been through the camp, combing the forest, sniffing out everything, seeing how the land lies.'

'Where did they come from?'

'Parachute drop. Whole companies of Red Army partisans, organised on military lines.' He coughed. 'You need to know something else. We had to get on the radio, sorry, thought you might be a goner. Lots of urgent messages from our people back home.'

'I bet.'

'Ordering immediate return,' he said.

'Well, now we can, since we have all the goodies,' she said.

He nodded. 'Just be very wary of the Reds.'

How many more warnings would she get?

———

Beck welcomed her back to camp with a wide smile. No one was more relieved at her return than he. She knew he'd probably spent the whole period of her absence living on his nerves. 'You've done so well,' he said, patting her on the back, beaming at her. 'I feared for you, alone in that city. So brave. And clever. Great resourcefulness. You deserve a medal for this.'

'You've been busy?' she asked, anxious to shut down the plaudits.

'Of course, much progress, a complete dossier, all ready to go.' This was the sum total: a 4,000-word report on the workings of the rocket, eighty photographs, twelve drawings and eight large parcels of key components.

She knew Beck was anxious to prove his value, to garner her approval for the work he had done and she listened with close attention to his enthusiastic summary of conclusions. Crucially, she realised, there were two key facts that Whitehall needed to know: the rocket could easily reach London from the French coast – but it was a highly inaccurate weapon, not being guided by radio. This meant that the V-2 could not be pin-pointed on a target and could only land somewhere inside a wide circle of London and the Home Counties. It was a scatter-gun weapon – nowhere near being a guided missile.

Relief for the government! It meant the Germans could not realistically target a specific building, like Parliament, Buckingham Palace or 10 Downing Street. Its explosive power was also much smaller than first thought. This meant it would not now be necessary to organise the wholesale evacuation of London, as originally feared.

While concentrating on Beck's news, Helen was conscious of an atmosphere of foreboding. Everyone in the camp appeared to be on edge. Looking at the familiar faces she read worry and concern. Then she noticed the strange faces and the strange uniforms sprinkled among the trees: slouch caps, blue tops and grey trousers. She also spotted her least favourite man, Rozhkov, talking to one of them, identified by Lucas as the leader of the group, the Kommissar. They appeared to be in deep conversation.

She found the Bull behind the cook station, alone and downcast. He was cleaning a rifle. She asked him about their silent, insidious and somewhat threatening visitors.

He grunted and said in an unusually quiet tone: 'We have to be polite to these people. Try to make friends with them – even though I don't trust them.'

'Oh? Sounds difficult.'

'I doubt they'll deal fairly with us, given what's happened the past, but we have to try to make a connection, we can't fight the Red Army as well as the Germans.'

He cast a long glance in the direction of the Kommissar and added: 'He's probably NKVD, busily working with your friend over there to decide which targets to be picked off. They usually have lists of people they don't like... and I'm probably one of them.'

He laughed without humour and Helen began to glimpse the grim and difficult future Poland faced, squeezed between two enemies who didn't like one another but who agreed on just one thing: their distaste for the people in between. A prospect that, despite the efforts of Poland's Home Army fighters, the country could end up simply exchanging one tyranny for another.

'We can't be outright antagonists,' the Bull said. 'We can't be their enemy, so best make the pretence of joining them.'

Lucas and Silvers were in the Dakota making ready for the flight and she was arranging the sacks of rocket parts into a neat pile when Rozhkov detached himself from his new friend and breezily addressed her. 'You realise this is ridiculous, taking all this stuff back to the UK.' He was standing above her, cocky, brazen, challenging.

She pursed her lips and decided to say nothing.

'Russia needs this technology much more than the Brits,' he said.

She ignored him again. There was little use in pointing out his many court martial offences. She'd no intention of taking him on the return flight and since he appeared now to be playing for the other side he could stay with his new friends in the forest.

'Did you hear? It's a scandal. The Russians are taking much more punishment than the English. Huge battle damage, destroyed countryside, shattered people, so they must have priority. They deserve it. Give them the knowledge of how to build these rockets.'

She looked up at him. 'Your opinion on these matters counts for nothing.'

'We'll see about that.'

She stood up when he saw the other man approaching, clocked his sullen and suspicious dead-eyed expression, the facial scars and the confident swagger. 'Perhaps you could ask your friend,' she said with a certain acidity of tone, 'what is his purpose in being here?'

Rozhkov snorted and grimaced. 'I can tell you that. The real partisans – that is the Red Partisans – are an advance party to clear the way for the Red Army, to discover hidden perils and provide valuable intelligence. In fact, to clear the way for the forces of liberation.'

The Kommissar was now close up, looking intently at her and the rocket material. He radiated hostility. A thick voice uttered a long monotone and Rozhkov interpreted. 'He says we do not recognise allies from the capitalist world led by a man who made war on the Soviet republics.'

She straightened up, meeting aggression with aggression, staring into two pools of deep hostility. She saw fanaticism, aggression and a predisposition to violence. She said: 'This material will save the lives of thousands of people in my city. Ordinary people, women, children, workers...'

'What do you capitalists know of the workers?'

'I am a worker!'

Her outraged reply was met by a low growl. Rozhkov said, 'We're taking charge of this material, which will be very useful when we decide to bomb your cities and smash the enemies of the people.'

'Bombing our cities?' She was incredulous. 'Aren't we supposed to be allies?'

'Germany, they will be our first target... Britain comes next.'

'No!'

Rozhkov moved to block her, pushing her away, as three blue uniformed figures appeared as if summoned by intuition and began carrying the rocket material away.

'No!' But she was powerless to prevent the theft taking place. Two men held her arms and the other forest fighters just stared and did nothing.

She struggled, pushing and wrestling, and saw Lucas and Silvers approaching. Guns were produced. A series of clicks as safety catches flew off told of maximum hostile intent. She stopped struggling, sighed and looked directly at her crew. Reluctantly, she shook her head.

Chapter Forty

'What are you going to do about it?' she demanded of the Bull. 'Are you going to just let them walk off with it?'

'They have guns. We don't want a shoot-out in the forest. They'd cut us to pieces.'

'Then what?'

He looked down at the highly polished rifle, then up at the expectant faces of his men. The Kommissar and his group had already marched off, horses loaded with her material.

'Are you going to let this happen?' she demanded again. 'After all the effort that's been put into this, you and the scientists? After my men have put their lives on the line? So the Reds can just walk away without you doing anything about it, is that it? To hell with London, the Germans can bomb it flat.'

Some of the fighters now crowding around the Bull knew what she had said. The others didn't need to. They could read her tone.

There was a long silence. It was a deeply humiliating moment. Then gradually the Bull began to nod and his tight lip line told a different story. He'd been shamed by his compliance and passivity. He could see his authority and leadership draining away with each moment's hesitation.

He put down the rifle and drew himself up. 'To the truck!' he called.

———

She raced with the others for a place in the old Fiat. No way would she be left behind. She had set this in motion and it was up to her to see it through. Her crew were looking querulously in her direction but she waved them away.

The Fiat wobbled under the weight of so many fighters and she knew she'd been right to put her faith in the men who'd survived all these years against the worst the enemy could deliver. The Bull was now acting against his own policy of collaboration with the Soviets.

As the vehicle got under way she realised that Beck was also squashed in among the throng. She reached out and touched his arm. 'I didn't have you down as a fighter.'

'I'm not. I'm a non-combatant.'

She blinked.

'You'll need a fetcher and carrier,' he said. 'If we're to get the stuff back, someone has to lift and carry.'

She looked away and noticed they were not following the main road. She caught the attention of Aleksy and said, 'This is not the way the Kommissar went.'

'Of course not!' He gave her a grin. 'We're not going to announce our arrival. We need to get ahead of them. This is a parallel route to where we're heading.'

'And where's that?'

'You'll see.'

The journey continued, skirting giant potholes and ruts with the fighters grimly checking weapons and ammunition, until finally they arrived at a small town next to an ancient river bridge. The men disembarked and seemed to know exactly where they were headed. She had the strong impression they had made this move before. The Bull was still wearing his pre-war Polish Army uniform. That was fine in the splendid isolation of the forest and where, if necessary, he could fight a conventional action. But in a town? The sight of the three-sided Polish cap was a lightning rod in a shoot-out if they came up against opposition.

'Duck down here.' It was Aleksy again, directing her to crouch below the parapet of the bridge. It was an old stone crossing leading to a narrow street in the town. Refuges had been built into the sides of the bridge to keep 16th century walkers safe from galloping horse traffic and now these acquired a rather different 20th century purpose.

'What is this place?' she whispered.

'Best you don't know.'

She grimaced and peered cautiously out at four-storey brownstone blocks, at barred windows, closed doors, shuttered balconies. No signs of life were visible. It was as if the town had gone to sleep, its inhabitants taken to the cellars. Not a cart moved, no cars, no horses, the streets empty, leaving only curious stray dogs for company.

The truck had been hidden away and she was accompanied to the refuge by Milosh and Borys, armed, ready and careful to conceal themselves. She also watched Grachev, Sayenko and Vasilyev hide in buildings at the far end of the street.

Time enough to study these fighters at close quarters; at the brutish machine pistols slung across their chests, at the long stick grenades at the belt, at strings of ammunition wound around shoulders like deadly necklaces. She was close enough to see the suffering in their pasty faces, observe their watchful gaze, smell their breath and know what they ate at the last meal.

'Now we wait,' Aleksy said. 'The Sovs are a slow marching column and they've got all that stuff to carry.'

This was her make-or-break moment; the mission to obtain the secrets to Hitler's weapon now hung in the balance. If the Soviet partisans got away with her V-2 material it would represent total failure of the mission. She'd risk all to prevent that.

Despite her strength of purpose, she wasn't attuned to the waiting game. A chill wind blew across the bridge even as a large drop of sweat dripped from her brow. Fatigue was catching up with her. Eyes flickered and her legs and knees ached from the cycle marathon. She was hungry, impatient, angry and weak. Only now did she acknowledge how much the long ride had drained her.

Then the doubts.

Would this end in a deadly shoot-out? How could she justify it? In her desperation to save the vital evidence had she set up a bloodbath, risking these men's lives as well as her own?

A pale-faced Beck was crouching within whispering distance.

'You may regret your decision to come,' she told him. 'This may end badly.'

He gave her an encouraging grin. 'I want to be here. I feel safe when I'm with you.'

She snorted and looked away. Foolish man. An image of her son's face swam into focus and she could hear Peter's questions and the long litany of whys. Like, *why are you doing this, Mummy?*

Resolve quickly returned. Her answer would have been forceful and strong on conviction. She would not let the Kommissar walk off with the secret of the rocket. His was an outrageously cynical act of plunder. She envisaged clouds of smoke and dust over a stricken London because she could not thwart this man. *I'm not a sit-at-home mother.* She could hear herself saying it.

At this, thoughts immediately switched back to her son and she felt an acute longing to hold him close, glorying in the anticipated picture of a shock of spiky hair, the dishevelled wayward socks, the penetrating voice, the big grin and the perpetual quiz. She was eager to hear his latest escapades and news of school. It was her choice but she still felt the pain of their separation. Was Mother still going easy on the homework? Was he still dozing at the back of the class? Like a counterweight to Helen's instinct for an ambitious future, she recalled another of her mother's precepts: *Don't hurry him through his youth, don't make him grow up too soon.*

She looked up at the bridge but still no person moved in the town. Flies buzzed and dogs prowled. Another picture came to mind: the village mother urging her to take the children. An extraordinary request. Helen fervently wished she could do something for those poor kids. Guiltily, she thought about what she had to do next, flying away and leaving the children to their terrible fate. It seemed like a brutal abandonment.

But it wasn't her job – she could hear the crew saying it, and they were right. Her task was to get the plane home safely with both crew and vital evidence.

She glanced at the river. Swans swam in sedate serenity, ducks fussed and water slid quietly over a weir; a deceptively peaceful scene masking a deadly trap. Would the Kommissar, a stranger to these parts, assume a cowed population dare not walk the pavements? Or would he realise he was walking into danger?

Time ticked by in frustrating tedium. No one stirred. Cats crept into corners and there was an unnatural stillness in the air. Finally the noise of many feet and hooves on cobbles heralded the approach of the column. The rhythmic pounding of boots on stone set her on edge. Was this how it felt before a battle? The approach of an enemy, the imminent clash of brutal cold steel, the visceral fight for survival? A chill went to the bottom of her stomach. She was a vast pool of conflicting emotions.

A whisper: 'Wait for the signal.'

The noise of those feet came on and on. Pounding, marching, relentlessly getting nearer until they seemed to be right on top of her.

Then a piercing toot. A trumpeted signal meaning the head of the Kommissar's snake had reached the bridge while the tail had passed fully into the narrow street.

The trap was sprung. The Bull's fighters appeared, weapons trained and ready, blocking off both ends of the column. Guns in front of the marchers, guns behind them, guns above from balconies, all followed by a raucous megaphone broadcasting an uncompromising message of defeat. 'Down, down, faces to the road, hands over heads.'

Without hope of escape, the Soviet partisans were penned into the narrow confines of the street, sitting ducks if shooting were to break out.

They knew it. The Kommissar knew it.

Confronted with this turnaround in fortunes, he made a desperate ploy to avoid defeat. When the Bull and Helen approached to take possession of the rocket material Rozhkov, still acting as spokesman, called to her: 'Perhaps we were mistaken about you.' He moved closer. 'Perhaps you could, after all, be a steadfast friend.'

She wrinkled a brow. 'What?'

He tried again. 'Are you a steadfast friend?'

She looked at him, at his new inquiring, even hopeful,

expression, and wondered about the stilted nature of this phrase. There was something familiar about it. Clearly this was some kind of test. Or trial? Or code?

'What kind of impertinence is this? A traitor asking me about steadfast friendship?' She picked up the rocket material, heaving it on to the truck.

At this there was an immediate change of attitude; from inquiry to outright jeering bravado. 'You might have got yourself a minor victory today... but you won't last!'

She ignored him, but he persisted: 'Soon we'll be everywhere and sweep you away. You're on the wrong side, the wrong team.'

'I think,' she said, turning her back, 'that statement more accurately describes you.'

But he wasn't done. 'We have people at the very top feeding us what we need to know. Right at the top. Your best technical people. Key people who are on our side.'

Long after they had left the bridge and were well on the way back to camp, with the Reds lying face down in the road, Helen was turning over in her mind Rozhkov's boasts about information coming from high places. She was also replaying those strange words. Was she a steadfast friend? It sounded as if Rozhkov expected a formula response, perhaps another strange phrase, as a means of covert authentication.

Clearly, those in the sway of his conspiracy required a method of recognising and validating one another. A steadfast friend? Surely it would be more natural to say a sincere friend? Steadfast was such an old-fashioned term, as if it came from a previous century. A steadfast friend... a steadfast friend? She turned the words over in her mind. Where had she heard the phrase before?

Then suddenly she had a chilling moment of recall.

She swallowed. And now she knew where the phrase came

from. It was a dagger to the heart. It was the moment she began to put together several unrelated and mystifying events into a pattern. A terrifying pattern. The stilted phrase, Rozhkov's treachery and the Kommissar's last-minute hope that she would betray her mission: putting these together with a long-forgotten incident in London caused her to blink away a spasm of painful tears.

It was a pattern of events that caused her acute personal distress. She had been savouring their victory over the Kommissar and his plundering partisans with a fast return to shores of safety.

Now she knew she would be flying back into a storm.

Her mood darkened when they reached the forest camp. The day had become overcast and gloomy. It was raining and the woods were a dripping wet sponge, water spilling from the trees, forming hidden puddles in the undergrowth and deepening the glutinous swamps. Not the welcoming sanctuary the Bull and his forest fighters found it in warmer times.

Like the rest of her crew, she would be glad to be away from this place, back in the sky where flyers belonged, and back to safer territory with their vital cargo. She nursed the unspoken dread that they had stayed too long on the ground and that their luck was running out. Nerves were ragged, activity driven by a frantic urgency for an immediate return. Then there was the added burden of the deadly insight she had gained at the Kommissar's bridge.

To add to her trepidation strange faces were appearing between the glistening trees; adults who did not look as if they belonged. That was bad enough, annoying, an irritation which she tried to ignore, but worse was to come. A child's face, tiny, white and frightened. And then another. Two of them dressed not for the forest but for travel.

This caused her almost to stumble while carrying another of the scientists' sacks of evidence between the Bull's van and the aircraft. Anxiety welled about the advice she'd given at the village. It was her message that pained her – to send the children to distant relatives – advice she now regretted. She'd been conducting one of her son's 'why' inquests ever since. She heard that little voice in her head. *Would you send me to a family who didn't want me? Would you leave me behind?*

Against this, she'd formulated a justification: the children would be best with their own people; best in their own country.

She looked at the tree-line. Damn it! More young faces.

A voice cut into her thoughts. 'Somebody wishes to speak with you.'

She turned. It was Aleksy. Next to him a shrivelled female form looked out at her from hunched shoulders and sad appealing eyes. Helen noted the ragged coat, the tight headscarf and the battered shoes.

'She wants to know,' Aleksy said, 'if you're the flying lady.'

The woman put her hands together as if in prayer.

He said: 'She thanks you for warning the village and now implores you to save her child.'

Helen said, 'Aleksy, this is ridiculous, you should have told her...'

The woman was turning, beckoning, and a young boy ran forward. He had on a coat much smarter than the woman's, a satchel and a brown paper parcel under one arm. 'She wants you to fly him to safety and a better life.'

Helen, still clutching her heavy sack, sighed, turned to the woman and said: 'The aircraft is full up with stuff for the war. This is a military flight. No passengers, no children.'

The woman, understanding immediately the tone of rejection, began hyperventilating, swallowing hard, rolling her eyes, struggling for breath.

'She's desperate to save her child,' Aleksy said.

'She's going to have a heart attack any minute,' Helen said.

By now the woman was on her knees, gasping noisily, hands wide in appeal.

'Oh my God!' Helen grounded her parcel in one swift movement, stepped forward and reached down to haul the wailing figure to her feet. Grasping the slender body, she felt the trembling touch of a scrawny hand, the desperation of clutching fingers. It was a choker. *This could be me*, Helen thought, *if the tables were turned.*

'She's desperate. Since you warned them, they're all desperate,' Aleksy said. And to add credence to his words two more women appeared, tearful and pleading, and behind them three young figures. By now the gathering had attracted the attention of the forest fighters. She had become the centre of a crowd.

She had no alternative plan to offer. There was none. Despite her misgivings, she tried to explain. 'I can't take them. You must send these children to your relatives in the country.'

'Impossible,' Aleksy said, responding to many shaken heads. 'Their relatives are so poor they can't take the children. These other families haven't enough food for themselves and they're frightened.' He pointed to one of the women. 'Flying the children to a safe haven, it's the best chance of a future they're going to get.'

'But you don't know me,' Helen exclaimed, palms held aloft in a gesture of incredulity. 'How can you think of entrusting your child to a perfect stranger?'

'You showed them sympathy,' Aleksy said, 'they know you're with them in spirit, you warned them, and now you can save them.' He pointed to the gasping mother still clutching her arms. 'She says her son's a good boy and won't give you any trouble. She appeals to you as a friend and as a mother.'

A familiar voice behind her interjected. 'We can't take them.' It was Lucas. He too had put down the bulky container he had been carrying. 'Don't listen. No way can we take children on the plane. You know that.'

Helen nodded reluctantly, aware of many voices, a chattering hubbub of pathos, appeal and sorrow. More children appeared, more women. A gawky teenager pushed to the front of the throng; it was the girl with the widow's peak Helen had spoken to at the village. 'This is Julia, she wants you to take her brother Jan.'

A shy little boy peeped at her from behind his sister. Helen shook her head but this knowing teenager wasn't put off. 'She looks at you,' Aleksy added, 'says she sees health, wealth and happiness in another land. Her brother's been learning English, a perfect fit for you.'

Helen swallowed and lowered her gaze, stricken by the emotional force all around her. Her stomach was contracting in spasms. Like she was falling from a great height; a repeat of the terror felt on her very first flight.

Lucas was beside her, clutching her arm. 'Don't!' he said. 'You can't give in. They're playing on your heart strings.'

She turned to answer him, her voice sharp. 'Of course they are. Wouldn't you, if it were one of yours?'

He shook his head. 'You can't. We're already overloading the Dak. It would endanger the aircraft, wreck the mission, would probably kill us all as well as the kids. Do you want that? This is one time to be rock hard. Tough decisions. It's what command is all about.'

She bridled at that, being lectured on how to perform her duty, but Lucas wasn't done.

'Face it, we're risking our own necks. This flight tonight...'

221

He shrugged. 'Be realistic. We're pushing our luck. You know as well as I, we may not make it back. The odds are against us. The night interceptors are only just over those hills. We'll as like as not run into one of their killers.'

By now she was both angry and conflicted, torn down the middle by these women and children. There was no time for reflection. She was in the spotlight. An immediate decision was required. She turned on Lucas; 'Now you listen to me. Stop all this doom and gloom. We're going to make it back to Brindisi, I'll make sure of that.'

Jack Silvers, attracted by the noise, waded into the crowd and butted in. 'Excuse me, but you can't take those kids; it'll put the flight in jeopardy, there's too much going into the Dak as it is, it's already overloaded. We may not even get off the ground.'

'Believe in the trusty old Dak,' she said defiantly. 'She'll take off. These old crates take much more than what it says in the book.'

'Not in this bog!'

She dismissed his objection with a derisive wave. 'I'll do it!' She would not be dictated to. She was the boss. She made her own rules. And then she looked back at the crowd, confronting tearful families pleading for her mercy. Could she say *No* if it were Peter standing beside her as an endangered child, wide-eyed, innocent and sad? Her eyelashes flickered and she took a deep breath. Perhaps she was meant to do this. Perhaps it was her real mission. How could she refuse these children and live with herself; to look her son in the eye when she told him about this episode and justify her refusal? She acknowledged to herself that this was now her moral litmus test: the Peter Test.

Turning back to Lucas and Silvers she said: 'There are times to bend the rules, occasions to attempt the impossible. The Dak's a sturdy old bus. It won't let us down.'

It was like a dam breaking. With news of her decision came a flood of eager, expectant young faces. She saw clean clothes, well-shod feet, rucksacks, bags big and small, holdalls, raincoats, satchels, even a bedroll. Several of the younger ones already had name tags on cords around their necks: Beata, Damara, Henryk, Olaf, Tobasz, Eliza. The last clutched a tiny doll. Henryk had a home-made badge resembling an RAF roundel, a sign if ever there was one of how much their presence had become common knowledge in the village, emphasising the risk to their security. The families had clearly raided wardrobes and bottom drawers to kit out their children in caps and coats, making them demonstrably better dressed than when she had called at the village.

An immediate problem were the cases and trunks. 'We can't take those, they weigh too much,' Silvers insisted, and with 800 miles to fly using extra fuel tanks Helen had to agree. 'One small case only,' she told Beck, who she deputed to look after the passenger loading.

'Or equivalent? And a hand-held toy?'

'Agreed.'

She and the crew continued loading parcels into the plane, ignoring the rain, and she began to face up to the full implication of what she had done. As the commander of a secret flight into enemy territory she was flouting every operational imperative and regulation; and then there was the problem of how to provide for all the children. She knew well enough the enormous effort that went into raising just one child; all the caring, feeding, guiding, tutoring and nannying of parenthood. Now she had a tribe. Crazy! *But sometimes*, she told herself firmly, *you just have to do what is right.*

Lucas was still objecting. 'There's too many of 'em. We can't take all the luggage and those passengers we have on the schedule and the kids as well.'

'I'll speak to the Bull. A couple of guys will have to stay.'

'A couple?'

'Those little kids, they only represent half a man's weight, some of them a third.'

Silvers was a manual man. He was quoting from memory. 'Thirteen paratroopers is max and we have all that luggage on top.'

'Paratroopers!' She scoffed. 'With all their gear and weapons and uniforms, we can take three kids for every one of them.'

Lucas was still objecting. 'Look, be reasonable, even if by some miracle you get them to Italy, what then? You're just transferring them from one area of deprivation to another. There's nothing in Italy, you know how barren it is around the airfield, it's a brutal place, a hell-hole that everyone hates, a damned battleground.'

She looked at them. A picture of grim resolution, defiance and determination in spite of their objections. Then she said, as if this was the answer to all their worries, 'Don't worry, I have a plan.'

The Bull also turned out to be a sceptic. He wasn't happy at chopping two of his emissaries off the passenger list.

'They're important people we're sending over to negotiate more help for us from the Allies.'

'Negotiators!' She snorted. 'How many talkers do you need on one aeroplane. We already have three.'

'You're the crazy one!' he said, and managed a grin. 'Taking kids on a military plane? There'll be trouble for you at the other end.'

'Better than them staying with you.'

His attitude changed at this. He nodded. 'I know. They're a liability. Look at them. No hope in the wet and cold.'

'That's why,' she said. 'They won't last out here. Bad food, illness, no prospects, miserable and frightened. Children need sustenance and hope.'

'And you're going to give it to them?'

'Look at the ones already in the camp. Like little savages.'

'True,' he said, 'but it might be better to walk them out of the country.'

'Then YOU walk them out.'

'It might be possible.' He shrugged and didn't sound very sure. 'Across the frontier, maybe. Over the mountains.'

She looked at the hopeful faces scattered among the trees. 'With half the German Army on your tail? They stand a better chance with me.'

Chapter Forty-One

The whole camp was suffused with the energy of departure. Borys had brought out his sturdy horses once again to drag the Dakota from its hiding place in the forest; an exclusion zone was declared around the aircraft to prevent chaos and confusion from clogging preparations, and a key stage was passed when the engines, which had gone cold during the extended delay, burst into life without any trouble, to the great relief of all.

Helen insisted goodbyes were said well away under an awning, protected from the rain and policed by Beck.

'You make yourself useful organising the farewells,' she said. 'Are you good with kids?'

'I'm about to find out.'

'Don't let the family goodbyes go on and on. It's got to be a slick operation. When we're ready I want the kids straight away. You're the loadmaster.' Despite her stern words Helen was aware of the steamy breath of raw emotion. Here was the turmoil of mothers handing over their children never to see them again, of kids leaving home for ever, clutching for one last kiss. There were cries and smiles, brave faces and sad ones.

She tried not to be drawn in, given the urgency of her preparations, but a sudden concern caused her to look around for Marta. 'Has anyone seen the little kid with the long black hair?' Her plea was answered with shaken heads. Strange, she hadn't seen her all day, which was odd because she was usually under her feet.

'Where the heck has she got to? I can't leave her behind.'

'We can't hang about.' Lucas, arms full, was naturally on edge.

'The poor kid will be distraught, absolutely lost, if we leave her behind.'

'She'll have to take her chances, there's enough women down there to see to it. We've too much to do to worry about one kid.'

Helen took a long look round, acknowledging the point, but unwilling to make final preparations for the most important flight of her life until the child was found.

Then the cry rang out. 'We've found her!' And one of the camp women was hurrying the little girl over.

Ready to go; the moment they had all been waiting for. Her hands were on the controls, the engines run up, doors closed and sealed, their precious parcels loaded and all twenty-seven passengers, both regular and illicit, strapped in.

Sheepishly, she recalled the original RAF instruction for an immediate turnaround, counted in minutes, with promises that the rocket 'treasures' would be ready. It hadn't happened and she would make no apologies for delaying to deal with the resulting chaos.

She tensed. Fatigued or not, she would need all her nerve, concentration and physical endurance to get this overloaded aircraft off the ground and back to Allied air space – plus a huge helping of good fortune. Now was the moment, she told herself, to prove to everyone she was the top aviator they believed her to be. To justify everyone's faith; to ensure their safety and their futures.

Lucas glanced across at her from the co-pilot position, no longer apprehensive, now exuding encouragement and confidence, resuming his role as her staunch supporter.

She forced a smile in his direction, conscious that all eyes were on her; those watching from the ground but most of all the twenty-seven pairs of eyes now boring into her back.

She took out a piece of rag she'd saved for the purpose and wiped the sweat from her hands, kneading and flexing the fingers, afraid they might stiffen or lock with tension.

Her throat felt constricted and she tried to clear it, but that made the lump she imagined to be there even worse. *Is this how an actor feels*, she wondered, *when walking on stage and into the spotlight at the Palladium?*

She released the brakes and using her right hand eased the throttles forward. Both engines responded as anticipated – but the wheels of the aircraft did not. She could feel the airflow increase, the fuselage vibrating, buffeting and shivering with stalled effort. She increased the revs to maximum, the noise bellowing out dangerously across the countryside. But still the aircraft did not move. It felt as if the machine was trying to tear itself to pieces, retching and straining to free itself without success from whatever was holding it back.

Lucas frowned and shook his head. 'No use,' he said, 'we're stuck.'

Reluctantly, she retracted the throttles. They'd made enough noise to wake every German in Poland, let alone the artillery unit they knew had arrived just the day before on the far side of the forest. She leapt from her seat and went out through the exit leaving Lucas to soothe bewildered nerves.

Down by the undercarriage she pulled up short and swore. Rain had taken its toll of the grass airstrip and mud now engulfed the wheels right up to the axles.

———

The Bull's men were working up a sweat. 'Never fear,' he yelled, 'we'll dig you out.' Channels were dug and planks inserted while Lucas and Silvers, inactive for long periods of their stay in camp, now earned their pay performing the more delicate task of getting parcels and adult passengers off the plane with the aim of lightening the load. The children, many confused and anxious, were Beck's task.

'Expect the worst,' Helen said, gathering together all their flying documents – charts, radio call signs, flying instructions – ready to make a bonfire. 'You know the drill. If Fritz makes a sudden appearance everyone scatters to the forest and we torch the Dak.'

'Looks like the end of the road for us,' said Lucas gloomily. 'We'll be joining those partisans or doing that impossible trek over the mountains.'

'Keep the faith,' she said. 'Look at those diggers, going at it like crazy men.'

'Even if we do manage a take-off,' Lucas said, 'you may be forced into dumping the kids.'

'No way.' She was committed. 'Altogether or not at all.'

Once the aircraft had been dragged from the mud on to firmer ground the process was reversed with parcels and passengers ushered back on board conducted with a kind of restrained frenzy tempered by the necessity of dealing with little ones concerned over lost dolls and treasures. 'Aren't we going now?

Am I going back to Mummy?' There were only three steps up or down from the aircraft door but this was a bottleneck in dealing with small children needing to be guided or helped. 'I don't like that aeroplane, it was horrid, noisy and smelly.'

Finally, all was ready for another attempt at take-off. Once more she was at the controls, all eyes focused on her. Her face was taut but she no longer felt afflicted by nerves. The stakes were too high, doubts were an indulgence. The enemy could still make a sudden appearance. Instead, she felt grimly determined. She wanted to see her Peter again; she wanted all the little Peters behind her to be smiling again. Where was that uncertain Helen, the one who sometimes doubted herself or who'd been tentative in the face of fearsome Whitehall mandarins? That Helen, she told herself, was gone, replaced by a more resourceful personality. Who'd be scared of a rampaging Lord Cherwell when you'd confronted the forces of Hitler's darkness?

At the nod that all was set, she went again through the starting regime: engines, brakes, throttles.

She breathed out in disappointment. Nothing. Once again, maximum revs, violent shaking but still no movement.

'End of the road,' Lucas repeated.

'Never give up!' Her response was sharp, determined. 'We'll dig her out again.'

He shook his head. 'We can't do the same trick twice, unload this lot and expect them to scramble back a second time. It's just too much.'

She ignored him and slipped out of her seat and dropped down to inspect the damage. She went to the wheels, thinking in terms of more planks, sand, mattresses, gravel... and stopped dead.

She stared. The wheels were not stuck. No mud blocked the plane's progress. She frowned; so why no movement? The dial in the cockpit had indicated brakes free, but perhaps...

She turned to the Bull. 'Quick! Get me a penknife.'

'Third time lucky,' she announced several minutes later, bounding back into her seat, all smiles.

'What have you done?' Lucas, confused, had been anticipating an 'abandon ship' order.

'Slash, slash, slash!' She waved the penknife, still clutched in her hand like the saviour it was. 'Think Abbott and Costello driving down Hollywood boulevard in an old jalopy with no brakes.'

'You've cut the brake lines?' He was incredulous.

Her answer was to move the throttles forward once more, holding her breath, and this time there was a response. Slow at first but then gathering speed. They looked across at each other, open-mouthed.

'Yes, oh yes! Told you, never lose the faith.'

Euphoria quickly evaporated, however, the next test quickly upon them. It was dark. They needed a flarepath for take-off, but the delay with the mud and the brakes had created another problem: all the urchins with the flarepath torches had melted back into the forest.

She breathed in, determined not to be defeated, opening up the throttles to full power. The Dakota grumbled and bounced over the rough ground. Peering into the gloom, she sensed the aircraft's leaden weight and willed it to lift, watching the speed indicator. Not enough, not enough...

'Hey!' Lucas pointed ahead. A hedge at the end of the field was looming. She grimaced and took the only available option, closing down the revs, slowing her bulky charger and turning to taxi back to the start point. As they passed the awning where the mothers had gathered, worried faces peered up at them, doubtless fearing an imminent disaster and wondering if they'd made the right decision to put their children aboard this lumbering monster.

She turned, angling the aircraft on a different path, desperate to find a longer run. She opened her up again, rumbling down this new track, engines screaming to attain lift-off speed, willing the overloaded machine to lift.

And finally it did, clearing another hedge with scant space to spare, wallowing and sagging back towards the ground like a machine taking off from a sea carrier, before staggering slowly upwards.

He looked across at her. 'Does nothing daunt you?' Lucas said.

But she wasn't listening, yanking at the undercarriage lever. 'It's not coming up.'

'Of course it's not, you've cut the brake lines.'

She nodded. It was the price they'd paid to get off the ground, the brake lines also operated the hydraulics to raise and lower the undercarriage. But wheels-down meant a terrific drag on flight, slowing speed and using up precious fuel.

'Got another trick up your sleeve?'

She accepted the challenge. She'd always been independent minded, coping with all kinds of mishaps in those early aviation years, given to sticking-plaster solutions to get her home. That's why she was sitting in this seat. They hadn't wanted someone who obeyed the rules and thought in straight lines.

'Hold her straight and level for a few minutes, will you?'

She climbed out of the seat and peered inside the hydraulic filler tank. Half empty. She stood looking at it, thinking, remembering all those jokes back at base about using it as a place to empty lousy cookhouse coffee. She took a couple of steps to check the drinking water reservoir kept high up on the opposite side of the fuselage. Full.

'Here's what we do...'

'It won't work,' Lucas said. 'However much you pour in that tank it will just drain out of the hose you've ripped.'

'Not if we work fast. There's still enough in the system to make it work. The holes I cut are quite small. It will take quite a while to drain out.'

He didn't believe her but had no better solution, so they reversed positions, Lucas removing the drinking water reservoir from its position and pouring the whole contents into the hydraulic tank while Helen worked the undercarriage lever, pumping furiously.

'It's working!'

They changed positions again, hand cranking continuously, and slowly, very slowly, the undercarriage came up.

For the next few minutes they sat exhausted, breathing heavily.

Tension was still high but a semblance of normality gradually returned to the cockpit. A parcel containing apples, a hunk of cheese and potato pancakes appeared, thanks to the scavenging abilities of Lucas and Silvers, which was just as well as Helen had been running on empty.

The Dakota continued on its most direct course for the base in Italy and after a while she turned to see what was happening at the back of the aircraft, concerned at how the smallest of the children would cope with the experience of flight in a rough transport aircraft. She smiled in relief when she saw Beck hard at work.

From somewhere he had produced a harmonica. 'All sing!'

she'd heard him call before the engines began to bellow their terrifying tune and then again later during the flight when little voices flagged, 'Keep singing!' She wondered just what they were singing.

'The Polish anthem?' Lucas suggested.

'All sing and rock with the plane.' Beck's young audience did their best to roll and sway with the aircraft.

'It's a game... see if you can keep pace. When it dips you dip...'

Beata and Petra were sick despite his exhortations and the sharp stench of their stomach contents added to the ordeal.

'Don't worry, you'll feel better in a minute... all sing!'

'The man's a damned genius with those kids,' Lucas said.

Dolls and teddies soon formed a bizarre contrast to the bare and uninviting khaki green of the Dakota's interior. There were two brown leather music satchels, a violin case and innumerable cardboard boxes. When the flight levelled out and attained an acceptable calmness other items appeared: playing cards, quizzes, a book of quaintly drawn pictures of houses in garish colours and fan photos of Marlene Dietrich and Ingrid Bergman.

Gradually fear and unfamiliarity were conquered and some of the older ones expressed excitement at looking through the porthole windows and seeing the ground shrink away. Beck, sensing the continuing need for reassurance, embarked on a tour of encouragement. Helen, trusting 'straight and level' flight to the ever-reliable Lucas, joined the tour, anxious to ensure the children were holding up despite their ordeal.

Where are we going? A frequent question, this time from Eliza, a chatty teenager with a white bow in her hair that complimented white socks.

'Somewhere safe,' Helen said, Beck translating, 'where you can be yourself, where you don't have to guard what you say, or watch who's listening.' She looked again at the young face and recognised Eliza as one of those she had seen at the village. This girl had evidently left all that worry and dislocation behind. Now she was bright-eyed, looking out on a new world with wonder.

'Will there be people like me where we're going?' she asked. 'I want some fun.'

'Of course!'

A brave girl, Helen decided. If they made it back to Italy she would have to be introduced into a new social milieu. Her friend Isabelle at the Bury orphanage sprang to mind; a person well practised in the art of opening up the reclusive traits of wounded fledglings – once the language barrier had been crossed. She smiled back at the girl and speculated: what possibilities lay in store for this thirteen-year-old? Higher education, a career, a life of adventure, motherhood?

Little Gabriela was clutching a doll. Helen addressed her, through Beck. 'That's a nice case you have there. Very smart. Lots of little treasures inside?'

Gabriela, eight, drew herself up and answered with a serious face. 'Sandwiches for when I get hungry, needle and cotton, my dance shoes, the tutu...'

'You're a dancer?'

'Yes,' she said, her serious expression unchanging, as if she really didn't like answering his questions, but then her brave face suddenly crumpled into sadness. 'My Mummy... never seeing her again, never seeing any of them again...' Tears were close.

Helen swallowed. Enough to make anyone cry. This poor little thing would need protection from a cruel world and lots of help and reassurance to face a future in a different country, a new culture and a strange language. A momentary doubt: had she, Helen, done the right thing by this little child? She drew in a deep breath. Only now was she realising the full implication of what she had taken on. But having taken this thing on, it was her responsibility to ensure Gabriela found a peaceful place of safety. A warm image came to mind: a big house with a reassuring sense of security, empty fields to play in – except at harvest time – and a vision of England that contrasted with all that these children had known.

Hope for an upbeat prospect next? Surely she could connect with Zofia, eight, the girl with the big check coat down to her knees and a protective arm around the violin case. 'Your favourite subject at school,' she suggested, pointing at the case.

Beck translated and Zofia replied, 'My teacher says I should concentrate on the violin, but I love the piano.'

Helen glanced down at Marta, curled up asleep beside the older girl. 'Well, you don't have to make up your mind. Enjoy them both.'

Once again Helen's thoughts turned to her home town, this time to the active amateur operatic and symphony companies and to Miss Ogilvie, her old piano teacher. Was she still in business?

As she later recounted to Beck, she became aware during this chaotic tour of a cluttered fuselage that they were probably talking to the musicians, mathematicians and opera stars of the future. They had managed to fend off the anxieties of the small ones: pleas to go home or a return to Mother.

So far, she observed, Beck was coping well as her appointed 'uncle' to the children. Later, as the long journey progressed, it would become more challenging.

Silvers appeared in the cockpit, almost wrapped in a cluster of charts. 'Next problem,' he announced. 'We've wasted so much time on the ground we can't follow the safer way home.'

The plan had been to fly back over Austria in the hope that enemy air activity was lighter there, but they needed to be cloaked all the way by the protection of the night. Austria would require a big detour and longer flight, leaving them exposed at daybreak still well out over enemy territory.

'Better the shorter route, direct,' Silvers said. 'Get back still in the dark.'

'Straight over the top of their night fighter station, you mean?' A nightmare image flashed into her mind of the fearsome Junkers JU88 with a forest of wires like stunted radio aerials protruding from its nose, the antennae of the Lichtenstein radar that would relentlessly seek them out.

But Silvers was confidant. 'It's only a school. Not operational.'

'Then let's hope they only train between nine and five,' she said.

'They're probably in the mess now,' he said, 'downing steinhägers and shouting *Prost!*'

'We hope.'

Conversation died at this point but wary eyes continued to scan the night sky. Lucas was busy with star shots, pinpoints and radio beacons, navigating them back to Allied air space. She had every confidence in him. Her role was to spot and avoid their deadly foes: Focke-Wulf 190s, ME410s or the 110 night fighters. She and Lucas were calculating their chances of making it back without interception. Every minute was one more closer to base and safety. Prospects seemed good; the night sky empty of other aircraft. She was beginning to enjoy a period free from continual crisis, but it was far from being a quiet moment. She'd been aware of an increasing hubbub behind her, hoping Beck and the other adults would cope.

A stern face appeared in the space between Helen and Lucas. She took off her head set. 'Yes?'

It was Nagorski, a grim-looking AK plenipotentiary, one of only three of the Bull's official representatives who had survived her hugely resented last-minute passenger cull. And he wasn't smiling. She wondered if he ever had.

'Your attention is required.' The voice was gravelly, laden with contempt. 'Those children of yours are creating chaos... but what they're doing on a military aircraft I cannot understand.'

She switched her gaze from the night sky ahead to the craggy, high cheek-boned features glowering at her. She noted the uncompromising uniform and stiff collar. Here was a man consumed by the dignity of his position to whom the proximity of a collection of noisy children was clearly an affront.

'Can't you deal with it? I'm rather busy just now.'

The sarcasm had no effect. 'I am the representative of the Polish government on official business, not a nursemaid to this unruly mob.'

'Mob?' Her voice rose higher than usual. 'Mob, you call these little ones we're saving a mob?' She was out of her seat, telling Lucas, 'Call me if there's a problem,' and pushing her stiff emissary unceremoniously towards the rear.

Past the radio shack and the navigator's tiny place, confronting the packed space at the rear.

There they were, some lying on the floor, some children sitting, others standing. Several were tearful, one little fellow sobbing noisily. The Dakota was an ugly beast and there hadn't been time to make it child friendly. The best they could do was to acquire several sleeping bags and make use of the built-in casualty bunks for the smallest children. Beck was doing his best, arms around a huddle of young figures, singing some sort of lullaby that sounded vaguely like 'Silent Night', but he was clearly being overwhelmed. Here was the effect of sadness and distress. Loss of parents, banished to a distant land, bereft of touch, comfort, reassurance.

She clapped her hands and spread them wide, a gesture that cut through the hubbub although she still had to shout to overcome the noise of the engines. 'I want us all to be friends, to look after each other,' she told her audience, Beck translating. 'We're going on a lovely journey... I want us all to be happy...'

Some of her words were being lost to translation, distraction, vibration and noise, so she cut to the nub of her message. 'I need you to help me. I want the older ones to be my little mothers, my helpers. Will you do this?'

She pointed appealingly to a girl of ten and another of eight and this was answered by uncertain nods. 'Everyone pick a friend. Older ones with young ones. Hold hands and smile.'

She followed her own prescription and beamed while friends were selected and pairings achieved. She waited, with shortening patience, until every child was linked to another, Beck facilitating the process when awkwardness prevailed. 'Time to sleep.' She put two hands to one side in a posture of the night.

When calm had been restored she turned to look at Nagorski. He was a representative for the AK, the Home Army, the official resistance, and the government he served was the Polish exile regime in London. Maybe she should forgive him his intolerance; he'd been living for years under German occupation, enough to blight anyone's equilibrium.

'All quiet,' Lucas reported when she took back control and she hoped it would stay that way. The human noise behind her abated and in the ensuing calm her thoughts went back to the fraught scene they'd left behind at the airfield. How did those women know she was a mother? She snorted. Obvious when she thought about it! She and the others had been discussing families quite openly; word must have got around. And then her mind turned to what lay ahead when – and if – they made it safely back to base. Lucas had warned her the authorities would shuffle the children off to 'some godawful displaced persons camp in Italy', but she was determined to fight against that, repeating to herself the statement she had made to her doubting crew back at the airfield: 'Never fear, I have my plan.'

More scanning the skyline and a continued sad but watchful silence as she began to force herself to confront how her decision to save the children would change her life. It was clear that from now on, if they made it to Brindisi, her life would be dominated by children. How would young Peter cope? She couldn't wait to see his smiling face. This thought finally lifted her spirits.

A shuffling noise behind caught her attention and she heard Silvers say, 'Come on, you.'

Without turning, she said: 'Not another crisis, I hope.'

'Don't think so.' He chuckled. 'Just someone wanting to visit the pilot.'

This time she did turn and exclaimed, 'Good grief!'

A tiny hand crept around her neck and Marta's form attached itself to Helen. Then a full embrace sinuously accomplished despite the presence of the control column.

'This little thing! She can insinuate herself into the tiniest space.' Fingers were entwined. It was cheek to cheek, cuddles and closeness, a release of tension in the luxury and warmth of a little body. Helen couldn't afford to be tearful in front of her crew, even though she wanted to relapse, such were the horrors of the last few hours and days. Now she had to be both tender and strong; to hold on to the steely resources of her nature that had got her – and them – almost to safety and success.

'You'll never lose that one,' Lucas said.

And contrary to normal practice, as well as regulations and possibly common sense as well, the girl stayed in the cockpit, her tiny form finding space where no other could.

Finally they made it out of Axis air space unscathed and Silvers called up the tower at Brindisi to warn them to clear all obstructions from the vicinity of the runway. 'No brake lines, no brakes, need every inch to get her to stop,' he said.

There weren't enough straps for all the children so she had Beck organise a giant cuddle for the landing, each child clutching another, making a game out of a crisis.

And she did it, putting the Dakota down almost on the start line and rumbling off the end of the strip into the scrub, but without mishap. She taxied in and the engines died. The crew released belts and Silvers came forward, all formality gone, patting her on the back. 'Well done, skipper. Fantastic flying. Some take-off, some landing.'

Lucas sighed with relief. 'Very well done. I knew you'd get us home.'

Beck was crowding into the cockpit. 'Fantastic!' he said, then after a short pause he could be heard again, this time from the back of the fuselage.

'Three cheers for the flying lady!' answered by young voices managing a ragged cheer and other calls.

'Can we get out now?'

Lucas grinned. 'Well... what now?'

'Let the Poles take charge of the cargo. Get the children out, I want you to play uncle, find some safe space and let them run wild.'

'And?'

'I'm going to be tied up for a while sorting our logistical problems, and you can take our guests to the sergeant's mess tent and introduce them to the delights of some solid British cuisine.'

'I'm not sure...'

'Up to you to use your force of personality to overcome any little obstacles.'

'Like the mess sergeant, the orderly officer, the quartermaster...'

'Baked beans, spam fritters and corned beef hash, just the job for some hungry Henryks, but don't let them gorge on it, or they'll all be sick.'

'To celebrate a great victory,' Lucas agreed.

It was job done for the crew – back to base, home and dry – but she wasn't cheering. She knew she now faced the fight of her life. 'Some tough talk ahead,' she said, 'some serious deals to make.'

In particular, with a certain Mr Ashley Devereaux.

Chapter Forty-Two

Ashley Devereaux had a blank expression.

He was, she knew, disguising his surprise at her return. She didn't give him time to construct a lie. 'Didn't expect this, did you?' she said.

He feigned confusion. 'Welcome back, so glad you've made it, but what's with all these kids?'

'Never expected to see me again, or the V-2 parts, did you?'

'What are you saying? You've done extraordinarily well.'

'Haven't I just! Despite all the people trying to stop me – both over there and over here.'

'You're tired, it's no wonder...'

She poked an accusative finger at his chest. 'Stop pretending, Dev. I know who you really are, you and your viper in the co-pilot seat, did you really think I'd let him win? I've defeated him and now I've defeated you, because the V-2 stuff is back here where it belongs.'

He took a deep breath but she didn't let him speak.

'Don't deny it or try bluffing. You see, I've worked it out. Joined the dots. That's what you say in the spy business, isn't it?'

He swallowed. 'Really, Helen, you're being ridiculous.'

'You see, I've finally seen through you. It's taken a while, all my adult life, but now I've done it. At last. The man I regarded all these years as my best friend and my greatest supporter turns out to be a Judas. How gut-wrenching is that?'

He kept an even expression. 'Helen, how can you say such things?'

She pointed back to the sacks and containers being unloaded from the Dakota. 'You wanted the V-2 bits to go all the way to your friends in Moscow, so don't bother playing the innocent. Oh, and the friends tried so very hard. Destroying my credibility, trying to undermine my authority with the Resistance, hijacking the goodies, even trying to recruit me. That was the moment I knew—'

'I'm shocked and hurt—'

'At being exposed! I've always sensed there was something missing from this mission and now I know. Integrity. Yours. You are playing for the other side.'

He took a deep breath and looked around. There was no one within earshot. 'I don't know how you came to these absurd conclusions—'

'Remember that day last year when we met in London at the back of the Savoy? Doubtless you'd been schmoozing some sleazy contact. Well, we sat for a sandwich on that bench in the Embankment Gardens next to that funny statue, remember?'

'What statue?'

'Some old general.'

'You mean Robert Raikes, the Sunday school man?'

'No.'

'Lawson, the MP?'

'Don't obfuscate, Dev, an old general.'

He sighed. 'Lord Cheylesmore?'

'That's him. I remember it. Soldier, philanthropist, steadfast friend. You were laughing at the inscription on the old boy's memoriam. Steadfast friendship!' She gave him a contemptuous glance. 'So you used it as your password for all your dodgy friends, all your Soviet stooges over in Poland. You set that up: are you a steadfast friend?' She sneered. 'I remember thinking back there in the Gardens that your humour was a little strange. Ill-judged. Now I know why.'

Devereaux took a deep breath and looked as if he might concede. 'Where's all this going?'

'I'm sure a certain Mr Mingis of MI-whatever would be most interested in the duplicity of his master spy.'

'You're playing with fire. You don't know the damage you could do.'

'I've a fair idea. Civil servant?' She laughed. 'Some shadowy spook, a duplicitous spook, I could create very large waves in Whitehall.' Then, ablaze with contempt for his betrayal, she fired her most bitter shot. 'They hang traitors, don't they?'

He swallowed, looked as if she'd punched him. 'God, Helen, I didn't think you could be so brutal.'

'Neither did I – till I was betrayed by someone I'd spent so long believing in and trusting with my life, now to find not only the country was to be sacrificed in Poland but me as well...'

'No, no, that's not true, I was against you going in the first place.' He looked suddenly defeated, licked his lips and said: 'I suppose there's no point in appealing to your better nature, to our friendship, to our long history together?'

She didn't answer. Her manner dripped contempt.

He said: 'I picked up on that little phrase *could* create very large waves.' A smidgen of confidence returned and he looked at her searchingly. 'I can read an element of uncertainty here. So what happens now? What is it that you really want?'

She didn't answer directly. Looked at him with a new perspective. A perspective she didn't like. There was a chasm and a silence between them.

Then she said: 'Something only you can provide.' She paused before adding: 'You really are in charge here, aren't you, even though you don't like to spread it about, but I know you're the boss of the operation, and what you say goes.'

'Well?'

'I want authority that cannot be revoked. Cast-iron permission to do my thing.'

'Authority and permission to do what exactly?'

'A flight back to England for me and all the kids, plus a free pass beyond all the usual objections from immigration.'

He'd spluttered then and told her it was quite impossible. He could never assign one of the RAF's prize assets to a refugee mission. A child refugee mission! Especially not with a service crew involved. And how could she expect him to direct the civilian authorities back home to do such a thing? 'And for what? Why?'

Ah, she thought, the grown-up version of the 'why?' game and this time there's no doubting the answer. 'For saving the lives of children under threat of enslavement or death and to give them a better life in Britain, that's what.' She pointed. 'That whole bunch of them were going to be kidnapped by the Nazis, turned into foster kids or destroyed, used in medical experiments or sent into slavery.'

He shrugged. 'I can't help that. What you're asking is madness. I could never authorise it. The brass wouldn't understand or sanction it. The immigration people would object. It would be crazy. It would ruin my reputation.'

'You'd best decide then,' she said. 'Which are you going to sacrifice? Your reputation or your neck?'

He looked at her then, shocked and disconcerted.

It was a look that made her feel seedy, unclean, like a blackmailer. Could she carry this off? She hesitated, a bitter taste in the mouth, but desperation drove her on.

'They'd never believe you,' he said.

'Perhaps, I might even look foolish... but you'd still look treacherous.'

'They'd laugh you out of court.'

'Possibly, but you'd never live down the suspicion. The cloud would follow you everywhere.' She adopted a male accent, imitating two officers at an interview panel. 'Can't appoint him, old boy, strictly on the QT, dodgy past!'

'Such is revenge. Brutal.'

'Sorry, I don't like this.' She tried to keep her face stiff. 'Really, I hate this, but there's no holding back when it comes to saving children.' Then, flinging discretion to the winds, she almost shouted: 'Look, I have to get these kids to safety. Back home with me!'

When they next spoke it was as complete strangers.

He tapped her on the shoulder. 'You can't take a service crew. You'll have to recruit some spares from somewhere.'

'Don't worry, I only fly with volunteers, just me and Lucas.'

'He's service.'

'He's a volunteer.'

'I forbid it.'

She shrugged, ignoring him.

'Flying with just two of you?'

'Done it before. I'll find a third and a fourth, don't you worry.'

He shook his head at her attitude, then said: 'Seriously, what are you going to do with all these kids? Where are you going to put them? Who's going to take them?'

'Just leave that to me. Get us there. Including a bus to Bury.'

'Bury? Are you quite off your head?'

He looked at her expression, sighed and shrugged. Then he made sure they were out of earshot of any of the airfield workers and said: 'Look, you've got this all wrong. Wasn't I the one who warned you about Communist influence? Told you to be careful of your minister friend, that Ellen Wilkinson. Now why would I do that if I was pushing things Moscow's way?'

She smiled knowingly. 'Very clever, I thought about that. And nearly fell for it. What you spies call a blind, isn't it? Well, it didn't protect you from the obvious.'

He looked down, having given up trying to talk his way out of trouble. 'I have to say, despite all your angst, there are a lot of us about. A lot of people here think we're not doing enough to help the heroic Soviets.'

'What – at the expense of London... and me?'

'Turns out there's not much of a defence against these rockets anyway.'

She poked him in the chest once again. 'I want to make it clear; I'm only silent while I get my way. And that includes getting the rocket bits to London and not losing any of them along the way. Clear?' She gave him a sideways glance. 'And Chernyak, that's the man charged with guarding the treasure, he has orders to stab to death anyone who tries it on.'

When it was time to part from Beck, she gave him her personal details and told him to get in touch. 'Don't let them bully you, I want to know where they send you.'

'Farnborough most likely,' he said, 'same as last time. Bound to be a close examination of all the new evidence. I want to make sure they understand and take on board all the essential points, to prevent any more misunderstandings, such as that nonsense about solid fuel.'

'Well, don't let them hide you away. You must come and visit. Promise me that.'

'I will.'

She worried on his behalf and felt powerless to control what was in store for him. She didn't want the authorities to treat him like a prisoner; they would doubtless throw a ring of security around him. It would be like a form of house arrest; a bird allowed to sing but not to fly. At the same time she wondered if they would find him a suitable job inside the big technical tent at Farnborough. It would be foolish to waste his talent.

He touched her elbow. 'I want to thank you for all your support.' His expression was earnest, almost intimate. 'I owe you everything,' he said. 'My opportunity for redemption, my role with the scientists. And when I'm in your company I have the feeling that everything will turn out well.'

She looked away, knowing she was dealing with a personality still conflicted by wounds from childhood; the boy in the middle of a parental war, not knowing who loved him, variously tolerated, protected and exploited.

'I'd love to visit you,' he said, 'especially to meet this very special young man who keeps demanding big answers from his mother.'

She chuckled at the thought of the questions her Peter would ask.

'Another thing,' he said. 'What you're doing for these kids...' He pointed at the aeroplane crowd, shaking his head in a gesture of incredulity. 'It's just fantastic. You have a big heart. A great humanitarian spirit. But how are you going to cope? How will you manage?'

She gave him a wan smile. 'I've just fought one battle,' she said, 'and now I'm just about to fight another.'

Chapter Forty-Three

It was a potent mix: relief and joy to end the flight in the safety of Allied territory, but tension and anxiety at having arrived. The question was: would Devereaux bend to her will?

She was sufficiently angry at his betrayal to continue playing it tough. She now had in her hands the futures of fifteen young people and she vowed to do whatever it took to keep them safe.

First step was to retain her crew, the second to have the Dakota repaired and the third to get a flightpath to the UK.

Pensively, she watched progress in the workshops, checked the crew duty rosters and the flight board, growing in confidence as inquisitive base officers backed off at the mention of Devereaux's name. In the meantime there had been another fraught session with her old mentor.

'Do you really think you can just walk into the UK with fifteen Polish kids, just like that?' He shook his head. 'Not heard of immigration control then?'

'They let in the Kindertransport kids,' she said. 'They were refugees from the Nazis. Winton, the man who brought them over, he's a hero.'

'That was by special arrangement and each child had to have an adoptive parent who paid the government £50. Where are your adoptees? Where are your fifties? Times fifteen, let's see, that's £750.'

'They'll let them in,' she said with utter conviction.

'No they won't. They'll just end up in some awful reception centre, like Brownsea Island or even worse the London Reception Centre, where they weed out spies.'

'For goodness' sake, they're just kids, they don't need screening.'

'You won't get them past immigration control,' he said flatly.

In answer, she gave him The Stare. The Stare that said *he* would have to arrange it.

On the third day she had her wish. Her old crew were back in the Dakota, the children properly accommodated in new seating and appropriate harnesses, and their destination was Northolt, an airfield on the outskirts of London that was home to a Polish fighter squadron that might be expected to be flexible on the matter of immigration controls.

This time she was a passenger. A new captain, Bob, was at the controls and would be taking the Dakota on to new horizons. There was no opportunity for extended goodbyes to her crew – they were fully occupied and she couldn't keep the children waiting while she said heartfelt farewells to Lucas and Silvers and thanked them profusely for their vital support in Poland, so she had done this the night before in the bar tent at Brindisi.

'Couldn't have done it without you two,' she said.

'Won't forget this trip in a hurry,' Silvers said.

'Wouldn't have missed it for the world.' Lucas couldn't keep a straight face at this, so added: 'Hairy, definitely very hairy. Expected it to be dodgy in the air, but not in the jungle.'

'Forest!'

'Felt like the jungle.' He grinned again. 'And give our

regards to that boy of yours and tell him he's got an outrageous mother.'

The flight to Northolt went without incident. With two fuel stops on the way the children were becoming seasoned travellers and on landing she was relieved to find that Devereaux had kept his word and could still work his magic. Her charges were directed away from the main control buildings to a small hut where minimal formalities were observed. A blind eye was being turned by officials whose arms she was quite sure had been twisted.

She used the telephone in the adjacent orderly room to put in a quick call to her mother. She knew she had to be speedy – not only to assuage the temper of the grumpy duty sergeant but also to trump objections from the other end of the phone line.

'Got a surprise for you, we're on our way, see you later this afternoon,' she announced to her mother, moving speedily on. 'And tell Dad to clear out the big shed, will you?'

'Why, whatever for? And who's *we?*'

'Tell you later.'

She and the children were directed to a waiting bus, as if officialdom was glad to be rid of an embarrassing affront to proper procedure. Inside she located a heavy cardboard box of supplies; another plus from Devereaux. It contained drinks and a hamper of sandwiches, introducing her brood to another set of British wartime staples: corned beef, Spam and pickle, fish paste and eggless pudding.

It was going to be a long journey from the airfield and conscious of the need to lift the prevailing mood of uncertainty and fear she embarked on a comprehensive game of I-spy, directing attention to every possible passing object of interest while introducing some basic English nouns: a house, church, car, field, child, dog, donkey. She was perhaps only just beginning to glimpse the task she set herself: coping with the psychological fall-out of children who had abandoned home, parents and country for a foreign land.

On the Dakota's flight out from Poland she had been busy with the business of flying, leaving Beck and the others to play mother. Now, however, she was on her own with her new brood; she had all their attention and she was the sole point of focus.

As the bus got under way she walked the aisle making eye contact, smiling, making encouraging noises and trying to read their thoughts as they peered with evident incredulity out of the windows. Everything, of course, would seem alien: fearsome figures in tall helmets, strange vehicles travelling on the wrong side of the road, red boxes in the street, some with glass in them, vast roadways of immense blackness but no cobbles, low brick houses, sheep and cows grazing in the fields, horses and dogs aplenty, people in strange clothes... but where were all the trees?

Some of her charges sat sad-eyed as if in a dream, their armour against hurt, heartbreak and loneliness. The youngest didn't want to look outside, squirmed down in their seats, hunching shoulders against this strange new world. Others were puzzled that the people seen outside did not shrink into the undergrowth as the bus passed. The people here walked boldly, without caution or craven posture, as if they had little to fear.

Soon Helen had used up all her childhood songs, had recited poetry the words of which they didn't understand, becoming hoarse with the effort. She went quiet – and in a brief contemplative moment all her moral qualms returned about the manipulation of Devereaux. Did it amount to a form of extortion? An ugly word, a criminal offence when sought for monetary gain. She thought about her action in lesser shades of grey; gaining an advantage, having a hold over him, twisting his arm – all for the very best of reasons, a high moral purpose.

Instead, should she have laid the facts of his disloyalty before the authorities? By failing to do so, was she leaving the country open to more of his betrayals? And the bigger question: could such manipulation ever be justified, even by a cause as pressing as hers? She sighed. The urgency of the mission had been so immediate she had acted instinctively. She couldn't allow her tribe of embattled kids to end up in the chaotic and uncertain world of a refugee camp. She was responsible for getting them out from under the Nazi peril, so surely she had the right to fight their corner. And now, with the reassuring world of the Home Counties and the rural splendour of Suffolk flashing past the bus windows, she came to a conclusion.

In her world children always came first. Every time.

Five hours later the bus pulled up outside the farm, by which time she was both hoarse and tired but knew that her biggest test was only just beginning. As the vehicle came to a stop a chorus of voices erupted. Jan said: 'What's this place?'

'My home.'

'You live in this big house?'

Helen laughed, staring out at the familiar pink facade and long sloping roof of the farmhouse. It was solid and welcoming. What could go wrong in this place? This house had seen it all, had passed the test of centuries; it was voluminous and expansive, a maze of rooms, nooks and crannies, a house capable of absorbing all your troubles. If she had a problem, she instinctively expected to find the solution here.

The bus driver pulled open the sliding door and Helen led her chattering troupe out into a section of the farmyard that contained relatively clean concrete slabs, using downward movements of her arms to plead for calm and quiet.

Calm, of course, was difficult, since the farmyard dogs were running around the group barking and wagging tails, producing shrieks of concern from the young ones. The spaniels were wildly prancing, eager to engage with all these new friends, a couple of noisy mongrels simply barked and a friendly Labrador nosed close, looking for approval. 'Sit!' Helen commanded Bella, her favourite.

Meanwhile young Petra was entranced by the gargoyle fixed to the farmyard wall. It had a human face on a monkey body and the intrigued child was trying to rearrange its stone tail.

Helen's mother, standing at the open kitchen door, wore a predictable pattern of emotions: surprise, confusion and incredulity.

'Hi!' her cheery-faced daughter called. 'Here's my surprise!'

By this time hands were firmly on hips. 'Who are all these kids? What are they doing here?'

Helen came up to her mother and gave her a big hug and smile. Then she turned to the watching youngsters. 'Listen. This is Auntie,' she called, repeating slowly, 'Aunt-ie.'

'Aunt-ie!' they all cried.

'Helen, what have you done?'

'Don't worry, there's plenty of room – the spare room, my old room, Thomas's room, and Nat's rooms – and Dad can use the big shed as an overflow. It's only for a short while, just till I can get them settled.'

'You mean to stay?'

A nod of the head which produced an explosion of incredulity from her mother. 'Don't be silly, they can't come in here, we can't take all this lot.'

'Yes we can.'

'It's impossible. What do you expect us to do with them all?'

'Just be your normal kindly, homely, welcoming self.'

'But we haven't got the places or the food.'

'You can do it; I know you've got plenty of stuff stacked away.'

'Helen... I could kill you for this.'

'No you won't.'

Just then, the driver turned his vehicle and drove the bus away.

Of course, Helen would admit later, the situation was verging on the chaotic. She had to keep her newcomers amused with sweets, crayons and Christmas paper hats while filtering the upstairs rooms of their present contents. It was simply a matter of removing to the safety of the back shed Thomas's banjo, his lovingly painted model ship mounted on a stand and his collection of Dinky cars. Then Nat's gramophone, jazz collection and a pair of motorbike rider's big boots.

'Don't forget his skates and his tennis racquet. He'll never forgive you if...'

'Worry not, being done,' she said.

Finally, clearing the junk room. That was a haul. An old sewing machine, a wash basket, a shopping trolley, some suitcases.

Her mother was still agitated. 'Are you serious? I can't believe you've done this. This is not the right place for them! You're always bringing home waifs and strays but at least it's usually only a dog or some lost animal...'

'Just for a day or two until I get things sorted out.'

Her mother was still shaking her head. 'Have you thought this through? How are we going to feed them? And sleep them? I bet they haven't any ration books.'

'Mum, I know you, I've watched you. You've been stocking up ever since Mr Chamberlain came back from Munich. Somewhere out here you've got the biggest tin can hoard in the country. You've been putting stuff aside for years for the worst the war can throw at us.'

'You take too much on yourself! You should take them to the council.'

'No,' said with the kind of finality that brooked no argument. Helen was reassuring. She would improvise; she'd call at the Red Cross depot for spare blankets and mattresses and get her father to organise bedding. 'Where is Dad, by the way?'

'Oh, go and find him, out there somewhere. In a world of his own.'

In the interim the children, tired of being confined to the kitchen, large though it was, decided that exploring was the name of the next game. The doors upstairs were large and forbidding. That made them even more tantalising.

Helen, who returned speedily enough after locating her father and acquainting him with her requirements – no need to worry about objections from him – found herself staring at a most strange apparition. The top of a tiny head peeped out from what appeared to be a rumpled but flowing floral dress. The tips of two high heels could be seen beneath.

Her mother arrived just in time to stand aghast at this sight.

A small voice piped: 'Look, Auntie!'

Helen held her breath, awaiting the expected explosion while trying not to laugh, but her mother surprised her.

'Never did like that dress.'

After this, it had been necessary to declare some juvenile exclusion zones; in particular, the display cabinet containing a highly prized hand-painted Hungarian coffee pot and best Doulton china and the gaily decorated china ducks arranged around the hearth.

Her mother naturally demanded some sort of explanation for the arrival of so many unexpected guests.

'You know I can't tell you that,' her daughter said. 'Just that they've had a very hard time, so please be indulgent as well as organised.'

'It's all very well for you to say that... all very well to make these grand gestures, but who is it that always picks up the pieces?' A question answered by pointing at her chest. 'And if you think you can float off again to that airfield and leave me with this lot on my own...'

'No.' Helen was firm and quelled such fears. 'Don't worry. I'm here to sort it.'

Helen was the first mother to arrive at the school gate just after three in the afternoon, knowing news travelled fast and determined that her son should learn of it from her.

'Hear you've got quite a party going down at Vale Farm.' She knew that Sybil Quare wouldn't hold back, neither could the others who crowded round demanding details.

'Just a temporary thing, on their way to another destination.' She knew that wouldn't satisfy, fending off questions as best she could and was glad when the bell rang and the usual home-going torrent emerged. She grabbed Peter, pulling him to one side, away from the clamour and set off back towards the farm at a fast pace.

'It's a race,' she said, 'to see who can walk the fastest all the way home.'

Halfway there, when they were quite alone and their progress began to flag, she announced that she had 'something to tell'.

Inevitably, this would play out as another 'why?' game – the who and the why. How could it not, with the arrival of a bus-load of strange children? She introduced them as 'a new set of brothers and sisters we're going to be looking after for a short while'.

First, she had an appeal to her aspiring young adult. 'I want you to be my helper. You're a big boy now and I want you to help me make them happy, not sad.'

'Why?'

'Because they're poor children who've had to leave their homes and mummies and come away without any of their things to a strange place and a strange country.'

'Why?'

'To save them from danger.'

'Why?'

'Because some bad men were going to take them away.'

'Why?'

'Because they were very bad men.'

Here the quiz paused. 'Did you see them, these bad men?'

'Yes.'

'But you got away?'

'Yes.'

At this Peter was silent. She could see him thinking about his mother getting the better of some very bad men and after what seemed like a very long minute, he looked up at her and smiled his approval.

She swallowed deeply then, almost cried, wrapped in the warm blanket of her son's pride. Better than any adult plaudits; better than any medal.

———

Her next most urgent task was to speak to her friend Isabelle. No telephone today; this was something she'd do face to face, walking out from the farm into an overcast morning hoping this wasn't an omen, navigating Westgate Street until she was climbing the steps of the building that had become a familiar port of call over the years.

Isabelle was a childhood friend; plump with a round smiley

face, a matronly figure before her time. They had grown up together jiving to Fats Waller's 'Ain't Misbehavin'' and '12th Street Rag' and singing along to Paul Robeson, but their adult lives had diverged. Isabelle's steady boyfriend was away in the forces and her predecessor at the Westgate Street orphanage had been bombed out and moved away, leaving the young deputy to run the place on her own. She was a natural with children; kind, authoritative and immensely practical. Helen and Peter were welcome regulars as Thursday lunch-time helpers, but today was different and both women knew it.

Helen returned all the waves and smiles from familiar young faces as she weaved her way through the day room and into the kitchen to find her friend hands deep in a sink of steaming water, plates and bowls piled up ready for the suds. The wan smile of greeting was indicative. Word of Helen's sudden deluge of refugees had clearly gone before her.

A shrug of the shoulders, a resigned facial gesture began the conversation. 'Issie, I've gone and done something slightly crazy.'

'So I've heard.'

'And I'm floundering.'

Isabelle didn't immediately reply. She took her hands out of the sink, found a towel and proceeded methodically to dry her hands. Then she leaned back against the sink and slowly shook her head. 'Sorry, Helen, I'm really very sorry about this, but before you even ask I have to say no.'

Helen blinked away a tear of disappointment. 'I was hoping...'

'Of course you were... but can't you guess? Look around you. Full up at the inn, I can't take any more, I'm short of space, short of food, short of supplies and short of money. In fact...' A deep sigh. 'I was hoping you'd help ME.'

Helen's shoulders slumped. Rejection was a hard blow. She

had been counting on Isabelle, had regarded her friend as a stalwart, as her secret weapon; had reckoned that if anyone could understand and find a solution to her problem it would be the person who'd spent her life succouring the town's waifs and strays. This was a woman who always found a way.

Isabelle put out a sympathetic hand. Of course she was sympathetic – because sympathy was all she had. 'Honestly, you must know this, I would if I possibly could.'

Helen swallowed and nodded. 'I know.'

'But how the heck have you got yourself lumbered with so many?'

'Long story.'

'Who are they all?'

'Ssssh!' A finger to the lips. 'Mum's the word.'

'You can say that again. Mum times fifteen is how I heard it. And I bet *your* mum is just loving it.'

Helen stayed to help finish the dish mountain and hang out sheets from a couple of bed-wetters and then lug in some precious coke supplies for the stove. Isabelle had meanwhile disappeared and eventually emerged from a store cupboard proffering a couple of threadbare blankets. 'Can't see you go home empty-handed, but honestly these are the only spares.'

At the door she asked, 'So what are you going to do now?'

Helen made a face. 'Desperation stakes. Worst possible choice.'

The front room was set out as if for a meeting. After much marshalling and cajoling, Helen had them all sitting, quietening them, some on chairs, others on cushions, and announced: 'We're going to have some nursery rhymes and some songs.'

Jan, who had some words of English, gave his own version of

this message, producing excited, expectant faces and a welcome silence.

Helen began with favourites from her own childhood: 'Hey diddle diddle the cat and the fiddle', producing a rough sketch of a cat to illustrate, earning several giggles; then 'Hickory Dickory Dock' and 'Cock a Doodle Do!' Later, she vowed to herself, when they had conquered the language gap, she would expand her repertoire to *Jack and the Beanstalk*, the *Three Little Pigs* and all the others from her formative years.

But for now, a singsong. Even though scant meaning would be attached to the words, she counted on the verve of their delivery to produce the right effect, recruiting Jan and her mother to help with 'Run Rabbit Run' and 'You Are My Sunshine'.

Then Ada, a smooth-skinned black-haired girl nearing womanhood, responded in kind; had them singing a traditional Polish song they all knew.

Helen smiled and clapped, happy that she had succeeded in reaching into the hearts of her charges through the joy of music, even though the words would have to come later.

This was her formal attempt at organisation and control, and at correcting some of the chaos that had proceeded it. But she had to do more than this. With Isabelle and the orphanage unable to help, she was thrown back on her earlier option, one that gave her pause and considerable qualms of conscience.

Mother was in the yard, pegging out washing, the children were quietly occupied for once and no one was within earshot of the alcove in the hallway where the telephone stood in splendid isolation, an instrument used on rare occasions and therefore linked to moments of great news, crises or disasters.

Helen drew in a deep breath, found her scribbled note and dialled the number she'd been given for emergencies.

'I'm sorry,' said the person at the other end, 'Mr Devereaux is no longer with us.'

She put down the receiver and stared hesitantly from the window. Pressure was building; she couldn't delay. This was a last resort. She put in a call to the big house out on the Newmarket Road, fearing a frosty, possibly hostile, reception.

An unfamiliar voice, probably a new domestic, said a message would be passed on and she was left standing impotently and alone in the hallway, suspecting that this was merely a routine put off. Where was he? Italy, Britain, some other posting, in trouble?

It wasn't until late afternoon that she heard the instrument's strident summons and almost ran to answer, cupping the mouthpiece with her hand.

'Hello.'

'You called.'

It was him. 'Where are you?'

'Thanks to you, in Bury.'

'Oh?'

'I told you you'd wreck my career. Well, now it's happened, I'm off the case and kicking my heels back home.'

She breathed out, deciding not to be commiserating or sympathetic. His present location could only be a boon.

'How bad is it?'

'Smoothing your path has cost me.'

'Nothing else? Well, that's very convenient,' she said, 'because I need your help.'

'Again? Haven't you had enough? Done enough?'

'Unfortunately not. You see, the situation is urgent. I need a home for my little brood.'

'A problem I recall warning you about.'

'The Bury orphanage is busting at the seams and can't take any more.'

'What do you expect me to do about it?'

'You still owe me. You owe the children.'

'You've got a nerve.'

'Your family, the oh-so-well-appointed Devereauxs, has properties all over town. Bound to be some spare accommodation somewhere. Work the family. Give me a property.'

He snorted. 'You don't want much, do you?'

Next day when the telephone rang Helen, fast on her feet, was quick to answer. And this time Devereaux's tone seemed less abrasive.

'Could be you're in luck. Mother thinks I've taken leave of my senses, of course. Why have I got myself involved and so on. This is just a maybe. Nothing definite. She thinks the idea might be good for the family reputation, boost our standing in the town. But the question is, for how long would you need this?'

'For as long as it takes.'

Despite all her other worries Helen had been quietly confident all along that the old farmhouse would swallow up her juvenile invasion without difficulty. Vale Farm had been a fixture in Bury since 1300. It had a pitched gable roof with huge dormer windows, massive double chimneys and decorative stone hares dancing along the ridge tiles. Out in the yard there were barns and sheds galore and on the other side of the house a walled garden with a fancy monument. The interior included a granny flat and a wide sunroom.

So far they had converted the dining room into a playroom: crayons, pencils, blackboards, paints. Lots of paint splattering wallpaper and carpet. She inspected the artistic results, saddened by some of the scenes: men with guns and ruined houses, scenes of horror played out from young minds, though some of the younger ones had managed carrots and cakes. Hopefully, the presence of farm animals and the peace of the Suffolk countryside would in time generate more placid artwork.

After the school pick-up she had to field another of Peter's quizzes. He'd looked put out by having two boys bedding down in his room and they'd been leafing through his manual of past FA Cup winners kept in pride of place on his bedside table. 'You mustn't mind if they touch your things,' she said. 'They haven't anything of their own, they're not lucky like you. You have to be ready to share.'

He looked uncertain of this answer and she waited for the inevitable reaction. 'Why don't they speak like us?'

'Because they speak another language.'

'Why don't they remember their manners at the table?'

'Because their mummies didn't teach them.'

'Why?'

'Because they come from big families with no time to teach them good manners like yours.'

'Why?'

'Because they like lots of children.'

'Why...'

From the corner of her eye she saw her mother's frown, then took a deep breath and said: 'Because we like to have small families so we can give our boys and girls lots of attention. That's why you're lucky and they're not.'

There was a long pause before Peter said: 'You should tell their mummies that.'

This produced a chortle from the direction of the sink and Helen began to suspect that her mother did not regard the shock of her child invasion in quite the negative way her dour manner suggested. Maybe there was a little part of her that enjoyed the challenge, though she wouldn't admit it. Already she had called in favours from neighbours – extra blankets and sheets – though she was careful to guard from prying eyes her special wartime stock of baked beans, spaghetti, tinned sausage and soup.

'You're a farmer's wife,' her daughter said, 'and farm wives can cope with anything.'

'I'm not a farmer's wife.'

'Yes you are... as good as. You cope with Dad and all his old sheds and cars, Eddie and the farm girls, don't you?'

'That I do.'

It was like a prompt. Some strange noises emanated from one of the sheds in the yard and Helen hurried out, worrying that her young ones' desire for exploration and adventure could be the cause of damage to any of the valuable and shiny cars her father lovingly restored ready for the peace – whenever that might be.

She opened the door with some trepidation but found her father laughing heartily as three tiny ones bounced up and down like yo-yos on the dickie seat of a Dolomite roadster.

'Is that all right?' she asked, eyeing the rather swish looking red and silver coupe.

'They can't hurt, it's solid enough,' he said, and she realised her father was actually enjoying the invasion. He'd always been good with children, had given her Peter tractor rides around the farm and encouraged his efforts with a hammer and nails. Three of her brood now took turns at the steering wheel of a Vitesse Tourer.

'The boy's next door,' he said, pointing.

Another door, another shed. And when she entered she was immediately proud of her young son. She had already explained to Peter the reason for this deluge of strange children and why he should be especially kind to Marta because she'd lost her mother. Now she watched him being the little man showing the wide-eyed waif around his den of shed-made wooden swords, his cricket bats, toy cars and football boots.

'Helen!' Her mother was calling. 'Your favourite person has arrived!'

Back in the newly designated playroom – all breakables removed – a queue of youngsters was forming. At the head of the queue was a chair and leaning over it and the young form seated below was a tall land girl dressed in the usual uniform of beige breeches and green jumper. The sound was unmistakable; scissors clicking hard at work.

Sue the Snips the family dubbed her; in civilian life a hair-dresser and still determined to keep her hand in. 'Lots of lovely new customers,' Snips announced. 'All eager for a bit of hot styling.'

'You've given the dog a breather then?'

Normally she and her companion farm worker Diane would be seen from afar in the fields. They drank at The Plough and lodged at Sycamore Cottage at the end of the drive, but the attraction of being around so many exciting new youngsters was like a magnet. Diane was in the kitchen making sandwiches. Welcomed help; extra mother-figures on tap.

The immediate hurdle of finding sufficient bedding for the night was solved by a combination of the second-hand shop, the Red Cross, neighbours and the deep recesses of Mother's wartime treasure trove. The odd detached car seat also did service.

'Where's Peter?'

It began as a calm inquiry and, when no answer was forthcoming, became louder and more insistent. 'Has anyone seen him?'

Helen realised she had been busy for too long dealing with the mountainous pile of laundry created by keeping the children freshly clothed. She had also been working out her answers in readiness for the next inquisitorial session. The questions would keep coming and she anticipated the most likely: why he had to go to school when the others did not, why don't we all speak the same language, why he had to eat fish when he didn't like the taste and why the war was taking so long.

Now, however, she abandoned her thoughts and her task, leaving a great blob of wet clothing on the top of the wringer, and anxiously checked all the rooms in the old house, the barns and the yard. Her sense of alarm rose when Gabriela volunteered the fact that she had seen Peter playing with his bike.

This was a tiny Fairy cycle her father had fitted with stabilisers.

'I'm on my adventures.' She could hear Peter's explanation in her head.

All the children had been warned never to stray into the town because of the danger – also, lest their exuberant chatter and conspicuous appearance be noted by officialdom with potentially disastrous consequences. Perhaps Peter thought this didn't apply to him.

By now the alarm was in full cry. Grandpa was deputed to scour No Man's Meadow and the bridge over the river, Mother to re-check all the rooms and corners of the farmhouse and Helen, fearing the worst, running as fast as she could along Oasthouse Lane, past the Linnet tenements and into the main thoroughfare at Raingate Street. Perhaps she should call out the farm girls to help scour all the streets.

Which way to go – left or right?

Then an inspired thought: what places had he known in the

town? That sent her running afresh towards Isabelle's orphanage, her hair askew, breathless and badly dressed as she was for the street. An elderly woman in a turban hurriedly vacated the pavement, frowning at such haste, and a coalman, a heavy sack on his back, stopped in midstride to gape at her.

She rounded the corner into Westgate Street and almost collided head-on with her son travelling in the opposite direction.

She gulped, speechless and out of breath, and lent against a brick wall.

Peter stopped the bicycle and looked cross.

Eventually, she managed, 'Where have you been? On your adventures, I suppose?'

He shook his head. 'To see Auntie Isabelle.'

'Why?'

'To give off some of my toys. An engine and two trucks for the children.'

A sound bubble had formed around Vale Farm: yells, laughter, cries and tears. Days of high-pitched juvenile chatter, banter and exclamation had transformed the place from its previous quiet routine into a school-level hubbub and gradually Helen's decibel tolerance had become attuned to the new normal.

It was not therefore with any great surprise or concern that she heard young voices telling her that soldiers had appeared in the farmyard. Another game? Or another nightmare, an imagined scare from their old life?

Several young ones clustered around her, grabbing her legs, seeking protection and she put her arms around shoulders in an instinctive gesture of reassurance. Her attitude changed, however, when Ada appeared, blinking and pointing, an unusual state of apprehension for the normally calm teenager.

Helen walked to the big window in the playroom and was momentarily startled by what she saw: a half hundredweight khaki truck with canvas sides. It dominated their prize piece of brushed concrete driveway. And by the front door stood a six-foot uniformed figure with the red cap and a face rigidly set with some, as yet, unrevealed purpose.

Her mother's voice betrayed a similar uncertainty. 'Helen, is this something to do with you? Why have we got the Army on our doorstep?'

Then, of course, she got it – and her face lit up with hope. 'Don't worry, everything's fine,' she told the children and opened the front door.

'Captain Fairfax? Helen Fairfax?'

She nodded. The bark did not intimidate, remembering the old adage never to show fear – either to an enemy or even the military police. 'That's me.'

'We have a Mr Beck who has been granted permission to visit these premises for twenty-four hours.'

'Fine, bring him in.'

'First, you have to agree to be his conducting officer for the said period, in which case you will be solely responsible for his security.'

'You make it sound like he's a prisoner.'

'He will then be released into your custody. Pick up will be at 0900 hours tomorrow. Is that agreed?'

'Is all this rigmarole necessary?'

The clipboard was extended from a rigidly straight arm. 'Sign here.'

They sat in the best chairs in the bay window at a table set out with Mother's Sunday teacups and a plate of prized McVitie's chocolate biscuits. The children had been schooled to keep their distance – but eyes were wide and singularly focused as never before.

After so much worry – and so many telephone calls – fearing that she might never see him again, Helen was overjoyed finally to have Leo sitting opposite. At first, they didn't speak, examining each other carefully for signs of change, as if they'd been reunited after a great disaster. Eventually she smiled and he grinned.

'Was it awful?'

'Not really. A little regimented, that's all.'

'I can imagine.'

'Hard work. Documenting and explaining everything, convincing them, killing all Farnborough's preconceptions. Did it in the end, though.'

'So, where are we on that? Or are you forbidden?'

But Beck was too consumed by the minutiae of his work to hold back and she was conscious again of his compulsive grasp of the technology, confirming what she already knew from Professor Nowotny: the scatter-gun effect, the fuel, the smaller-than-feared size of the rocket and its warhead and the lack of any defence. The best hope, she already knew, would be the coming invasion, the Second Front they all wished would sweep the Nazis away from their launch pads in France.

'Enough of that!' Beck said suddenly, looking round for the children and wanting to know why they had not been sent to a home. 'It's just astonishing, you having them here, how you're coping...' He looked at her earnestly. 'I think you're both doing a wonderful job but I can't understand why your government has not arranged something; you can't do this all on your own. You're under siege.'

She shrugged and looked away. This was something she dare not share: her manipulation and hold over Devereaux, the favours called in, the dark secret of her mentor's betrayals but more than that: her own shame.

He grasped her hand. 'When I've finished with them–' and here he pointed vaguely in the direction taken by his retreating military escort. '–I want to help you. With the children. The young, they're the future. They're what we should be doing in the peace.' He blinked several times in a sudden outburst of emotion. 'A new purpose and direction in life, for me atonement, a redemption and a new beginning.'

Later, standing in the kitchen and insisting on helping with the washing-up, he told her mother: 'Your daughter is a true humanitarian. It's been a privilege to know and serve with her.'

Over-hearing this Helen looked away, her confusion and doubts stabbing an already troubled conscience. Could she ever confess to Beck her acts of brazen manipulation?

The children had jumped all over him, calling 'Uncle Leo', causing great hilarity but later her mother arranged things so the youngsters were kept from the living room. That's when Helen quizzed him about conditions at Farnborough.

'Accommodation a bit spartan,' he said. 'Canteen meals, no recreation, no literature, no music, just work.'

She was still curious. 'Tell me about your life in Germany.'

He looked reflective, even apologetic. 'As you know, I was very keen on the idea of getting into space. A shot at the moon, now that would be something.'

'Yes, but life here down on earth?'

He sighed. 'The rocket station I worked at, Peenemünde, it was an academic refuge, insulated from the reality of the rest of the country. A place run by scientists for scientists. Easy to ignore the outside world, easy to ignore the potential for killing lots of people.'

'So what changed?'

'Going home on leave to see my mother. Very unhappy. Tells me all about these brown shirt thugs roaming the streets. Father angrily rebutting it all, telling her to shut up, his diatribes against enemies of the country. Gradually I realised what victory for the Reich would mean. More people like Father, more bullying, more killing.'

She put out a reassuring hand to him. 'I'm sure your mother will be okay. Friends will do the right thing, you'll see.'

He nodded and she decided to lighten the conversation, remembering his preferences, selecting a 78 from her stack of records and playing a selection of polkas, the Strauss sound replacing the normal childish hubbub on her father's HMV wind-up gramophone.

'Music filled with hope and optimism, a calming antidote to our present world,' Leo said.

Remembering his passion for biography she purloined her brother Thomas's old school volume, *Great Orators of the World*, which had somehow defied the big clean up. He riffled through the pages: Socrates, Cicero, Luther. 'My favourite was Pericles and of course Lincoln and the Gettysburg Address,' he said.

'Take it with you,' she said, 'bedside reading at Fort Dismal.'

He laughed. Later he was found a mattress and blanket for the night and in the morning was collected as expected by the unbending escort. It seemed a cruel twist that his stay was so brief, a mere twenty-four hours. She resented the brevity of the visit and the shortness of their time together. She also feared he might still disappear into some security black hole; he had a ring of security wrapped around him so that his position appeared almost like house arrest. She stood awkwardly on the doorstep, unsure how demonstrative to be, a brief hug and squeezed hand sufficing for their farewell, as the military once more claimed him. No light was forthcoming on her inquiries about the prospect of a further, and longer, visit.

After his departure Helen found a rare quiet moment in her room and gave herself over to daydreaming, intrigued and captivated by Beck's declaration that he wanted to help with refugee children. She saw in him kindliness, empathy, quiet courage and renewal. For one filmy, pink-flecked dream-like moment she saw them as representatives of a new international order – the Englishwoman, the German-American, the English boy and the Polish adoptee – living a perfect life in a world finally at peace.

Then she told herself to stop being ridiculous.

That was how her mother found her, propped up against the bedboard, looking sad almost to the point of tearful.

'He's more than just a friend, isn't he?'

No reply.

'He's certainly smitten on you. Got a funny accent though.'

Helen blinked. 'Because he's had a very difficult life. Just don't pry.'

Chapter Forty-Four

She was a little round blob of a woman, bulging out of her WVS greens, with an expression set in a permanent pout. Not the traditional smiler from the canteen truck offering a steaming cuppa; more the angry bee from 'the department'.

Helen had been treading warily, staying well clear of the town hall. She dare not make a fuss with official agencies lest they question the children's refugee status, declare them illegals, intern them or even expel them from the country. No way would she risk any of that. 'I was hoping you were going to help,' she told the woman.

'That's the problem, the irregular way these children have been brought into the country. They don't seem to have been screened or approved. You can't expect to have ration books issued for them without identity cards and you can't have identity cards for persons who are not registered.'

'They're just innocents, fleeing from dangers abroad.'

'That's as maybe, but procedures should have been followed. Proper immigration procedures.'

'You mean sending them to some distant camp full of other displaced and unsuitable people?'

'I'm not sure I can be of help in this case.'

Helen's fears continued: scenarios that gave her bad nights. Dreadful images in which she failed her charges, making their situation worse instead of better.

Later there would be more prosaic problems to deal with: falls from swings, scrumping apples from old Tom's orchard, a constant honking from the car shed and mysterious 'treasures' that appeared in a new den she located in the adjoining copse. She was drawn there by unrestrained giggles and found to her consternation much small-boy booty: a bird table, a hammer, chisel, pliers and most worryingly of all, three gnomes in all their gorgeous red and green gaudiness – none other than Dopey, Bashful and Sleepy. Thank goodness her coterie of young garden thieves had missed Snow White. Some unfortunate gardener, doubtless proud of his front lawn display, was now short of three of his set of Disney characters.

There was even a tiny statue of Lady Godiva, her nakedness the cause of all the giggling.

Only one proper response was open to her: immediate restoration – 'but don't get caught!'

Some kind of routine had to be established; meal times certainly, then everything must stop at six o'clock when Father insisted on gathering round his greatest treasure, the Pilot 650 six-valve receiver with the braded effect loudspeaker, placed on a table next to the fireplace, the first wireless to have a magic eye tuning indicator. Though only some of the audience understood the words – 'Here is the BBC News and this is Alvar Lidell reading it' – total silence was understood to be the inflexible rule.

'Uncle' Eddie, the man who lived in the town and did the actual farming at Vale, found ways of supplementing food supplies: potatoes, eggs, chickens and oats, countryside 'extras' all strictly off ration.

At the weekend Helen's brother Thomas arranged leave from his army unit and arrived in a state of high amusement at the family's strange invasion. 'Only my sister could arrive out of the blue with half the world's lost children in tow.'

His mischievous contribution was to take a gaggle of the more likely children on a country walk, creating an enormous kerfuffle by imitating sheep noises. The children had been peering through a fence at the flock when Thomas began to imitate the animals' bleating. Seeing this was an acceptable joke, the rest of the party took up the noisy refrain and joined in, provoking the whole flock of sheep to an even louder response. Soon their b-a-a-a-ing echoed across the countryside, causing 'Uncle' Eddie to come running, fearful of a fox attack.

Dressing up had become a children's favourite so Helen, with the earlier incident in mind, decided she had to make a gesture, passing over with some regret several cherished jumpers, skirts and high heels, creating near-fights over who should try the heels first. Despite the sacrifice, dressing up then returned to bite her. Petra, blonde and funny but far too small for the outfit, next presented herself wearing a uniform jacket, Sam Browne belt and skewed officer's cap.

'This joke's on you, I think,' her mother said.

Next came the peach rayon knickers with elastic – the only item allowed by wartime regulation to use elastic – looking simply huge on Petra.

Mother pursed her lips and coughed. 'You'd best get her out of them – before one of the men sees her. You don't want your smalls advertised to the world.'

Helen could see Peter frowning. He clearly disapproved of the girls dressing up in his mother's clothes. His 'whys' gradually became 'whens': 'when can I have my things back?' And 'when are they leaving?'

More rescues had to be performed to save Max Factor

lipsticks and father's best Homburg hat. 'He won't be laughing quite so loud if he sees that,' Mother said, and Helen wondered again, as she often had, about the difference in temperament evidenced by her parents.

Throughout her time at home she had a shadow: little Marta, like a cling-on, following her everywhere, almost in her shoes, almost falling over her on the stairs, those big staring eyes appealing for touch and attention.

'Sorry, Helen.'

It was Devereaux again. 'I tried, I really did, put pressure on Mama but she's come down against it, won't have it. And once she's said No...'

'This is hugely disappointing.'

'Well, I don't know what else I can do.'

The ensuing silence seemed like a black hole to Helen. A toxic mix of conflicting feelings; disappointment, fear, regret and guilt swirled around and eventually Devereaux spoke again. 'Look, I can't do the impossible and I rather think our arrangement has time lapsed.'

'If that's how you want to put it.'

'Too much water has flowed since you arrived back in Bury, I don't think anything you might now say would have much effect. The urgency of the matter has passed.'

She could hear the fear and the hope in his voice and she felt seedy and unclean, like a blackmailer. Her conscience had been troubling her and she knew she would be ashamed if she were forced to explain to anyone – Beck or her mother – that she had been turning the screw in this way.

She swallowed and said, 'Okay, I won't hold it over you. I've hated doing this anyway. So I simply appeal to your good nature. It's just that you have it in your power to help. I'm desperate, I must find somewhere for my kids.'

Another silence. A long one and she wondered about his reaction. Perhaps he would be scornful; she wouldn't blame him if he were. Maybe hostile; maybe he would reject her, ignore her and end the call.

Then his voice came again, even and without rancour. 'Just an idea,' he said, 'but what about Grove House out on the Haverhill Road? Why don't you try Lady Russett? She's all alone in that big old place.'

Her mother was hanging bedding out to air – 'another bed wetter last night' – and Helen knew that Marta had some way to go before she became anything approaching settled. The man with the orchard had been on the phone again, complaining that his apples were still disappearing and Mother's skills at first-aid had been called upon to repair damage sustained in a fall from a tree. Father had fixed up a swing from a stout branch down by the stream; paddling and fishing for tiddlers, frogs and tadpoles were features of the day as the children had equipped themselves with nets on sticks manufactured on the farm.

Eventually a woman delegated from the London Polish Committee arrived to begin English lessons, although several small figures could usually be found hiding from these sessions in one of the many sheds.

And all through this bizarre period Peter had continued to go to school.

Helen reached out to take the proffered cup of tea and smiled her gratitude. Beautiful china, probably incredibly expensive, Meissen or something like that, and the old lady positively creaked when she served it.

'Go and see Lady Russett,' Devereaux had told her. 'I'll fix it.' Another of his desperate suggestions. 'She's over ninety, last of the line, sitting in that vast old hall, far too big for her, only occupies a couple of rooms, draughty old place but ideal for what you need.'

Helen looked gratefully at Lady Russett. 'So nice of you to see me,' she said, conscious of the fading finery, the chintz and the cobwebs.

'Yes, well, I've spoken to your friend Mr Devereaux and I gather you have designs on Wetherby Hall.'

Helen blinked. 'Oh, I wouldn't put it quite like that, we just wondered about a possible arrangement.' She swallowed and instantly regretted using the phrase. It suggested a financial arrangement whereas Helen was hoping for the free use of the premises. Where could she possibly find finance for any rental agreement?

Lady Russett put down her cup. 'I've been thinking about it,' she said. 'I admit it would be a fitting legacy to my family's good name and my own life, providing needy children with a refuge.' She lifted the cup, hesitated and put it down again. 'But difficult, breaking with tradition, parting with, or dividing up, the family seat...' She looked hesitantly around the room. 'Perhaps I should consult my solicitor about it.'

Helen could see her hopes slipping away.

'I'll sleep on it,' said Lady Russett.

'Another vague straw in the wind,' she told her mother, 'one that's likely to blow away.' A gloomy silence settled over the kitchen and Helen wondered if she had backed herself into an impossible corner. In Poland saving the kids seemed absolutely the right thing to do – but was it? She couldn't saddle her mother with this chaos for a moment longer but now she had reached the stage of desperation, bereft of ideas, stripped of options.

An outbreak of crazy mischief didn't help. The more adventurous of her tribe had been exploring every corner of the farmhouse, all its nooks and crannies, and had even taken to chasing over the rooftops, climbing over ridge, gables and dormers and sliding down to the balustrade with the inevitable trail of damage.

'This can't go on,' her mother said, examining another pile of shattered roof tiles that had landed in the yard. 'It's been an experience, I'll say that for it. I admit there have been good times in all this... but really, Helen...' She brushed a stray hair from her eyes and winced with fatigue as she stepped back into the kitchen. 'It can't go on.'

Mother and daughter eyed each other in a moment of desperate frankness.

'I know.' Helen was stung by regret at having caused so much aggravation. She owed her mother hugely for her indulgence and generosity and vowed to make it up to her.

Just then the telephone trilled in the hall and Helen, inert and drained of energy, stumbled out to answer. A female voice with a strange accent announced itself but Helen wasn't sure she caught the correct title. The voice continued that it had heard about her 'commendable act of charity' and her difficulty in placing children.

At this she began to worry. Was this interest, sympathy or gossip? Perhaps a sympathiser; perhaps a time-waster. She wasn't in the mood and if the caller represented a newspaper this would be dangerous. She didn't want the story getting out about her 'illicit immigrants'.

'I'm sorry,' she said into the mouthpiece, interrupting the flow, 'I didn't quite catch your words earlier... who did you say you were?'

By this time her mother was also standing in the hallway, staring at her. Telephone calls were a rare occurrence, prompting a querulous expression.

'I see,' Helen said.

Silence.

'Yes, that's right.'

More silence that seemed to stretch and stretch.

'Correct.'

By this time her mother's expression was demanding of an explanation. So much talking that she couldn't hear.

'Thank you. Yes, I'll do as you suggest.'

At this point the receiver was replaced.

'Well?'

Helen let out a long pent-up breath and wrinkled her brow. Before the call she'd been feeling beaten up. Now she was simply surprised. 'Someone from the Polish government in exile in London.'

Mother's expression transformed rapidly from gloom to intrigue and then to hope. 'And?'

Finally, a smile, a sense of relief. 'They think they may be able to help.'

'Thank God, snatch their hands off.' Mother looked as if she had just received a telegram from the winnings department of Littlewoods Pools. 'What else did they say?'

They sat at the old dining table to discuss the details. The exiled government of Poland had arrived in London after the fall of France in 1940. They were soldiers, statesmen and others who had escaped the German invasion of their country. Several came with families, some with children, and now a body calling itself the Committee for the Education of Poles had set up a boarding school for children aged five to eleven.

'It's a new thing, apparently,' Helen recounted, 'just starting, still searching for textbooks and teaching materials, just five teachers, but already they're thinking about a chapel and a choir and hope soon to have a small library.'

'Yeah, yeah, but what about our children?'

'They think they can fit our children in. I'm to visit tomorrow to discuss the arrangements.'

It was the saddest of days and it was also the most joyful of days, the most moving and the most tearful. Helen, determined to keep smiling, had a lump in her throat and her eyes were moist. Her people, her little ones and those not so little, were singing the national anthem – 'Poland has not yet perished so long as we still shall live'.

Young voices, tiny piping voices and those not yet broken. It had been an emotional day. Mrs Wojcik, the headmistress of Finchingate, had greeted the party with arms wide.

'Welcome Helen's People, you're safe now! You've arrived, you've reached your safe haven, your long journey is over. All those difficult times and the long harrowing trek are behind you. You're home, children! A big welcome to our little piece of Poland.'

There were flags, the white and red of the national colours, bunting and festive balloons. And a spread. No more Woolton

Pie, Spam fritters or parsnip pudding; instead pierogi dumplings, potato pancakes, blueberry buns and noodles with cottage cheese.

As the children feasted an accordion provided a soothing backdrop. After the meal there were games: hopscotch, or *klasy* to give the proper name, was being played on the yard outside amid chalked squares on the tarmac. Inside the young ones laughed to Polish versions of 'Twinkle Twinkle Little Star'; 'Head, Shoulders, Knees and Toes' and 'Once I Caught a Fish Alive'.

Helen caught Wojcik's eye and was reassured by a smile and nod that she had done the right thing. This was the boarding school, the end of a very long road. True, it was a spartan affair, but Wojcik, a comely and homely figure, was clearly the right person to take charge of those who until this day had been Helen's People.

They had set out early from Vale Farm, the same bus appearing in the yard, sharp at nine, as requested, courtesy once more of Devereaux, and they had all climbed aboard taking with them the reluctantly repacked satchels, rucksacks and cardboard boxes. Helen rode the journey to ease the transition. She couldn't just wave them goodbye with an instant cut-off and vanish from their lives. She would not break the connection. She would commit to a continuing presence.

'But we don't want to go,' complained Beata. 'We want to stay with you and Auntie and Peter and Marta. It's fun at the farmhouse.'

'Can I take the kitten?' This from Gabriela.

Helen knew there would be reluctance. She, her parents and the land girls had opened up the old farmhouse, with all its many creaking rooms and intriguing corners, and had done their best to ease the children's pain of leaving their homeland.

'Where are we going?' An echo of that earlier worry.

'To a new home specially for you. You'll have other children there who speak your language. And teachers too. Lots of new friends, proper lessons, just the place for growing up.'

Her honeyed promises took something of a jolt when they arrived and she surveyed the Nissen huts and barrack blocks of a former army camp recently released to the Polish exile group as the premises for their new school. An outside wash house and separate mess hall were standard military items. A fresh coat of paint failed to hide the words BASTION BARRACKS. In the schoolroom a blackboard was propped up on a wobbly easel and the smelly coke stove created wafts of heat and condensation at the Crittall windows.

'Don't worry,' the headmistress told Helen, 'not as cosy as your farmhouse, I'm sure, but we're about to put in lots more creature comforts. They'll be fine. Children are eminently adaptable, as I expect you know.'

But the presence of more native Polish speakers, far from providing reassurance, merely reminded several of the children of what they had lost, prompting the inevitable question from Gabriela: 'When will I see my mummy again?'

Others, however, were demonstrating developing talents. Petra, who'd been an eager listener to Beethoven's Fifth and other symphonies on the farmhouse radio, was all smiles when she spotted an ancient Crane piano in the corner of the room. And Beata, discovering a plentiful supply of coloured pencils, was creating quirky cartoon stick men she called Mr Gloomy, Mr Grumpy and Mr Funny.

'I think we have several budding geniuses here,' Helen announced, then in a moment of skittishness, asked, 'What's a collective term for our group of geniuses? A coven, a cohort, clique, coterie, gathering or gang?'

Despite her industry Beata was still anxious. 'Will you stay with us?' she pleaded and, 'I wish you could stay.'

Helen promised to be back, to keep in touch, to continue to be a visual presence to her little tribe. She wasn't about to vanish from their lives. She had plans to make a career working with children as soon as the war was over and this was clearly the place to start. She'd already promised 'to be around as much as I possibly can'.

Did her new life start here?

'Put me down on your rota,' she told the headmistress, who was recruiting volunteer teacher assistants to supplement her permanent staff.

'For how many days?'

Helen swallowed. Crunch point. Could she really volunteer, given that the military might reclaim her? Even married women were now expected to do war work. What was her work status and immediate future? Back to ferry flying, a full-time mother to Peter and Marta, or school staffer to Helen's People?

Chapter Forty-Five

I t was an opportunity to put things right; to restore normality to Vale Farm and to put back the order of how things were in the kitchen before Helen introduced fifteen young persons to throw her mother's household routines into chaos. Now the oven was being taken apart, scraped, brushed, cleansed; cupboards spring cleaned, tiles burnished.

However, an engine noise in the yard interrupted this domestic industry and her mother stopped to peer through the window.

'Looks like an official sort of car,' she said – then sighed and turned to her daughter. 'Helen, you promised me, you gave me your word, no more flying, no more leaving me to deal with everything. You said you were finished with all that...'

They both stared at the large car carefully manoeuvring around the tree in the centre of the courtyard. Two heads could be seen; one in the front seat, the other in the rear.

'I *am* finished with all that.'

'Well then?'

'Something to do with the kids, I expect. Prepare for war.

Put on your armour plate, more questions about who the children are, where they're from, why they're here...'

'Haven't you done all that?'

'More official nonsense, no doubt, these people never give up.'

Two sets of eyes ready for a fight... then a gasp as a tall figure stepped from the car.

'Oh, good grief, it's him. Bloody Dev, of all people, what a nerve!' Helen whipped her tea towel angrily against a table. 'I don't want to speak to him. Say I'm out.'

'This doesn't sound like the new positive you.'

'Big falling out. Can't stand him.'

'Well, he's seen us, he's coming this way and he's smiling.'

'Smirking, you mean.'

'You go,' her mother said, 'I'd have to invite him in if I answered the door. Only polite.'

But the new arrival had not gone unnoticed by the other occupants of Vale Farm. Peter had been paying close attention to the detail of this strange vehicle. Strange, but not so strange, as he was to demonstrate. Both he and Marta were ready and waiting when Helen reluctantly pulled open the big oak door.

'That's a Humber,' Peter announced loudly before another word could be spoken.

Devereaux, standing on the doorstep, looked down and smiled. 'Quite right, young man, it is a Humber. A Super Snipe in fact.'

Helen was frosty. 'Why are you here?'

'I thought all the whys were your son's prerogative,' he said.

She shook her head. 'I don't have anything to say. And I'm certainly not interested in a social visit.'

'I was rather hoping we could have a conversation.'

'Rather not.'

He smiled broadly. 'It's a nice day.'

'You didn't have yourself driven all this way to discuss the weather.'

Devereaux put his head on one side and said 'Helen!' with the kind of tone that begged indulgence between two people who were once close.

'All right, but not here.' She snorted, whipped a coat angrily from a peg, told the children to stay inside and stepped into the courtyard. 'In the car?'

'Best not,' he said. 'A private conversation.'

With undisguised reluctance, she stepped toward the footpath alongside the farm that had been their meeting place many years before. They had lingered on this path in more congenial times when relations were on a more amicable footing. Despite her antipathy, she took a proper look at him for the first time in many months. At Brindisi she'd been too angry to pay him more than scant attention, but now she gave him a close examination: a well-cut blue pin-striped suit, a watch chain from a waistcoat pocket and Brilliantined slicked back hair. He'd also put on weight. How could this be? She looked again. He didn't demonstrate the demeanour of someone who'd suffered disgrace, humiliation or demotion. He still retained his familiar quiet confidence; the aura of authority had not been flushed out of him.

'Thought you'd be occupying a cell right now,' she said.

'You sound as if you'd like that.'

'Nothing more than you deserve.'

Before he could say more, she came to a decision. She wasn't going to give him an inch on whatever it was he wanted – but her conscience was still troubling her over the way she had exploited him – extorted him – into giving her a flight and free entry into the country for her little tribe.

'Just one thing,' she said. 'I have to apologise for the way I forced you into doing what I wanted. I used the situation to get my own way. A form of blackmail. In retrospect, it was wrong of me. So, for that, and that alone, I'm sorry.'

He shrugged and smiled. 'Gracious of you.' A cough. 'What I actually came around for was to give you this.'

She looked down and realised he was holding a slip of pink paper. A cheque. She looked closer at all the noughts: £1,000.

She swallowed. 'Look, I'm not holding this over your head anymore. You're free of this, I shan't say anything to anyone...'

'Doesn't matter,' he said, 'doesn't make any difference, I want to give you this as a contribution to the children... and to that orphanage you're involved with in the town.'

She shook her head. 'I can't take it. I've twisted your arm too much. This is a guilt offering.'

He grabbed her hand and pressed the cheque into it. 'Take it. For the children. That's what this has all been for, isn't it? Your love and devotion to these kids. It's for them.'

She swallowed, stunned into silence.

They carried on walking without further comment, past the big old willow tree and the pond by the woods, until he said, almost casually, 'There is something else I'd like to explain.'

'The big car and the chauffeur?'

He nodded. 'About what happened after Brindisi. I was spot on about the consequences of that flight of yours to Northolt. Certainly put a stop to my rise through the ranks. Big ticking off, taken off the team. Certainly blighted the career. Going nowhere, so I took another big decision. Thought, even if it means going to that prison cell you'd so love me to occupy, even if... well, I'm going to confess. Tell all. Tell them everything.'

He turned to her and she looked at him, confused and uncertain.

'The amazing thing is,' he said.

'Yes?'

'I did it, I did confess.'

'And?'

'I've been forgiven.'

She was startled. 'I don't believe it!' She shook her head violently several times. 'Forgiven? No, no, this cannot be. Another of your outrageous farrago of lies!'

'Absolutely true,' he insisted, 'as true as I'm standing here, and being chauffeured around in that office car.'

———

The full details emerged slowly, after several references to the Official Secrets Act and the need for complete discretion.

'The thing is, they chewed the cud for a while and then decided they wouldn't bust me after all. Instead, it's more useful to our side to keep me in place and still send stuff to the Sovs – only the info provided is what our lot want them to know. Probably duff gen, I shouldn't wonder.'

She spent some time absorbing this.

'A double agent then?'

'If you like.'

'I'm surprised you can be so flexible.' The last word was delivered with a certain asperity.

'Look, things are changing. Early on, Stalin could do with everything we could send him. Not just armaments, information too. The Sovs were under tremendous pressure from Hitler. But now everything's changed. They're on the up. And Uncle Joe, well, he doesn't any more look quite as white as the driven snow.'

She stared at him for more silent minutes. 'How does anyone know you're just a double? You could be a treble agent. Or a quadruple.'

He shook his head. 'No chance, and that's why I'm here, speaking to you.'

'What now?'

'They've given me a new job. I'm putting together a team to cope with the next crisis or emergency that crops up.'

'Like what?'

'Who knows? We're just training, setting up, getting ready to be available.' He looked appealingly at her. 'The thing is, I want you to come back.'

'What?'

'We want you back, the brass are mightily impressed with your performance, what you did in Poland and all, so we want you back on the team...'

His words tailed off as he saw her expression of incredulity, then he pressed on: 'Look, you'll get a letter quite soon inviting you to a ceremony, they're going to give you a medal, full recognition of your heroics in that forest...'

'No thanks to you!'

'They want you back, Helen. I want you back. You're simply the best.' He sighed and looked for a moment quite vulnerable. 'And I was also hoping that, in spite of everything that's happened, you might be in a forgiving frame of mind.'

Responding to this was a hurdle. All this confusing turn-about of events, all this dubious information, all this topsy-turvy craziness, was too much to take in. After a long pause all she could manage was this: 'Lots of brownie points for owning up, Dev, forgiveness will take a lot, lot longer.'

The Humber had driven away and the two women were back in the kitchen. Spring cleaning, however, was largely forgotten and Mother was straight to the point.

'What did he want?'

Helen, still startled and conflicted by this confusing encounter with her old mentor, didn't answer directly, merely gave a non-committal shrug.

'He wants to involve you again, doesn't he?'

'Still trying to get my head around it. He's very insistent.'

'You promised me! You said you were finished... finished with him and finished with anything that meant you going away again.'

Helen made an anguished face. Before leaving, Devereaux had pressed her again. Not once. Twice. Would she come back? Join his new team? Now she let out a deep breath. 'It was all too sudden,' she told her mother. 'I had to say something... a spur of the moment sort of answer.'

'So you said...'

'That I'd have to think about it and let him know.'

Her mother plunged a pot that didn't need cleansing into the sink and crashed shut a cupboard door, causing something heavily metallic inside to crash to the floor. 'Really, Helen, you can't go back on your promise,' she said in a voice several octaves higher than normal. 'Peter and Marta need you. They deserve a full-time mother.'

They'd had this exchange before. *I'm a grown woman*, Helen insisted to herself, and took a few reflective moments before replying. She hadn't defied the enemy and people like the Soviet Kommissar to finish up under her mother's thumb. She was her own person with her own agenda for life. There had been constant discord over Peter's upbringing since the death of her husband. Despite this, she recognised that she was now closer to her mother than she'd ever been. 'Peter's got the perfect set-up here,' she said, 'with me, a great home, a great place, two loving grand-parents...'

'And a weekend mum. A mother more like a weekend auntie.'

'Nonsense. Anyway, I'm here now.'

'Good!' Pursed lips, a tight expression. 'Make sure you mean it. We don't want Peter turning into a young fogey, old before his time, parroting attitudes and ideas that sound like me or your father. He's got to talk and sound like other boys of his age.'

Helen attempted to lighten the moment. 'You're not old-fashioned, Mum, well, not much anyway.'

'Don't try soft-soaping me... just keep to your word.' She opened the cupboard door and began to sweep up the remnants of a broken torch. 'And you've got a whole lot more kids to worry about now, even if they have gone to that school.'

True, how very true, Helen decided. Devereaux's unexpected visit had merely unsettled her, although she could not deny that his offer – and the prospect of another active role, perhaps involving some flying – did not have strong appeal.

She sighed. It was time to acknowledge the big change in her life. The future, as she had realised during that fraught flight back from Poland, would now be all about children.

Chapter Forty-Six

She was deep into the story of the poor country boy who traded the family cow for a handful of magic beans, anticipating the questions that would surely follow from Peter in the inevitable quiz about poor Jack. But there was a part of her mind that was elsewhere, roving in anxious circles over her immediate future.

She smiled at the tiny girl perched on her knee. Marta hadn't joined the others at Finchingate. It had been clear all along that this little mite was a fixture in the Fairfax household.

Fee-fi-fo-fum! I smell the blood of an Englishman.

Their attention was rapt as Helen elaborated on her version of the beanstalk story, but again part of her mind was elsewhere. It was all very well deciding that her future lay with children, but her prospects were in a highly fluid state. The war raged on and the military would surely reclaim her. She asked herself again, as she had several times in the last days: should she return to flying as a ferry pilot, or stay grounded as her mother insisted, or think again about Devereaux's extraordinary offer? Part of her craved a new challenge and the devious Dev had known it.

Her thoughts were a jumble. So many possibilities. And

then there was Leo Beck. She'd promised to be his protector, had been continually harrying Farnborough to discover news of his progress, worried that once his work on the rocket had been completed the authorities would decide he had outlived his usefulness. He was in danger of being discarded. It would be a grave injustice if he ended up in some displaced persons camp or was given a hard time by some secrecy-obsessed security department or, even worse, turned into some kind of espionage asset. Duplicity and deceit were not in his nature.

She had the unfortunate experience of Devereaux's trickery and she didn't want Beck's pure spirit debased by covert activity or misused by some outfit specialising in the twisted and the soiled.

'More!' demanded Marta at the end of the beanstalk tale, even though her grip on the story had to be strengthened through lavish illustrations in coloured chalks on a blackboard. Peter's expression seemed to be demanding more substantial fare.

Still thoughts of Leo Beck troubled Helen. He was not a commanding or military sort of person and hid his bravery behind a retiring nature. That's why she liked him. He was willing to act and stake all on his beliefs, as he had in the Polish forest. A loner who had rejected his previous life and was now intent on inventing the new. Such a person would find friendship hard to forge. All the more intense then when he did.

Thankfully, it was bedtime for her two avid listeners and she reflected that in the days since Devereaux had delivered his £1,000 cheque she had overcome her guilt at accepting the money and divided her time between Finchingate and the Westgate Street orphanage, dispensing this unexpected largesse equally between the two. An ecstatic Isabelle had expansive plans for using the cash and it was a pleasure to be the bearer of such good fortune.

Next day the telephone rang in the hall, her mother calling her once again. When she took the receiver she was overjoyed to hear Leo Beck's voice. He was calling from the station to say he had been released by the authorities at Farnborough and was on his way over.

'Leo, how lovely to hear you,' she said. 'I'll get Dad to drive over and pick you up.'

'No,' he said, 'I'll make my own way. Got to call at the police station first.'

So he was still on a tight leash.

When he arrived on the doorstep she saw no reason to hold back to an earlier sense of formality, flinging her arms around him in a massive hug. And soon they were sitting in the farmhouse conservatory in deep armchairs with slices of her mother's speciality carrot cake and cups of real coffee – none of the usual treacly liquid out of a Camp Coffee bottle.

'They're still keeping tabs on me,' he said, 'they've loosened the chains but I still have to report in to the police station at ten every morning.'

'Ridiculous,' she said. 'What are they expecting?'

'I think they're working towards building a British rocket. Not in so many words, as yet, but of course, I don't want that. If I'm to work in science I want it to be for peaceful purposes.' He sighed and looked at her earnestly. 'Actually, I want right away from all that. I really want to work with children.'

'I'll introduce you to Isabelle,' she said. 'In fact, we can go there at lunch-time and help serve the children's dinners. Hands-on! It'll be a revelation.'

Her mood was buoyant. She felt like celebrating, brought out the old gramophone and selected her favourite 78, a pre-war recording of the New Year concert in Vienna, another Strauss fantasia of waltzes and polkas. She even managed, to the accompaniment of the *Blue Danube*, to entice him up for a few steps around the space between the armchairs.

Later they peered out at the grassy slope leading to the waterfall and the wooden bridge over the stream where swans swam in stately procession. It seemed so very remote from the ugliness of war and the ever-present threat of the V-2 hanging over London. They had both played their part in the effort to neutralise that peril.

'This is a rural idyll,' he said. 'You're so lucky to live in this place, to have had the perfect childhood here, brought up by loving parents...'

'You haven't met my father. Absolutely crackers about cars.'

'I love cars.'

'He'll bore you rigid about his treasures,' she said and reeled off a few of the motoring gems that lay in wait for his attention: the Austin Ruby, a Lancia Augusta, the Alvis Drophead Coupe and a fiery red MGTB. She knew Beck was comparing her family with his own fractured background. Being in the midst of a parental war and witness to bullying and aggression was torture; not knowing his mother's fate – whether she had managed to extricate herself from the grip of the Third Reich – was a form of grief.

'Any news about your mother?'

He shook his head.

'I'll get Dev to make inquiries through the Red Cross.'

He looked at her closely then. He seemed to be gathering himself and she sensed he was about to say something of significance.

'When this is all over – when this damnable war is finished – I want to work with children,' he said. 'And I want it to be with you.'

This was almost an outright declaration of love and remarkably direct for a man usually as reticent as he. In her mind it was a decider. Up to this moment her head had been awash with possibilities – flying, intrigue, children. Now there was a clear pointer.

She thought about the difference in their worlds and then about what they had in common: his Thomas Mann to her *As You Like It*; his fascination with jazz to her love of Strauss; their shared love of countryside and animals. There would be other interests to discover. There were so many aspects of their backgrounds and personalities to explore. She would not race into a relationship but allow it to develop at its own pace.

However, at that moment she knew she had crossed a bridge. Her own mother had rightly placed great emphasis on the importance of parental influence for Peter. There was also her little waif to consider. Marta had already climbed on and clung to Beck; he was a natural with her, as with every child. They both knew there would be enormous problems to deal with at the conclusion of the fighting; the peace, whenever it came, would create millions of displaced persons and vast numbers of lost and homeless children.

Sitting together in relaxed mood in the sunlit room she looked at Beck, a smiling, amiable, gentle figure, and knew that he, like her, saw their role together in this vision of the future.

It came to her again, what a cosy family unit they would make. The boy with no father, the girl with no parents and the man with no settled country.

She was the one who could make them gel together.

Epilogue

London, Saturday 1st January 2000

Just a quick final word from me, Zofia. Remember me? I was the one on the plane with the violin. Anyway, we three girls, Gabriella, Eliza and me, we've stayed friends all these years and Helen's party is by far the most important date in the diary for many a long year. And wow, what a party!

The cake is a fifty-pound, six-layered monster – a three-day cooking marathon from Henryks, a favourite among Helen's People – and the cutting of the first slice is a delicate operation performed with an electric saw. Now he's a chef at Claridge's and the cake is his ultimate achievement.

He's dripping icing and pride at all the cheers and accolades – and applause from this audience really counts. They're all survivors or survivors' children. Indeed, three of Eliza's young brood are zooming around the studio floor with toy cars to keep everyone on their toes.

Now that the cameras have been turned off we're in proper party mode and have forgotten we're in a TV studio. Alex Hunter, the host, has, in any case, disappeared, off no doubt to another studio.

Helen's celebrations become unrestrained – balloons,

bubbly, kids and catch-up. We're all finding out the latest news on our contemporaries – and then the woman herself is wheeled into our midst to meet her 'people' close up. You'd never think she was retired. There's no let-up to her campaigning. We've all followed her post-war career – working in dozens of DP resettlement camps and a litany of succeeding organisations that came with the United Nations umbrella: UNRRA, IRO, UNHCR. Then there was helping the villagers back in Poland, her Kids Cave charity, parliamentary lobbying and the latest: campaigning for a children's commissioner, ombudsman or government minister.

'Either one or all three, I don't care,' she quips from the middle of the scrum around her chair.

Her eyes light up when she sees Gabriella, Eliza and me once again. We like to think we've done things to justify all that effort and danger to get us out of wartime Poland. We swore we'd validate our rescue – by sticking together and carving out careers, as it happens, with the Philharmonic, Sadler's Wells and the Beeb.

We grin back at her and ask, 'Helen, after all that effort down the years, after all that you've accomplished, what would you say was your greatest achievement?'

She gives a hearty laugh and points. 'Darlings, that's you! You flourished and made something of yourselves and made a significant contribution to society. You,' she repeats, 'you are my greatest achievement. You didn't just disappear into a corner and lead miserable inconsequential lives. You didn't simply survive; you grabbed life by the throat and did not let the chance slip.'

Another round of applause at this, then more memories. And more familiar faces – there are fifteen of us originals, mostly female and now representing a slew of high-profile women ambassadors, British diplomats in all the most important places – Berlin, Washington, Tokyo and Moscow. Plus Ada, Petra and Beata who went back to Poland to make it big in arts and culture over there.

'You validated the whole operation,' Helen says proudly. 'You are the stars of Operation Skyhawk.'

Lots of cheers at this and then news of Helen's post-war brood: Cleo, on the board of the National Trust and Jonathan, something in the City. And then of course there's old Leo. He's a bit shaky on his pins these days but he's had a long career in international law and is campaigning for the new International Criminal Court at The Hague. He's in America right now drumming up more funds for Helen's charity.

We look around the room and there is Marta. Who'd believe the waif would come out of her shell and make a name for herself at the law: Lady Justice Bury – the town name because no one knows her true forbears. And Winter is present too – the man from Jersey, the son of the ambassador to London, hence his facility with all things English.

It has to be admitted, of course, that despite our best efforts with Skyhawk we didn't stop the V-2s coming over during those dark days of the rescue flight, though the intensity of the bombardment was much less than feared.

'What happened to Devereaux?' Gabriella wants to know, since Helen is still talking about her elusive erstwhile friend, but it's all a great mystery, the family denying any knowledge of his whereabouts. Seems he vanished back in the shadow world.

But this is not the end of our story. Oh no! A group of us are about to head out to Poland to attend the opening of a new social and sports centre and a hugely anticipated reunion with the people of our special village.

However, I have to admit several unresolved matters are at the forefront of our minds: three divorced husbands, a big silly

Labrador and several stray cats later, life is definitely on the edge for us.

As the party frenzy tones down eyes are beginning to stray across the room, away from our mentor to where her son is sitting, and we're all looking wistfully into the future and thinking about Peter.

He's now the subject of intense interest to Gabriella, Eliza and me.

Our clever history professor. As a boy, a constant presence and concern in the mind of his mother throughout Operation Skyhawk and now, in the maturity of his later years, a figure of some stature and touched by fetching flecks of grey.

He enjoys his spot in the limelight. Much sought-after in the worlds of academia and literature.

Unattached.

And very much still available.

THE END

Also by David Laws

The Martyr of Auschwitz

The Fuhrer's Orphans

Her Private War

Acknowledgements

In loving memory of our wonderful and kind father who completed this book before he passed away on 9th October 2023. We are grateful to Bloodhound Books for their support in publishing *For the Children*, and for their support of our father over the years.

A note from the publisher

Thank you for reading this book. If you enjoyed it please do consider leaving a review on Amazon to help others find it too.

We hate typos. All of our books have been rigorously edited and proofread, but sometimes mistakes do slip through. If you have spotted a typo, please do let us know and we can get it amended within hours.

info@bloodhoundbooks.com